THE LAZARD LEGACY

A NOVEL

THE LAZARD LEGACY

by William Rawlings, Jr.

HARBOR
HOUSE

THE LAZARD LEGACY
By William Rawlings Jr
A Harbor House Book/April 2003

Copyright 2003 by Willliam Rawlings, Jr.

For information address:
  HARBOR HOUSE
  629 STEVEN'S CROSSING
  MARTINEZ, GEORGIA 30907

  www.harborhousebooks.com

Jacket and Book Design by Fredna Lynn Forbes
Author Photography by Smith's Studio, Sandersville, Georgia

Library of Congress Cataloging-in-Publication Data

Rawlings, William, 1948-
The Lazard Legacy: a novel / by William Rawlings Jr.
    p. cm.
ISBN 1-891799-23-1
1.French Americans-Fiction   2 Rich people-Fiction   3.Physicians-Fiction   4.Georgia-Fiction   1. Title

PS3618.A96L39 2003
813'.6--dc21
                              2003000620

Printed in the United States of America
10 9 8 7 6 5 4 3 2

For Beth and the girls

Acknowledgments

Writing a work of fiction is never easy and rarely done in isolation.
Many have contributed in one way or another to this novel.
Here are a special few:

The elusive Laura Ashley inspired me. Dorothy Vincent encouraged me.
My family made it all possible in more ways than one.

Assistance from my "readers" was greatly appreciated, with special thanks
to Layne Kitchens and Helen Tarbutton.

Randall and Anne Floyd of Harbor House Publishers have been
most generous with their faith and encouragemnet.

The various villians and scoundrels that I've known over the years
helped make the bad guys all the more real.

Any mistakes are mine.

CHAPTER
ONE

"Latrodectus mactans."

The voice swam out of the blackness. Ortega struggled to reply and began to move his lips, realizing at that moment that the words were in a language he didn't understand.

The voice appeared again. "Ah, ha! Looks like our friend is trying to wake up."

Ortega opened his eyes. He tried to sit up—but found himself bound spread-eagle to something. A table? No, the open back of a wagon. He turned his head from side to side. He was in a tractor shed, a simple pole barn shelter with a large tin roof supported by creosoted posts and open on all sides to the surrounding fields. He could smell oil and diesel fuel.

"Welcome back, Señor Ortega—or whatever your name is," the voice continued, "I apologize for my associates. They've been rather crude in their efforts to get to know you better. I've tried to convince them that rubber hoses and electric shocks may be fiine for your part of the world, but this is Georgia, where heritage and subtlety are appreciated. Hence, my friend here."

He held a small glass jar, bringing it close to Ortega's face. Ortega's swollen eyes grew wide when he recognized the black insect scurrying around inside.

"*Latrodectus mactans*," the speaker droned. " The scientific name for the black widow spider. They're really quite common down here. The venom of this spider contains a neurotoxin that has the effect of stimulating every pain receptor in the body. You can achieve the desired effect of producing pain without all the messiness of having to physically inflict it. One can obtain so much more cooperation without all the—damage. There is an antivenin, provided, of course, the unfortunate victim receives medical care soon enough. Whether or not that happens will depend on how much you have to tell us. Do you understand, Señor Ortega?"

Ortega stared back, silent.

The speaker smiled, continued. "Here's a story you might appreciate. Down here, used to be that when a fellow had to do his business he went to an outhouse. Can you imagine what it was like, a fellow sitting over one of those little holes, his penis hanging down in the dark? Can you imagine a more tempting target for a black widow—a dick dangling down there in front of her face?"

He laughed as rough hands tugged at Ortega's belt and trousers.

Ortega felt his pants being yanked down past his knees, saw the stranger unscrew the lid of the jar. Moments later, when he felt the first sudden flash of pain as the spider buried her fangs deep within the tip of his penis, Ortega began to scream.

The scream held for less than a full minute, a detached, agonizing shriek that shook the barn and mingled with the wind sighing through the pine forests beyond.

CHAPTER
TWO

THE PERSISTENT BUZZING of the telephone awakened him. He fumbled for the receiver in the darkness. "Hello?"

"Dr. Pike?"

"Yeah."

"This is Rob Mitchell at the emergency room. I'm one of the ER techs. I know you're not on call. I'm really sorry to bother you, but don't you speak Spanish?"

"Yeah. Some." Ben Pike reached for the bedside lamp. "What time is it?"

"Just after midnight. Dr. Steed asked me to find some-body who speaks Spanish. We need a translator down here for a patient."

Ben Pike was beginning to wake up. "What can I do for you?"

"About an hour ago some farmer brought in a man he says he found lying in a ditch on some dirt road off the Mitchell highway. He was in bad shock, but Dr. Steed has got him stabilized. We got some of the fellows he works with down here, and none of them speaks much English. We're really not sure what happened and we're looking for somebody who speaks Spanish so we can get some history. Can you come down and and talk to him?"

"I'll be there as soon as I can."

Fifteen minutes later Ben hurried across the still damp parking lot toward the red and white emergency room sign. The evening's earlier rain had stopped, but the humidity made the heat of the warm August night oppressive. The automatic doors of the Ambulance Entrance opened before him. Standing in a knot in the wide corridor were three rough looking Hispanic males—farm workers he guessed—who stared with fixed eyes toward the trauma room. He rounded the corner and saw half-a-dozen figures in white uniforms busy over a prostrate form on a stretcher. A stocky, fortyish blond man in a long white lab coat was standing at the patient's left side, defibrillator paddles poised over the still form. Dr. Steed, presumably.

"Looks like he's back in sinus rhythm," a nurse who was watching a cardiac monitor called to the figure with the defibrillator. "No, wait. Damn! He's going back into V-tach. Rate is about 180. You want more lidocaine, Doctor?"

Dr. Steed nodded. "Give him another hundred milligrams IV, and follow that with another amp of bicarb. Then we'll shock him again."

"Lidocaine and bicarb's in. His pressure is down to 55 palpable," one of the techs called.

Steed raised the paddles. "Everybody clear?" He glanced to be sure the defibrillator was charged and applied the paddles to the patient's chest—the one in his left hand to the right upper side and the other to the patient's left chest below the heart. He called again, "Clear!" and pressed the buttons on each paddle simultaneously. The shock produced a powerful muscle contraction, causing the supine form to jerk as if it had been kicked in the back by an unseen force. Steed withdrew the paddles and looked toward the monitor. "What we got?"

"Looks like normal sinus with a rate of about 110," the nurse replied. She squinted at the automatic blood pressure monitor. "BP's up to 145 systolic."

"Good." Steed replaced the paddles in the racks on the defibrillator. "Let's just hope we can keep him like this for a while." He glanced over his shoulder, and seeing Ben Pike standing in the doorway, walked over and extended his hand.

"Hi. I'm Carter Steed. I'd heard you were starting practice here. I'm really glad to meet you, but sorry about having to get you up in the middle of the night to do it."

"No problem. I got the word you needed somebody who speaks Spanish."

"That's right," Steed replied. He looked back over to the patient on the gurney, satisfying himself that the situation was stable enough for him to be away for a moment. A respiratory tech was wheeling in a ventilator. "Looks like this guy is okay for the moment. Let's go sit down in the staff lounge and let me fill you in."

They walked down the corridor to the *Lounge*—an over-sized janitor's closet equipped with a worn sofa, two chairs and a small table on which sat an industrial size coffee maker and the detritus of spilled sugar, empty creamers and stained spoons. Steed flopped on the sofa and motioned for Ben to take one of the chairs.

"Jesus, it's been a night! Typical Saturday." Steed reached for a half-finished cup of coffee. "I've been trying for two hours to finish this cup. Two wrecks, an overdose and now this guy."

"Well, you got me out of bed and I'm here. You must have wanted me for something."

"Yeah, sorry." Steed glanced at his watch. "About an hour-and-a-half ago—we'd just finished pumping the stomach on some teenager who OD'd on aspirin—this pickup pulls up to the ER door and some guy in overalls rushes in hollering that he's found a body by the side of the road. Said he thought the man was dead, but then his son noticed he was breathing, so they threw him on the back of the truck and brought him here. Anyway, we bring him in, and he's really in bad shape. To make a long story short, he was shocky, acidotic and barely breathing. We intubated him, got a central line started, bolused him with Lactated Ringers and started him on dopamine. He came around pretty well—he must be strong as an ox—and I thought he was looking pretty good. Right before you got here he had several runs of V-tach and I had to shock him a couple of times. We didn't have any history at all, but when we examined him, it was evident he'd been beat up pretty bad. He had bruises all over him, and some broken ribs, but not much else. I thought maybe he was a drunk, but his blood alcohol was zip."

"A hit and run, maybe?"

"No. Not enough trauma. Looked more like he'd been beat up bad and dumped in the ditch. Maybe left for dead.

The fellow that found him said it was just luck. He was look-ing for a lost dog. The road is not traveled that much, and where he was, you couldn't really see him from a passing car. Anyway, the only thing he had in his pocket was a paycheck stub from Lazard Farms in the name of Carlos Ortega. We called out there, but the housekeeper said Dr. Lazard was out of town. She said she really didn't know all the names, but they did have some migrant workers from Mexico or some-where in that area and that she'd call the bunkhouse and ask about anybody named Ortega."

"What about Ortega? Did he ever wake up?" Ben inquired.

"Oh, yeah, he was doing pretty good by that time, it looked like. He was intubated and couldn't talk, but he seemed alert. About ten minutes after I hung up with the woman at the farm, those three guys you see out in the hall came rushing in the door. Babbling away to one another in Spanish. Looks like they were arguing about something. Apparently they know Ortega, and apparently he works with them. I got that much from them, but beyond that it's all been 'No comprendo' and 'No hablo inglés.' That's when I remembered reading on your resume that you spoke Spanish and I had one of the techs call you. How about seeing what you can find out?"

They approached the three men in the corridor who had now become silent. Ben introduced himself and ques-tioned them about Ortega. They agreed that they knew little about him except that he said he was from El Salvador and had been working at the Lazard Farm for a couple of months. The apparent leader of the group, who identified himself as Fuentes, said Ortega kept to himself but was bad to drink. Since it was Saturday, he'd had the day off and had been drink-ing heavily when he was last seen at the farm about 6 p.m.

Fuentes said he and his companions, Garcia and Martinez, were originally from Guatemala, but had been working at the Lazard farm—legally he added—for about two years.

Ben noted that their accent was a bit strange, but was not certain that he could identify a Guatemalan accent anyway. He turned back to Steed. "They're not very helpful. Maybe Ortega's alert enough to get some history from him."

They walked back in the trauma room. Two techs were busying themselves over the form on the gurney, while a nurse watched the monitor and a respiratory tech adjusted the ventilator. "How's he doing?" Steed asked.

"Just OK," the nurse replied. "He's having a lot of arrhythmias. Multiform ventricular ectopy mostly."

Steed bent over the patient. A breathing tube connected to a hose that snaked off to the ventilator emerged from his mouth was held in place by adhesive tape. "Mr. Ortega. Can you hear me?" He paused and tried again. "Carlos!" Ortega opened his eyes. Steed turned to Ben. "See if you can get some information from him."

Ben moved close to Ortega's bruised face. Ortega flinched and tugged at the restraints. *"Tranquilo, amigo. Soy un medico. Estás à hospital. ¿Que pasó?"*

Ortega raised his restrained right hand making a sign with his thumb and forefinger indicating he wanted to write a message.

Ben asked the nurse to get a pencil. "OK. Look, we're going to untie your hand so you can write, but don't pull out your IV's or your breathing tube. *¿Comprende?*" Ortega nodded affirmatively. "I'm going to ask you some questions, and you just nod or write an answer." Ortega nodded again.

The nurse interrupted. "Dr. Steed, he's having a lot of PVC's again, with some couplets and triplets."

Steed replied, "Let's watch him close, but get on with this. I still don't understand what happened to this guy, and if we're going to keep him alive, we need more information."

Ortega again waved his hand to indicate that he wanted to write a message. The nurse placed a pencil in his right hand and held a clipboard with a piece of paper for him to write on. Slowly he wrote in block letters:

As he was starting the third letter, the pencil suddenly trailed off the edge of the clipboard as the nurse yelled, "He's in V-fib!" Steed grabbed for the defibrillator as one of the techs began compressing Ortega's chest. Ben stepped back while the ER team aggressively pursued cardiopulmonary resuscitation.

Half an hour later, with the failure to restore a sustainable rhythm, Ortega was pronounced dead.

Drs. Steed and Pike emerged from the trauma room to tell Ortega's fellow workers. They were nowhere to be seen. The clerk said that while they were trying to resuscitate Ortega, Dr. Lazard had arrived and was talking with them in the parking area outside. She volunteered to go out and get them. Through the glass doors they could see the three men engaged in what appeared to be a heated argument with Dr. Lazard. The clerk went to the door and told them Dr. Steed wanted to talk with them. They entered, Dr. Lazard in the lead, followed by the Latinos.

Steed spoke. "Troup, I'm sorry, but we couldn't save your man. I saw you talking with those guys. I didn't know you could speak Spanish."

"I can't," he replied. Dr. Troup Lazard was in his late fifties, with jet black hair graying at the temples, and exhuding an air of comfortable wealth. He was dressed in khaki pants with a white shirt and blue linen blazer that he wore despite the heat. He stared at Steed and Pike.

Steed continued. "I really don't know what happened. He was in extremis when he came in, but I thought we'd be able to pull him out. I guess he's going to be a coroner's case. Oh, I'm sorry. Troup, let me introduce Dr. Ben Pike. He's our new internist who took over Dr. Powell's practice last week. Ben, I'd like you to meet Troup Lazard, one of our prominent local citizens, in case you didn't know."

Steed smiled. Pike and Lazard looked at one another. After an almost imperceptible pause, Ben extended his hand.

"Good to see you again, Troup."

"Hey, you guys know one another?" Steed interjected.

Silence. After a moment, Ben spoke. "In a sense of the word. We're brothers."

CHAPTER THREE

"YOU'RE BROTHERS?"

Steed looked incredulous. "Troup, you never said anything about a brother. Besides, your last names are different."

Ben smiled. "We're half bothers, actually. It's a long story."

Lazard was agitated. "Where did you find Ortega? Did he say anything? Tell me!"

"Calm down, Troup," Steed countered. "We did what we could. They found him somewhere off the Mitchell road—not far from your place, I think. He was intubated and wasn't able to tell us much. He tried to write a note, but he arrested just as he was getting started."

"The note. What did it say?" Lazard demanded.

"I don't know. D-E-Something." Steed turned to Ben. "What do you think?"

"Here it is. See for yourself." Ben was still holding the clipboard. "Looks like 'deo'—'god' in Spanish. Maybe he was asking for last rites."

Lazard grabbed the clipboard. "That's all? Nothing else?" He glared at the two other physicians.

"Troup! Dammit, calm down!" Steed shot back. "I know this guy worked for you, but you're really getting worked up."

Lazard relaxed. "I'm sorry. This guy, Ortega…he was kind of a trouble maker. I've got a big farming operation in addition to my medical practice, and I can't let somebody like him get all my employees upset. He probably just got drunk and passed out somewhere."

"His blood alcohol level was zero," Steed said matter-of-factly. "It looks like he was beat up pretty bad. I've got to call the coroner and the sheriff. This may end up as a murder case."

Lazard stiffened.

Twenty minutes later, Hoke Brantley, the chief sheriff's deputy arrived, followed soon after by Elmo Kantt, the coroner. Ben Pike had started to go home, but he was wide awake and decided to stick around to see how things were done.

Dr. Lazard grabbed both the deputy and the coroner as they arrived and engaged them in whispered conversation before they examined the body.

Ben had not seen Hoke Brantley in nearly twenty years but recognized him instantly. He still had the same massive frame of the high school fullback, and the same red hair, now receding at the forehead. They were the same age, and had been best friends in school when Ben and his mother left town after his father's death. As chief deputy, Hoke had become the *de facto* law in Adams County. The sheriff, Gardner Ulrich, had been paralyzed and confined to a wheelchair for nine years since he tried to intervene in a domestic dispute between a husband and his very drunk wife who was armed with a .25 caliber automatic. He'd taken a bullet in the stomach which severed his spinal cord at the level of the twelfth thoracic vertebra, leaving him without feeling or control of his muscles below his waist. Rather than retire on disability, he ran for reelection from his wheelchair, and used Hoke Brantley and the other deputies as his eyes, ears, and strength throughout the county. Hoke had done well, and the general consensus among voters was that it was a good arrangement. Ulrich could look forward to reelection as long as Hoke kept the crime rate down.

Hoke greeted Ben warmly. "Good to see you, man. It's been a long time. Lot of changes around here. Why did you decide to come back? I thought when you and your mom left here we'd never see you again. How is she, by the way?"

"She and my stepfather were killed by a drunk driver ten years ago, just about time I started medical school," Ben replied.

"I'm sorry. I didn't know..."

"Don't apologize, there's no way you could have known. But since you asked, that's probably why I decided to come back here. I don't have any other family, and this is the one place I feel like I can call home. When Dr. Powell died a couple of months ago, his widow called me and made me an offer that was too good to turn down. Academic medicine was getting old."

Elmo Kantt interrupted. "Hoke, I need to talk with you about this case." He turned to Ben. "I'm Elmo Kantt. I'm the coroner. I understand you're Ben Pike. I want to introduce myself 'cause I'm sure we'll be working together quite a bit." He was middle-aged, of average height and dressed in a somber black suit. Thin to the point of looking malnourished, he wore his hair slicked back with Vitalis. He reeked of after-shave despite obviously not having shaved in the last 24 hours. "I run the biggest funeral home in town, and as you know, the coroner investigates all cases of medical misadventure, so we may be seeing a lot of each other."

Ben immediately disliked him. "I hope not," he replied simply.

Kantt walked back over to confer with Dr. Lazard.

Hoke Brantley saw the look on Ben's face. "He's not one of my favorite people either. But you've just got to deal with him. Three quarters of the deaths in this county end up using his funeral home, and I swear to you, he spends as much time politicking at funerals as he does comforting the bereaved. The only way he could lose an election for coroner would be to get caught screwing a corpse. Looking at him, you kinda get the impression he'd like that."

They both laughed.

"What happens now?" Ben asked.

"Well, we've got a dead man who died under suspicious circumstances after arriving at the hospital. Technically he died while under medical care, but if I understand things right, he died despite the best medical efforts. In this case, it's the coroner who makes a formal determination of the cause of death. He can call a coroner's jury to hear the evidence, or he can make a determination on his own. If he decides the case warrants investigation, he'll refer it to the DA and the sheriff's department, otherwise, he can just sign the death certificate and that's the end of it."

The chief deputy rummaged in his pocket for a cigarette only to have a nurse stop him with a curt, "No smoking in here!" He grudgingly stuffed the Marlboros back in his shirt pocket.

Hoke continued, "Usually, the ER doctor will collect blood and urine specimens for drug and toxin analysis and give them to the coroner. He in turn will label them, prepare a chain of custody form and send them to the State Crime Lab."

"I presume you'll want an autopsy. Whose place is it to order that?" Ben asked.

"Like I said, since this has become a coroner's case, that's up to Kantt. He'll take possession on the body until a determination about what to do is made."

Elmo Kantt was hunched over the counter filling out a legal-sized coroner's Report of Death form in his stilted left-handed script. Carter Steed emerged from the Trauma Room and handed him several tubes of deep red and clear yellow fluid—blood and urine specimens Ben presumed. Kantt had Steed sign a chain of custody form, and then he in turn initialed the vials and signed the form.

Steed walked over to Ben and Hoke. "Looks like that about wraps it up. Kantt's taking the body to his funeral home, and I guess he'll get the crime lab pathologist to come down in the morning—I should say later *this* morning—for an autopsy."

Ben glanced at the clock on the wall. 2:45 a.m. "I'm going home. I'm going to try to make rounds at the nursing homes tomorrow. Good old Dr. Powell had quite a few patients, and I'm having a hard enough time convincing them that anybody other than him could really ever understand their problems. Dragging in with bags under my eyes won't help. See y'all in the morning."

Ben had nearly reached the door when an ancient RN who apparently had been waiting to speak to him touched his arm. "Dr. Pike? I'm Emily Coxwell. I'm the night supervisor here—have been for nearly forty years now. I just wanted to tell you how glad we are to have you in practice here. I've known and admired your family for years. In fact, I was the nurse on duty when you were born—what?—thirty-five years ago now?"

"Thirty-six." Ben smiled at the old woman.

She gazed at him for a moment. He was tall—about six feet—with sandy blond hair and sharp brown eyes that seemed to take in every detail. "You know, you look exactly like your father did when he was a younger man. You've got Lazard written all over you."

"So I've been told," Ben replied. "My father died when I was so young that I always felt like I never got to know him."

"Your half brother is different. He looks more like his mother. I scarcely remember her, but she was dark, moody. Your father was always so generous. He'd send gifts to all the patients in the hospital at Christmas. Little remembrances, he called them. Helped me out right after my husband died and I didn't have anything. Loaned me the money to go to nursing school so I could learn to do something to support myself. Wouldn't let me pay him back. He was a great man. I know he's been gone for years, but I still miss him"

"You're most kind." Ben was embarrassed.

He said good night and walked out into the still heat of the August night. Maybe his decision to come back home was the right thing to do after all, he told himself.

CHAPTER
FOUR

IN 1824, GENERAL MARIE JOSEPH PAUL YVES ROCH
GILBERT DU MOTIER, Marquis de Lafayette and aging hero
of the American War of Independence, accepted the invitation of Congress to visit the United States as "The Guest of the
Nation." Arriving in New York in August of that year, he and
his party spent the next thirteen months traveling more than
four-thousand miles through each of the then-twenty states.
On March 19, 1825, he arrived by steamer in the port city of
Savannah. After a tumultuous welcome and banquet, he traveled overland to Augusta, then through Warrenton, Sparta,
and on to the State Capital of Milledgeville where he arrived

on Sunday, March 27. His party was pressed for time; twenty-five miles travel in a day required two sets of horses in relays, and delays from poor roads and swollen rivers were frequent. From Milledgeville, he was scheduled to visit the last outpost of settlement at Fort Hawkins, and then proceed on across Creek Indian country to the Alabama border where the governor of that state was to meet him on March 31.

Among the notables in the general's party were his son, named after Lafayette's friend and mentor, George Washington, and his personal secretary, M. LeVasseur, chronicler of his journey. Also accompanying him were various aides and assistants, including one Augustin d'Ayen Lazard, the intelligent but dissolute twenty-two-year old son of his wife's second cousin whose joining the journey to America had been prompted by certain "difficulties" in Paris, the exact nature of which were never revealed. Unusually tall, as compared to the men of the day, he fell by default into the role of bodyguard and crowd handler to the frail and aging Marquis, who, by then, was in the sixty-ninth year of his life. Despite a good education and seven months in America, young Lazard spoke heavily accented English, although his elderly charge had commented privately to M. LeVasseur that it did not seem to impede his communication with the local mademoiselles.

As they approached the Capitol on the evening of March 27, they were welcomed by throngs of admirers and well-wishers who had turned out to see the last surviving general of the American War of Independence. When the general's party reached the far bank of the river opposite the capitol city, a canon salute was fired from the State House, followed by another as they crossed the bridge and entered town. Accompanied by the governor, Lafayette attended a church service, and then retired to his lodgings to receive visitors for the remainder of the evening. Somewhat bored by the endless welcomes, young "Jacques" Lazard set out on his own to explore the dirt streets of the latest backwoods village in which he found himself stuck for the next couple of days.

As he wandered from his assigned lodging, he approached the State House where preparations were under-way for a great banquet to be held the following evening. Recognized as one of the visiting dignitaries, he was immediately ushered in by a member of the Committee of Arrangements and given a preview of the decorations. The Committee was composed chiefly of the wives and daughters of prominent families in the city, a fact that relieved any reti-cence that Jacques might have shown toward such an endeav-or. A middle-aged lady (who he later discovered was the wife of the governor) conducted the tour of the ballroom, fes-tooned with wild flowers and garlands of evergreen, and dom-inated by a large banner reading "Welcome, Lafayette, Defender of our Country, Welcome."

Seeking to make his exit from such a boring exercise, Jacques was inching toward the door when he spied a young woman whom he would later describe as appearing *"comme un ange Américain"*. Breaking away from his tour guide he approached her and doffed his hat. She smiled, and from behind him he was shocked to hear her introduced as Elizabeth Marie Troup, daughter of the governor and of the woman who had been leading his tour. He bowed slightly, and was amazed to hear her reply in flawless, if accented, French, *"Ma plaisir, Monsieur."* She was seventeen, had striking brunette hair and brown eyes, and to Jacques's great pleasure, spoke French, having been tutored privately since her childhood. She was also, as her mother immediately pronounced in a stern voice, betrothed to Early Lamar Sheftall, son of a prominent and wealthy Savannah family who would be arriving the next day to accompany her to the ball.

Much to her mother's consternation, Elizabeth was quick to remind her that the young Frenchman was an honored guest, and furthermore, showing him about the community would provide an unequaled opportunity to use the language training that she herself insisted her daughter take. Reluctantly, the governor's wife agreed, but only if the couple were accompanied by her trusted slave and maidservant, Julia. Without further ado, Jacques and Elizabeth, followed by a huffing and puffing Julia, set out to see what few sights the rural capital had to offer. What happened that night is not known, but the diary of Governor Troup's wife records that Julia returned to the Government House at dusk, and that it was some hours before her daughter returned.

The events of the next day, Monday, March 28, had been planned in great detail. At ten o'clock the general was to review the local militia, followed by a reception hosted by the local Masonic Fraternity, and thereafter a great open air dinner and reception on the grounds of the State House. As always, Jacques Lazard was at the general's side during the receptions and seemingly interminable toasts and speeches. About noon, a black manservant dressed in the livery of the governor's house handed him a note on which was written (in French)

> *Dear M. Lazard,*
> *I have received word this morning that my escort for the evening has been delayed and may not arrive in time for the Ball. Of course, I must be there. I hope to speak with you again. I think of last night often...*
> *Yours,*
> *Elizabeth Troup*

More than five-hundred guests crowded the ballroom as the general was escorted about for formal introductions. The ladies were dressed in their finest silk gowns, all cut the Empire style of the day with high slender waists and short sleeves dropping off the shoulders. Jacques, dressed also in his finest, searched in vain for the governor's daughter. Finally, he saw her, and realized that she had been late, apparently awaiting her escort and coming only when it became evident he would not arrive. At about ten o'clock the old general bade the assembly adieu, the orchestra began to play, and the dancing began. Elizabeth and Jacques were inseparable, and soon became the talk of the ball.

Near midnight, Early Sheftall arrived on horseback. His carriage had broken an axle some twenty miles away, and he had walked until he came upon a farmstead that, for a price, gave him the use of a strong steed. Traveling through the twilight and then by the light of the moon, he had arrived just as the revelry was at its height. Elizabeth and Jacques had stepped outside through one of the open double doors of the ballroom and were so involved with each other that they did not see her fiancé until he was upon them. Sheftall would accept no explanation. He slapped Jacques across the cheeks with his gloves, hurled them at the Frenchman's feet and stepped back. Through the doorway, the trio could see the governor rushing across the ballroom toward them. After a short pause, Jacques stooped and picked up the gloves.

"You dropped these, I believe?" he said.

Sheftall snatched them out of his hand, snarling, "Tomorrow, across the river, at sunrise."

Jacques smiled grimly. "I presume that is a challenge, and, if so, I accept it. In my country, protocol allows me to choose the weapons." He paused. "Pistols."

This exchange had not been heard by the governor, and when he reached his daughter and Jacques, he reluctantly accepted her explanation that nothing of great importance had been said. She calmly reported that her fiancé had said he was not feeling well, and would be forced to miss the remainder of the ball.

The following morning, Jacques arose long before sunrise. He was uncertain if he had chosen the right course. As a red glow began to stain the eastern sky, he quietly slipped into the stable of his host, a prominent merchant who had offered lodging to the foreign dignitaries. Choosing carefully a chestnut gelding, he saddled the horse and led it quietly to the deserted street before mounting and riding toward the river bridge.

Waiting for him as the sun rose was a group of three men: Early Sheftall, his second, Asa Chandler, and a Negro manservant. "We had decided you were not going to show up," Sheftall taunted. "The sort of man who is so devious as to try to seduce the betrothed of another in his absence is also the sort of man who runs from a challenge."

"It appears that I've proven you wrong," Jacques replied in his accented English.

The manservant held out a boxed set of two smoothbore flintlock pistols as Sheftall explained, "I had to borrow these on short notice last evening, but I assure you that they will work adequately. Both are primed and loaded. Choose your weapon, Frenchy! It will be among your last acts."

Jacques removed his coat and lay it over the saddle of his horse. From the box he chose one of the pistols and checked the flint and primer. The rays of the morning sun painted the tips of the still barren trees red as the two figures stood back to back.

"Ten paces, turn and fire. I will count," Chandler, the second, called. "One. Two. Three..."

As he reached "Nine," Jacques felt a stinging blow to his right shoulder and heard almost simultaneously the report of a pistol. He fell to the ground as he screamed *"Bâtard!"*

Swiftly shifting his pistol to his left hand he rolled and fired as Sheftall was backing away toward his mount. The results of his shot were initially obscured by the smoke from the charge, but Jacques soon realized that he had apparently struck his opponent a dangerous blow. Dropping his weapon and clutching his bleeding shoulder, he approached the three others. Sheftall was lying on the ground, his head and shoulders supported by his manservant, with blood flowing from an angry gash on his left temple.

Chandler, who had been bent over the wounded man, leapt up and confronted Jacques. "He's wounded badly. He may die. We have two witnesses here who are willing to say you fired first and before the count. Sir, you will suffer the consequences of the laws of this state and will surely hang by the neck until dead!"

Jacques briefly considered his choices. With little hesitation, he picked up the empty dueling pistol, mounted his purloined steed, and set off in the opposite direction of that he knew the general's party would take.

He traveled as rapidly as his horse would allow for more than an hour, clutching his blood-stained arm. When he reached a small river, he left the road and followed it upstream for some distance until he came upon a spring flowing out of a rocky outcropping into a small pool that emptied into the river. Dismounting, he removed his shirt and inspected the wound made by the pistol ball. To his relief he found it was relatively superficial and should heal in a few days if infection did not set in. He bound the wound with cloth strips torn from his handkerchief and washed his blood-stained shirt in the clear water of the pool.

The sun was by now well in the sky, and the air began to warm. Jacques considered his situation. He had little more than the clothes on his back, his empty pistol, and a modest assortment of French and American gold coins in his purse that he fortuitously had stuffed his pocket as he left early that morning. He was no doubt a hunted man. Returning to Milledgeville would mean certain imprisonment. To keep moving was an uncertainty, but it offered hope. By putting his now dry shirt on and covering the remaining bloodstain with his jacket, he might pass for a traveler until fate or necessity gave him an opportunity. He remounted his horse and headed back to the road and away from the Capitol.

For two days and two nights Jacques traveled roughly east, following the sun by day and sleeping in the pine forests at night.. He avoided most farms and spoke only briefly to other travelers he met on the road. Twice he stopped to purchase food from the inhabitants of the occasional log cabin he passed. On the morning of the third day, tired, hungry and dirty, he arrived on the banks of a large river, across which he could see smoke drifting up from the cooking fires of half a dozen small houses. He hesitated and then prodded his horse to ford the river. A crudely lettered sign on the other side told him that he had entered Walkerville. The village was a rough-looking community of some five-hundred souls on the banks of the Opahatchee River. It had grown up around Walker's Store, an old Indian trading post that now sold everything from horses to meals and lodging. Jacques surveyed the muddy main street and concluded that the chief local industry must be whiskey production, as it seemed that every other establishment was a saloon.

Jacques weighed his next move. He was far enough away to be reasonably certain that he had at least one day, maybe two, before news of what happened in Milledgeville reached town. If he went to a larger city, it was likely that the search had already reached there, so perhaps he might give himself an extra day by hiding in this village. The fact that he was too tired and too hungry to run anymore without a rest helped him make up his mind. Tying his horse at one of the hitching posts on the main street, he walked into one of the saloons. To his relief, there were few patrons at this hour of the morning. He sat down at a table.

The proprietor ambled over. He was a rough-looking soul, adorned with a greasy bibbed apron and a week old stubble of graying beard.

"What'll it be, mister?" the proprietor blurted out.

It occurred to Jacques that he could count the man's remaining teeth on the fingers of one hand.

"Do you have food?"

"Of course, what do you think this is—a whorehouse? Where you from anyway? You talk funny."

The barkeep was suspicious.

"My accent is French," Jacques replied. "I'm from...er, New Orleans."

"Where you heading? We don't get many people passing through this town. If you got here you musta been heading here, or else you're lost."

Jacques thought quickly. "I'm looking for...a place to make some...investments."

The barkeep, whose name was Cowan, stroked his stubbled chin. "You're a gambler, ain't you? Yeah, that's it! Well, you may find a game here or you may not."

Jacques was silent. Let him think what he will.

"All I want is some food, a bed to sleep in, and a place to bathe. Can you provide those?"

"Listen, mister. For a price, I can provide anything you want. You got money? The bed will cost you fifty cents a day, and the bath is five cents extra. Full board's gonna cost you an extra quarter."

Jacques reached for his purse and spilled out a couple of small gold coins. He saw the proprietor's eyes widen. "Will these buy your silence as well?"

CHAPTER
FIVE

SOME HOURS LATER JACQUES AWOKE with a start. Remembering where he was, he lay back and surveyed his surroundings. He was in a tiny room entered from a storeroom behind the bar, furnished simply with a rope bed and straw-stuffed mattress, a crudely made chest with a washbasin on top, and a chair with a cowhide seat. Through a tiny window he could see that it must be just past sunset. A single wooden wall separated him from the main room of the saloon, and the sounds of raucous conversation filtered through, together with shafts of light from the lanterns that lit the room.

Suddenly he was aware that the conversation was about him.

"...and I tell you," he heard a gruff voice saying, "they said they were looking for a young blond Frenchie."

"Yeah, but are you sure they weren't Militia?" He recognized the proprietor's voice.

"I ain't gonna tell you again. No. It was something private," the gruff voice replied.

"Okay, tell us again what they said." A third voice this time. Higher pitched.

"This is the last time. They rode up and said good day, and they asked me if I lived around here and if I kept up with any strangers that might be in town. I said I did, and they said—or at least the one who was doing the talking said—they was lookin' for this Frenchman. He was about twenty-three or twenty-five years old, blond, and riding a chestnut gelding. Said he had something that belonged to them and that they wanted to talk to him."

The high-pitched voice interrupted, "The one that was talking, what did he look like?"

"In his twenties, dressed good. The main thing I noticed was that he had a big bandage around his head. Looked like it was covering up a cut or something on the left side."

Jacques smiled, silently relieved.

"What I was sayin'....They says this fellow was with Lafayette, and he was on the run."

"There! That's where you've got it wrong! If he was with Lafayette, he wouldn't be on the run." Cowan, the proprietor, spoke this time. "Listen to me. First, he's a foreigner, and he says he's from New Orleans. No reason to lie there. Second, he's carrying a pistol and a bunch of gold. I saw that. Third, he's on the run. We know that 'cause these people are looking for him and he thinks he paid me off to keep him hid.

You stupid ass, the man said Lafitte, not Lafayette. That's Lafitte the pirate. The Marquis of whatyoumacallit ain't gonna hang around with no dirty scum like the Frenchie. No siree! He's one of Lafitte's men who's done run off with some gold. Ever since he and his men got run outta New Orleans three, four years ago, they been casting about looking for a place to set up business. This fellow, he probably just took his share and some others, too, and went on the run. I done checked his horse. Ain't no gold hidden in his tack. He's got to have it stashed somewhere outside of town. If we play our cards right, it's gonna be us who end up with the gold. This is the plan..."

The saloon keeper went on to explain how he had the Frenchman convinced that he thought he was a gambler, and how he would let him play that role while he hid out for a week or so. Assuming he could play cards, they'd let him win some money, and then gradually up the stakes till the point he needed more gold for the bigger pots. All the while they would be telling him that men were in the area looking for him to keep him from leaving. When he finally had to slip out to get more gold, they'd secretly follow him and, "when he goes to dig up that gold, we'll put his body where the booty used to be."

They all laughed heartily.

Jacques realized he was in a dangerous situation, but luck had bought him a few days to think of a way out. Posing as a gambler would be no problem. Much to his family's dismay, he had extensive experience in the field gained in the salons and gaming halls of Paris. The seven months he had spent in America had given him more than adequate experience in this game called Poker which seemed to be so popular here.

His thoughts turned toward Elizabeth. He had been

willing to duel to protect her honor, yet he'd run at the threat of being arrested. At least Sheftall was alive, or so it appeared. If he were caught, the best he could hope for would be a charge of attempted manslaughter, plus horse thievery—both potential hanging offenses. If he tried to leave, even by stealth, he would be followed, as the barkeep and his friends would be expecting him to try to sneak back to his nonexistent hoard. His only hope was to contact Elizabeth. If she rejected him, he would either die sooner at the hands of the locals, or later for his crimes at the hand of the state. If she felt anything for him, perhaps—just perhaps—she might help.

Emerging from his room behind the bar he approached the three men at the table. The barkeep stood. "Ah, I see our friend is awake. Let me introduce my associates. This is Mister...ah, what is your name?"

"Teach, Edward Teach," Jacques replied.

"Well, Mr. Teach, this is Mr. Smith and Mr. Jones."

The gruff voice nodded and the high-pitched voice said, "Pleased."

The barkeep continued: "I've asked them to help me keep an eye out for you—no charge, of course. See, we run a little card game here most nights, the house takes a tip from each pot. Having a professional like yerself here can't do nothing but help business. Problem is, my friends say there was a gang of rough-looking men in town today lookin' for you. 'Course, we didn't say nothing. Your horse is in my stable; ain't nobody seen it. We'll be getting up some card games in your honor starting tomorrow night. Like I said, we're honored to have a man like yerself here. You do play Poker, Mr. Teach?"

Jacques nodded.

"Well, good!" the barkeep grinned. "Sit down so's we can get to know you better."

The following morning Jacques arose early and went to Walker's store, which in addition to everything else served as the local post office. He purchased paper and envelopes, and managed to find a new shirt to replace his blood-stained one, and a more rustic jacket with which to cover it. He wrote a letter to his hosts in Milledgeville stating that he had taken the gelding and offering to return the horse together with whatever amount they considered reasonable for its use, or to purchase it at their price. After thinking for a while, he wrote a second letter to Elizabeth. He apologized for all that had happened and begged her forgiveness. He told her that a letter to his hosts would soon arrive offering to pay for the horse. He told her his exact whereabouts and instructed her to either send for him herself, or, if her feeling deemed it appropriate, to have her father dispatch the Militia to whom he would surrender without resistance.

Taking both letters to the postmaster, he instructed him to send the one addressed to Miss Elizabeth Troup, Government House, Milledgeville, on the day's stage, but to hold the other and post it on tomorrow's stage. He reasoned that either letter could bring forgiveness or retribution, but by arranging for Elizabeth's to arrive first, the decision would be hers alone.

That night four prosperous locals joined Mr. Smith and Mr. Jones in a large gaming room in the back of the saloon. Lanterns were lit, whisky was set on the table, and the card games began. By midnight, Jacques had won a small sum, mainly due to the fact that the barkeep's friends kept throwing good hands. The other players seemed ignorant of the ruse, and two of them ended the evening with a significant net gain.

The next day, Jacques told his hosts he was going for a ride, but was warned that there were still rumors of men in the area searching for him. Mr. Smith generously offered to go along in order to vouch for him should he be questioned about his identity. It was even arranged for him to have another mount, lest the chestnut gelding be recognized. Jacques readily acceded to these conditions, and spent the next six hours thoroughly investigating the forest and farmland around Walkerville. It was not such a bad place after all, he decided. The land was flat and rich like his family's estates near Paris, and the vast virgin forest could be harvested and sent to market on the river. That night, the same group appeared for another card game, but this time the stakes grew higher. By the end of the evening, Jacques had won nearly two-hundred dollars, as had one other player, Solomon Cummings, a plantation owner with extensive holdings in cotton and timberland.

The next day was the second since Jacques had mailed the letter to Elizabeth, and the earliest possible time at which he could have receive a reply. He was waiting as the mail stage arrived, but there was nothing for him.

That evening, the card game started again as usual. Jacques had complained to the barkeep that if the stakes in these games kept getting any higher, he might need to "visit some friends" in the countryside to get more gold. His host feigned disappointment that he would have to be away, but offered to loan him a horse. After about two hours, the size of the pot had risen dramatically. Jones and two of the other players had dropped out of the game, leaving only Jacques, Smith, and Solomon Cummings who was hoping to repeat his success of the night before. After several more hands, Smith dropped out, leaving only Cummings and Jacques. Cummings was drinking a bit heavily, Jacques noted, but it did not seem to dull his abilities. The piles of gold coins shifted back and forth for the next hour.

Near midnight, most of the coins were sitting in front of Jacques, and Cummings was down to a small stack. The hand opened uneventfully. They both placed their antes, discarded cards and received others, and placed bets. In the lamplight, Jacques noted the subtle widening of Cummings's pupils.

"OK, Mr. Frenchman. I'm gonna have to raise you by a hundred dollars."

Jacques looked at his cards and looked at Cummings. "I'll meet that and go an extra hundred."

Cummings looked distressed. He counted his coins, and then shoved the entire stack into the pot. "Your hundred, plus what I've got, which is two-hundred-twenty more."

"I can meet that and raise you an extra hundred, but it looks like you're out of the game, Mr. Cummings," Jacques said softly.

"Wait a damn minute," Cummings retorted. "What you got in that pile? No—don't tell me. We've got, what, five witnesses here? I'll put up the Youngblood Place against whatever is in that pile to see your cards. It's got three-thousand acres of timberland and a good house. Here—give me a paper! I'll put it in writing."

Smith grabbed at Cummings's hand. "Sol... Hold on! Do you know what you're saying?"

"You're damn right I do! And I know what's in my hand! Well, Teach? Take it or leave it."

Jacques said calmly. "Write the paper."

Cummings grasped the quill and furiously scribbled a promissory note to Mister Edward Teach for the farm known as the Youngblood Place. Jacques looked at it and said calmly, "I must tell you my real name. It's Augustin Lazard. If you would be so kind as to make the note in that name we can proceed."

Smith, Jones and the barkeep exchanged knowing looks and nodded.

Grabbing another sheet of paper, Cummings rewrote the note, and after Jacques inspected it and handed it back, threw it in the pot. With a single stroke, he flipped over his cards to reveal four aces and a seven.

"Beat that, Teach, or Lazard, or whatever you name is."

"As I understand it, there are several hands that can beat that," said Jacques calmly noted. "Here is one of them."

He revealed a straight flush, ten high.

That night Jacques slept in his small room with the chest wedged against the door, a blanket covering the window and his reloaded pistol under his pillow. The promissory note was tucked inside a leather pouch which he strapped around his waist.

The following day was Sunday, and the saloon was closed until that evening. The mail stage ran daily, however, and he was waiting at Walker's Store when it arrived. He noted that, as he left the saloon, Cowan slipped out behind him and followed at a discrete distance. Again, the postmaster reported no mail.

The remainder of the day went quietly. He shared a midday meal with Cowan and his wife, a thin, harsh-looking woman whose hands were perennially red from the constant scrubbing required to keep the saloon clean. Cowan could not stop talking about Jacques's good fortune of the night before, and how, being from New Orleans and all, he might want to convert that useless fixed asset to cash. He opined that he might be able to make a reasonable offer, all in gold of course. Jacques remained noncommittal. No mention had been made of any card game that evening.

At five o'clock, the saloon opened for the evening, and the usual crowd of regulars streamed in. Among the first to enter was Solomon Cummings, searching for Jacques. He spied him at a table in the rear of the main room, and approached, smiling.

"Ah, Mr. Lazard, good to see you again this afternoon."

Jacques thought he looked unusually jovial for a man who had gambled away a farm worth a small fortune the night before. News of Cummings's loss had spread rapidly, and all eyes were on the two men.

"I was wondering if we might discuss my repurchasing the Youngblood Place?"

Cowan, who had been sitting at the table, stood up and confronted Cummings. "Now see here, Sol! You lost that farm fair and square. What my guest here chooses to do with it is his decision."

"I am well aware of that, my friend. But the transfer can not officially take place until the note is registered at the courthouse tomorrow, and a deed is prepared. Since today is the Sabbath, a day of rest and reflection, I thought Mr. Lazard might like to reflect on a large offer of gold coin."

Cummings flipped a modest-sized bulging sack on the table that clinked loudly as it struck the wooden top.

"Mr. Cummings," Jacques replied, "at this point I think I want to keep my winnings."

Cummings' eyes glowed. He hunched over and whispered in Cowan's ear. "As you wish, but perhaps some discussion of the alternatives might help you change your mind."

From his coat he drew a small pistol, cocked the flint, and pointed it at Jacques's heart. Turning to Cowan he growled, "You have something to get out of this, too, so why don't the three of us retire to your back room and help Mr. Lazard change his mind."

Cowan hesitated, and then, having apparently made his decision, got up and motioned for the other two to follow him.

The noise of conversation and clinking glassware that had resumed as the trio made it's way toward the gaming room suddenly stopped. Cummings half turned, concealing his pistol, but keeping it still pointed at Jacques's back. The cause of the sudden silence was two uniformed militiamen of the Governor's Regiment standing in the door of the saloon.

"Is this the establishment of Homer Cowan?" one of them asked.

Someone in the crowd called assent.

"We're looking for a Frenchman. Augustin Lazard. Is he here?"

By this time Cowan had unlocked the door, and Cummings tried to shove Jacques through it. In doing so he accidentally discharged the pistol, sending a ball into the wooden wall with a deafening explosion of wood splinters and smoke from the charge. The two militiamen were immediately in front of the three men. The older, a captain, looked at Jacques. "Are you Augustin Lazard?"

"I am, sir."

"Then you are to come with us."

The other officer took Jacques's arm as they led him away from the feeble protestations of Cowan and Cummings. They steered him outside to a carriage bearing the governor's seal on the door, and guarded by six more soldiers mounted on horseback. The captain opened the door and motioned for Jacques to enter.

Elizabeth, her mother, and the slave Julia were inside.

The governor's wife spoke. "We are here at my daughter's behest, Monsieur Lazard. Her betrothal to Mr. Sheftall has been canceled, and thanks to my husband's persistent questioning of his manservant, the truth about what happened in the duel has been revealed. As a sign of his contrition, the governor was able to prevail upon Mr. Sheftall to purchase for you the chestnut gelding. We would be pleased to have you accompany us back to Government House."

Elizabeth Pope Troup and Augustin D'Ayen Lazard were married on May 1, 1825, and were honored by the birth of a son, Lafayette Troup Lazard, on Christmas Day of that year.

CHAPTER SIX

FOLLOWING THE BIRTH OF THEIR SON, Jacques and Elizabeth returned to France. His mother, long widowed, had died, and as there were no other heirs, Jacques inherited extensive lands.

A second child, a girl, was born in 1828. With the Paris uprising of 1830, Elizabeth, concerned about the welfare of their children, insisted that they return to America to live. They sold the lands and houses, packed the silver and heirlooms and set sail for Savannah. After a brief stay in Milledgeville, they decided to move to Walkerville and live on the land that Jacques had won some years before. After months of searching, they chose a site on a bluff overlooking the Opahatchee River some five miles north of the village of Walkerville. The hill was surrounded by hundreds of acres of open pasture and beyond that thousands of acres of pine forests. On it they constructed a mansion of brick to Elizabeth's exacting specifications, and Jacques settled into the role of gentleman farmer with great relish. By the time of young Lafayette Lazard's marriage in 1846, the Youngblood Place, now renamed Marsellaise Plantation, encompassed more than twenty-five-thousand acres.

The mansion so lovingly constructed by Elizabeth Lazard did not survive General William Tecumseh Sherman's scorched earth policy of 1864. Lafayette Lazard served with distinction in the Georgia Guard, but returned home to find only his son, Elliot, alive, the other three children having died of diphtheria. Most of the family silver and some of the furniture originally brought from France had been saved by hiding it in the cabins of trusted slaves.

After the war, the plantation's lands remained intact, and Marsellaise Plantation prospered with the sale of timber and the production of cotton and corn. The town of Walkerville, which half a century earlier had been a rough frontier town, now boasted of shaded streets lined by the ornate Victorian homes of wealthy planters and merchants. In 1871 the ruined plantation house was reconstructed on its original site. In contrast to his mother, Lafayette chose the Greek Revival style, with huge Corinthian columns supporting the portico and an interior furnished with the finest woods, marbles and silks.

In 1877 Elliot married Mamie Campbell, daughter of a prosperous local banker, and over the next fifteen years they had five children. The youngest, born in 1892 and the only son, was named Lafayette after his grandfather, but, like his great-grandfather, was best known by his nickname, Jack.

Like his forebears, Jack Lazard was well educated, attending college at Emory College in Oxford, Georgia, and thereafter law school at Yale University in Connecticut. In 1917 at age 25 he joined the military, and saw service in the Adjutant General's office of the American Military Liaison in Paris. When he returned home in 1919, his father, by then nearing seventy, insisted that his son help take over management of the extensive family lands and business interests. In a compromise solution, Jack Lazard became a farmer, to which he devoted his mornings, and opened a law practice, to which he devoted his afternoons. As such, the compromise seemed to work well. Elliot Lazard had always employed several good overseers and managers, and Marsellaise Plantation almost ran itself.

A series of disastrous cotton crops in the 1920's caused by the boll weevil led to the decision to give up most row cropping, and concentrate on cattle and timber production. In 1927, Elliot Lazard died, and with his sisters all married in homes of their own, Jack inherited the plantation house and the vast Lazard lands, with his sisters each receiving a generous cash inheritance as their part of the estate. Two years later he married a young woman from Macon, Georgia, who bore him two children—a girl named Elizabeth, born in 1931, and a son named Troup, born in 1935.

Jack Lazard settled rapidly into the life of a gentleman farmer. In truth, the operation of Marsellaise Plantation required little of his time, and while he actively practiced law, he had sufficient income to pick and choose his cases at will. Conservative investment and practical management had made Jack Lazard a very wealthy man by the time of his wife's premature death from breast cancer in 1954.

Widowed at age sixty-two years of age, Jack Lazard was despondent. With his daughter married, and his son away at college, he felt utterly alone in the huge house. For a year after the funeral, he did nothing. The invitations and letters from well meaning friends went unanswered, and he found himself spending more and more time alone on the plantation, avoiding his law practice and contact with other human beings. The exact story about how Jack Lazard met Mellie McCranie has several versions, but there is no disagreement that, despite their age difference, they were immediately attracted to each other.

In June, 1955, Mellie Ann McCranie turned twenty-four and received a Master's Degree in Art History from the University of Georgia in Athens. Her parents lived in Walkerville, and she considered herself fortunate to be offered a position teaching history in the local high school. In truth, the job was entirely secondary to her love of horses, as she would have taken a position anywhere that allowed her as much time as possible with them. Her parents' small farm was adjacent to Marsellaise Plantation, and she had known the "Mr. Jack", as a kindly older neighbor when she was a child. She saw no reason why she should not be free to ride her stallion across his pastures and down his logging roads. She did this for months, seeing no one.

Late one afternoon in mid-October, while riding along the edge of a sagebrush covered field of head-high young planted pines, her horse was startled by the flurry of a covey of quail followed by two rapid blasts from a shotgun. The horse reared, throwing her to the soft earth, and galloped away into the waning daylight. Stunned, she found herself lying on the ground with two skinny brown-and-white hounds licking her face under the curious and observant eye of a distinguished gray-haired man dressed in a brown hunting coat and holding a smoking double-barreled shotgun.

"Are you hurt?" he asked anxiously. "My dogs were on a point, the birds flushed and I fired before I saw you. Who are you, and what are you doing here?"

Embarrassed but uninjured, Mellie leapt up, brushing the dirt off her riding pants. "Mr. Lazard, I'm your neighbor, Mellie Ann McCranie, and I was riding my horse until you spooked him. What does it look like?"

He stood for a moment, silently observing this defiantly beautiful young woman with flowing blond hair and flashing brown eyes.

Choosing his words carefully, he spoke. "Miss McCranie. Of course. No, I didn't recognize you. It's been a few years. Could I offer you a ride to the house? I'm sure you'll want to call your parents and let them know you'll be late."

From that instant, Jack Lazard became a different man. He suddenly developed a keen interest in horsemanship, and could be seen almost every afternoon riding across the fields in the company of his new neighbor. Mellie, on the other hand, was fascinated by her handsome and articulate companion, and by the art and treasures of Marsellaise Plantation. For years, the only visitors to the great house had been the doctors and nurses who had cared for the first Mrs. Lazard in her final illness. With the company of the vivacious Mellie McCranie, this all changed, and once again the ornate rooms echoed with laughter and happiness almost weekly at dinner parties and cocktail receptions. At an elaborate gathering on Valentine's Day 1956, Lafayette Lazard and Mellie Ann McCranie announced their engagement to be married that Spring. In January 1958, Mellie gave birth to a son whom she named

Benjamin Frederick Lazard in honor of her father and grandfather.

At first, Jack Lazard's friends had been leery of the union. But, once they came to know Mellie, they encouraged it. His own children, Elizabeth and Troup, were vehemently opposed to it, and did their best to block the wedding. They refused to attend the ceremony and, afterwards, visited only when protocol and holidays absolutely required it. Since both children now lived in Atlanta—Elizabeth with her husband, and Troup in medical school at Emory—they could find reasonable excuses for their absence.

The birth of young Ben changed all this. Even before Mellie brought him home from the hospital, Elizabeth and Troup angrily demanded a meeting with their father. They accused Mellie of being a self-seeking, money-hungry vixen who had married a tired old man for his fortune, and sealed her inheritance by having a child as soon as possible.

Jack Lazard listened to all this sadly, then calmly told his older children that the decision to bring another Lazard child into the world was a joint one between him and Mellie, and that he had been the one who had encouraged it. Two weeks later, he summoned Elizabeth, Troup and Mellie, now home from the hospital, to his law office.

The Lazard family, the husband with his second wife and two older children, sat in the oak-paneled conference room. They stared silently at one another.

Jack Lazard was the first to speak. "I have two things that I want to say first, and no matter what else we say here today, I want you to remember them. This first is that I love you all very much, and the second is that we, as a family, are very wealthy. In some ways I can understand how you all feel."

He turned toward his two grown children. "Troup,

Elizabeth, I know you must somehow feel that in marrying Mellie I betrayed your mother's memory," he said. "That is not the case. She knew she was dying for a long time, and saw that I suffered in many ways as much as she did. Before her death, she encouraged me to find someone else to be my companion 'in my dotage' as she said."

His voice caught, and he coughed. "When your mother died, part of me died, too," he continued. "And, no matter what else ever happens, that part of me and my life cannot be resurrected."

Turning to Mellie, he smiled. "And then I met Mellie. For the first time in so many years I realized that I might have a future as a member of the human race. She, and now Ben, have brought back to me so much of what I lost with my first wife's passing."

Jack Lazard paused and stared for a moment at his two children before continuing. "You, as my children, have treated Mellie as my wife and as your stepmother abominably. I cannot condone that, and it is only with great love that I can forgive it. You resent her for reasons that are invalid. You have accused her of greed and deception. Now, at this moment while I am healthy and sane, I want to tell you about my will. It has been written, signed and witnessed. There is a copy here in this office and one in the safe at the plantation. This is a summary of what the will says."

Reaching for his reading glasses, Jack Lazard drew a single folded sheet of paper from his inside coat pocket and began to read:

"First, on my death, I direct that I receive an appropriate burial, and that any outstanding debts be paid immediately. Secondly, I direct that the remaining cash and liquid securities in my estate be divided four ways, with one share to each of my children, and one share to my wife."

He looked up from the paper. "For your interest, if I were to die tomorrow, you would each receive more than five-hundred-thousand dollars in cash and securities."

He resumed reading. "For the land—roughly twenty-five-thousand acres—and the house, I leave this equally to my three children, but with a life estate for my wife. I direct that all expenses of the plantation and upkeep of the house be paid first out of income from the property, and those moneys above that amount be divided equally among my wife and my three child...."

Slamming his fist on the conference table, Troup leapt up, red-faced. "Dammit! Do you realize what you're doing? Are you some kind of a senile old fool? This woman...," He pointed at Mellie, "...is our age! She may well outlive Elizabeth and me both! Practically speaking, you're giving her the plantation. What if she remarries? Will they take over the house. I carry the Lazard name! It's mine, its my birthright, it's....!"

This time it was his father who slammed his fist on the table. "Troup! Sit down and shut up!" After a brief moment he consulted the paper again and resumed speaking. "There are a series of clauses in the will that state clearly that if any of my heirs contest the will or its contents, that person will automatically lose any inheritance that he or she might otherwise have received, and that share will be split among the remaining heirs. If any of you pre-decease me, again, that share will go not to your spouses or children, but will be split among the remaining direct heirs. That is the essence of it."

Removing his glasses, Jack Lazard folded the paper and replaced it in his jacket pocket. "I think I need to tell you one more thing. This is not necessarily the last version of my will. I am going to reserve the right to change it if I see fit, and feel absolutely no obligation to inform any one of you of that fact. I will base that decision, I suppose you could call it a threat, on your individual actions for the remainder of my natural life. If I do this, you will discover it at the reading of the will. So, be warned and act accordingly. You have much to lose."

He smiled mechanically at his family and, in turn, looked them each squarely in the eye.

CHAPTER
SEVEN

ON AUGUST 8, 1958, THE BODY OF TWENTY SEVEN
YEAR OLD Elizabeth L. Pope, nee Elizabeth Marie Lazard,
was found floating face down in the swimming pool of her
home on Collier Road in Atlanta. Her husband, one of the
younger partners of the law firm of Carter, McClendon &
Haynes, had left for his office at approximately 8:10 a.m. The
maid, Doretha Adams, arrived at approximately 10:00 a.m. as
per her usual schedule. Assuming that Mrs. Pope was not at
home, she let herself in with her key and began cleaning the
house. At 11:24 a.m., according to the records of the Atlanta
Police Department, a frantic call was received from Mrs.

Adams requesting an ambulance and police assistance at the Collier Road home of Broughton Pope.

The official report noted that Mrs. Pope was wearing a dressing gown over her nightgown, and apparently had not changed clothes after her husband left some three hours before the body was discovered. There were no signs of foul play or forced entry at the house. A broken mug containing coffee residue was found at the pool side.

According to the autopsy report, the cause of death was drowning. The body was unmarked except for a bruise on the left temple. Investigation revealed that, while the Popes were reasonably wealthy, she had carried no life insurance and was considered happily married to her husband, her only heir, according to a will prepared just after their marriage several years earlier. An interview with her brother, Troup Lazard, a medical student at nearby Emory University, established that he had visited Elizabeth and Broughton Pope the night before. He confirmed that she seemed in excellent spirits and had been planning a wedding anniversary vacation at Sea Island in September.

The medical examiner and coroner arrived at the conclusion that the deceased had been taking a morning stroll by the pool when, somehow, she slipped and fell in, striking her head in the process and drowning while unconscious. The cause of death was ruled accidental. Her husband remarked later that the only unusual thing was that he never knew that his wife had developed a taste for coffee.

Following the tragic death of his daughter, Jack Lazard seemed to sink into a deep depression. Mellie suggested a long vacation, and together with their young child, they left for three months on a round-the-world cruise. Spending so much time with his young son seemed to have a profound effect on the aging lawyer, and on their return, he appeared to have returned to his old self. Over the next year he turned over much of his law practice to his younger law partner, Crawford Matthews, and devoted increasing time to his family. In 1961, Troup graduated from medical school and announced his plans to pursue a career in internal medicine, eventually returning to Walkerville to practice. After three years of post graduate residency training at Cornell University in New York, he opened his practice in a building near the hospital on July 1, 1964. Unfortunately, one of the first diagnoses that he made was that of his father's inoperable kidney cancer.

Now seventy-two-years old, Jack Lazard spent his last months in introspection. He gave away large sums of money to local charities—$50,000 to the local hospital, $25,000 to his church, and a dozen or more gifts of $10,000 to various local organizations.

On a damp and cold Christmas Eve, 1964, he died quietly in the ornate bed that had been brought from France by his great-grandfather more than a century earlier and in which he had been conceived. His funeral was the largest in the memory of Walkerville, with the church filled to overflowing and mourners standing in groups in the church yard in a cold December drizzle.

In a codicil to his will dated four days before his death, Jack Lazard had named his law partner Crawford Matthews as the executor of his estate, and specifically requested that he have the specific responsibility to see that "all provisions of the will are strictly enforced in a timely manner".

On January 2, 1965, the heirs-at-law of Lafayette "Jack" Lazard, late of Adams County, Georgia, gathered in the same oak-paneled conference room of the law firm of Lazard & Matthews for the formal reading of his will. Matthews, now the executor, sat at the head of the long table. Troup Lazard, MD, sat on his right, and Mellie McCranie Lazard and her seven-year-old son Ben sat to his left. Many years later Ben would still remember the day vividly—his mother, dressed in black and weeping, his half-brother, dark and foreboding, and the attorney, thin, bald and very nervous.

Crawford Matthews began. "Mrs. Lazard. Young Ben. Troup." He nodded at each of them. "We're here for the formal reading of the will of your late husband and father. This will was written in February 1959, and has evidently not been changed since that time with the exception of a codicil added shortly before Jack's death appointing me executor. I understand that he had prepared another will about a year earlier, but this is apparently the latest version and, therefore, the only valid document. I have prepared copies for you to take home with you, but I would like to read the will in it's entirety first."

Picking up a thick sheaf of legal sized paper bound in a blue backing, he began.

"*I, Lafayette Lazard, being of sound mind, do make this Last Will and Testament...*"

For page after page Matthews read on, through the directions for burial, payment of debts, and half a dozen pages of small bequests to various individuals and groups that had won the late attorney's favor over the years. As he neared the end of the document, he paused and looked up. "The bequests I've just read to you, as well as the projected debts of the estate, are relatively small, amounting to perhaps twenty-thousand dollars. That leaves the bulk of the estate, including the land, the house, and approximately one point eight million dollars in cash and securities. Continuing with paragraph 48 on page 9, I want you to listen carefully to the following:

> *"With regard to the remainder of my estate, I make the following bequests. To my wife Mellie McCranie Lazard I leave the sum of twenty-five-thousand dollars in lieu of a Year's Support. If she chooses to object to this amount by force of suit, then I leave her nothing, and request that my executor use the full resources of the Estate to resist this challenge. To my son, Benjamin Frederick Lazard, I leave the sum of five-thousand dollars to be used for his support until such time as he shall reach the age of majority.*
>
> *"To my son Troup Warthen Lazard, I leave the remainder of my estate in fee simple for his exclusive use and that of his heirs."*

Mellie began to sob softly. "That's not what he said.... How could he leave us alone like this?"

Matthews interrupted her. "Mrs. Lazard, I'm afraid there's more. Let me read on.

> *"I furthermore direct that my executor seal and inventory my house within twenty-four hours of the reading of this Will, and that my current wife and her son be directed to vacate the premises within a period of no more than one week beyond this date."*

Troup Lazard stared at Mellie and Ben, his face expressionless.

One week later, a moving van backed up to the columned portico of the great house of Marsellaise Plantation and took the widow, her son and a few pieces of furniture and personal possessions to her parents' small home nearby, where she once again occupied the same bed in the same bedroom that she had as a child.

In the Fall of 1965, Adams County Consolidated High School had a new art history teacher, a youngish widow who had retaken her maiden name of McCranie. Two years later she married Myron Pike, an electrician who worked for one of the local manufacturing plants. He, in turn, formally adopted his stepson, Ben, who took his family name. When Myron was laid off some eighteen months later, the family moved to Savannah where he found a similar job. They lived in a modest neighborhood on Wilmington Island, and Ben graduated from Savannah Central High School in 1976.

Ben Pike was intelligent, aggressive and a natural athlete. He was All-State in football for three of his four high school years, and to everyone's surprise, turned down a football scholarship to the University of Georgia to join the Army. He told his friends he wanted to see a different part of the world. After completing basic training, he volunteered for specialized training in jungle warfare and counter-insurgency tactics. He was discovered to have a natural proficiency for languages, was trained in Spanish, and spent most of his four-year hitch in Panama as an instructor in the Army Jungle Warfare School.

After his discharge, Ben moved back to Savannah where he attended college courtesy of his GI benefits, and after being accepted to the Medical College of Georgia, was awarded a full scholarship on the basis of scholastic merit. After his graduation from medical school, he did three years of post graduate residency in internal medicine at Vanderbilt University in Nashville, Tennessee, joining the faculty in General Internal Medicine at the completion of his training.

Ben's first year in Nashville left little time for anything except work. The year began with the arrival of the newly graduated physicians on July 1, and ended in an indecipherable blur some twelve months later when he made the traditional transition from "intern" to "resident". He didn't remember the first time he saw Erica, but realized after a few weeks that he began to watch for her almost daily. She had just graduated from nursing school and was working the 3 to 11 shift on the geriatrics floor. He discovered that she usually went by the cafeteria for a quick snack after her shift, and he, in turn, begin arriving at the cafeteria every evening at 11:20 a.m waiting for her to come in with the other nurses some ten or fifteen minutes later. It was June, and for the hundredth time in nearly a year, Ben cursed the duties that kept him from having enough time to date, much less develop a viable relationship with a member of the opposite sex.

Erica was average height, with long brunette hair that she kept tucked under her nurse's cap at work, and let down as soon as she left the patient floor. She had bright blue eyes, and a too-loud silly laugh that echoed across the cafeteria. All this Ben observed from a distance and vowed to change his unwanted celibacy. By September they were sharing an apartment.

The subject of marriage had never really come up in a formal sense. Erica's parents, appalled by her living arrangements, finally came to accept Ben, and hoped they would formalize their relationship.

When Ben finished his residency, Erica flew with him to half a dozen medical schools across the country looking at and interviewing for faculty positions. In the end they elected to stay in Nashville, celebrating the end of his formal training (and the dramatic increase in his salary) by moving into a larger apartment in a better part of the city.

As the fourth year of their living together became the fifth, strains developed in the relationship. There was no one thing in particular, but many small things together. At one time Erica had had the bigger salary, now it was Ben. Their friends were no longer the beer, pretzels and football crowd of Ben's student years, but rather the silk tie, pearls and white Chablis group of junior faculty members in an aristocratic Southern medical school. Ben's work hours increased dramatically as he took on more and more responsibility for teaching and clinical research. They began to fight more often, and sometimes Erica would spend days visiting with college roommates in Atlanta or Memphis.

By June of their fifth year together they both knew things would never be any better than they were, yet neither had the courage to end the relationship. One morning after a particularly brutal argument the night before, Ben's beeper went off, signaling him to call the hospital paging operator. The familiar voice announced, "Dr. Pike, I've got a Mrs. Adeline Powell on the line to talk with you."

"I don't have any idea who she is. What does she want?" Ben replied.

"She said she thought you'd know her. I'll find out."

The line went still for a moment before she returned. "She says she's the widow of Dr. Paul Powell, from somewhere in Georgia, Walterville, I think."

"Walkerville, where I was born. Sure, I'll talk with her."

An elderly female voice came on the line. "Dr. Pike, this is Adeline Powell. You may remember my husband, Dr.

Paul Powell."

"It's been a long time, but I do remember his name. I'm sorry to hear of his passing."

"Thank you, Dr. Pike. It was all so sudden. But let me explain why I'm calling you. I knew your mother well before her death, and I remember her telling me that you had planned to go to medical school. My husband had been in practice here for forty-three years when he died of a massive heart attack last month. I've worked all those years in his office, and I've been trying to close out things, send the patients to new doctors, and all—you know. Let me get right to the point. The doctors here are all so busy that they just can't take on that many new patients. We need somebody to take over Paul's practice."

"Mrs. Powell, I'm really flattered that you called me, but I'm really not..."

"Please let me finish, Dr. Pike. I called you because I knew your lovely mother, and I remember what happened to her when your father died. You both were truly done wrong. That has bothered me all these years, and I see a chance to do something for you. I'd like you to have my husband's practice."

Ben paused. "Again, Mrs. Powell, I do appreciate your calling, but, to begin with, I have a good position here at Vanderbilt, and I seriously doubt if I could afford your husband's practice if I wanted it."

"Dr. Pike, you don't understand. I'm offering to *give* you my husband's practice in order to make sure his patients get taken care of. Money is not a consideration. I'm seventy-two-years old, all my children are grown and married, I have no debts, and my husband left me with a very comfortable nest egg. I want you to take over the practice, as is. You can have everything—the building, the equipment and the accounts receivable. I've been the bookkeeper and there's more than fifty-thousand dollars on the books, most of which should be collectable. I've even got a place for you to live until you find a place of your own. We have a cute little cabin on a lake just outside of town. I won't be using it much since Paul is gone. It used to be in the country, but you know how this town has grown. Anyway, it's private, and you can stay there as long as you like."

After a very long moment of silence Ben replied, "Mrs. Powell, maybe we should talk after all."

As he expected, Erica begged him not to move, and then refused to consider moving with him. She would not even travel to Walkerville to see the town. "Too small for a decent mall," she said.

Without saying so, they both realized this parting was inevitable and for the best. On July 24, Ben arrived alone in Walkerville, driving his faded blue Taurus and pulling his worldly possessions in a orange and white U-Haul trailer. He set up housekeeping in the late Dr. Powell's lake house and vaguely wondered what he would do with the rest of his life.

Chapter
Eight

EVEN WITH HIS YEARS OF TRAINING and exposure, he never quite grew accustomed to the smell. If someone had asked him to describe it, he imagined he would ask them in turn to describe the smell of a rose, or of rotting flesh. It was a unique and very specific odor, a nebulous combination of stale urine and diaper pails, vaguely disguised by the lemon/pine stench of industrial disinfectant. Ben wondered if he would notice it if he were, by some cruel whim of fate, relegated to wait out the remainder of his life in a nursing home.

As was the case with so many physicians, the patients in Dr. Powell's practice had aged with him. Unlike their doctor's sudden demise, however, many of them had outlived him only to await a piecemeal death in the celadon green rooms of Golden Age Manor. As one octogenarian had told him years ago: "When one finally realizes the inevitability of the end, you can only hope that the mind goes first so you're not forced to watch it take place."

Golden Age was his third and last nursing home of the morning. Adams County had five such institutions, but Dr. Powell had admitted to only three of them. He'd started at seven-thirty, and now by eleven had introduced himself to twenty-six of Dr. Powell's former patients who had chosen to stay under his Ben's care when he took over the practice. He hoped to be finished by noon when the weekly Sunday-after-Church flood of relatives came by for their obligatory visits. Dr. Powell had had only eight patients in Golden Age, and assuming no one had any major problems, he might be able to make it.

The RN on duty piled his charts on a stainless steel cart, and they set off down the stained green carpet of the first hall, past a changeable sign that read

TODAY IS SUNDAY
THE DATE IS AUGUST 14
THE NEXT MEAL IS LUNCH

He wondered if they posted the deaths with the same emphasis.

The RN was older, perhaps in her sixties, and truly seemed to care about the "residents," as the patients were called. She said her name was Mrs. Lewis and that she'd worked at the facility for fifteen years. She was a chatty sort, prattling on about how cute old Mr. Heldreth had been making goo-goo eyes at Mrs. Price, and similar such events in the necessarily fluid social structure of Golden Age Manor.

The first two patients were ladies in their seventies, but aged beyond their years with Alzheimer's Dementia. They shared a double room with a wonderful view of a large garden, but both stared blankly at a wall-mounted television set and the rantings of a white-suited evangelical minister.

"Mrs. Avirett and Mrs. Hawkins don't say much," the nurse explained. "They make good roommates. They haven't complained of anything in years."

Ben introduced himself but got no more than a cursory glance as the elderly pair continued to stare at the preacher who was now on his knees praying. With some annoyance, they allowed him to examine them briefly, then resumed staring at the television as he reviewed their charts and wrote a brief progress note.

"I'm sorry they didn't have much to say," the nurse apologized. "They don't get many visitors. But you'll like the next resident. She knew you were coming and said she was looking forward to meeting you."

They paused outside the next room before knocking. "This is Miss Ollie Duggan. She's one of our youngest residents. I think she's, let's see..." The nurse looked at the chart. "...sixty-five. Really, the main reason she's in here is that she doesn't have any family to take care of her at home. She's been blind with glaucoma for years, and has had diabetes and all sorts of complications from that. But she's really bright and spends her days listening to books on tape. We've got her in a private room because...well, she's able to care a little bit more than most of the other residents. Let me introduce you."

She knocked on the door and, without waiting for an answer, pushed it open. "Miss Ollie?" she called cheerily.

Ben saw a gray-headed figure in a wheelchair looking out the window. She turned at the sound of her name and smiled. "Janice, it that you? Where's my new doctor?"

She was a cherubic-faced, plump lady, with a wide smile and sightless eyes that gazed aimlessly through white-scarred corneas. As she turned her wheelchair around, Ben could see that both legs had been amputated above the knee.

"Right here, Miss Ollie. I brought him to see you."

Miss Ollie beamed. "Ben, it that you? Come here and let me touch your face. I still remember you as a little boy." She reached out for him as he sat on the edge of the bed and took her hand.

"Miss Ollie, it's a real pleasure to meet you," Ben replied.

"Meet me? You don't remember me? But then, maybe you were too small. You were the cutest little thing."

Ben blushed. "I'm a big kid now."

"Oh, I'd give anything to be able to see you. I hear that you look just like your father when he was your age. You know I was your father's secretary at the law office for nearly nine years? I finally had to quit when my sight began to leave me. I've got glaucoma, you know, and well, back then...." Her voice trailed off for a moment, then continued. "But I'm doing fine now. Being blind is not so bad if you've got good people to help you, like Mrs. Lewis here."

She smiled and reached blindly for the nurse's hand. "I loved your father. He was the most wonderful man. Gentle. Caring. I worked for him and Mr. Matthews until right after Elizabeth's accident. When you and your parents went on that cruise the work was a bit slower so I took some time off to have surgery on my eyes. They thought they could help me, but things got worse and I lost most of my vision. I stayed with my sister until she died about ten years ago. By then my diabetes was getting worse. They had to amputate my legs and I ended up here."

"Well," Ben said, flipping open the chart. "If I'm going to be your doctor, I need to check you over a bit."

With Mrs. Lewis's help, they lifted her to the bed where Ben quickly examined her and found no new or unstable problems.

As he was writing a progress note, Miss Ollie spoke. "You know, I'll never understand about why your father changed his will. I suppose you've heard the story."

"Probably a million times. But that was years ago, and all water under the bridge now. I certainly can't worry about it." He continued writing.

"But it was so unlike your father," she persisted. "He loved Mellie more than life itself, and you were the joy of his life. Lord, I'd worked for him for almost nine years. I think we got to be good friends in a sense of the word. I remember he came to see me at least once a month, for years and years, and never once did he mention changing the will, or having a falling out with Mellie. I just can't understand it."

"Like I said, neither can I," Ben replied. "But who would know? You can't raise the dead."

Miss Ollie turned to Mrs. Lewis. "Has he seen my next door neighbor yet?"

"No. Why?" she asked.

"Well, maybe you can ask him. Mr. Matthews. Your father's partner. He's been here for about a year now."

"Good God! Is that man still alive?" Ben exclaimed.

"In a sense of the word," Mrs. Lewis replied dryly. "His body still works, but I can't say so much for his mind. Alzheimer's."

Ben had last seen Crawford Matthews at the reading of his father's will. The lawyer had been in his forties at the time, and despite the nearly three decades that had passed, he still looked very much the same. He stood before the window, staring out toward the parking lot. Still thin, almost to the point of gauntness now, and even more bald, the sight of him still sent a shiver down Ben's spine. As clearly as if it were yesterday, he recalled his mother's sobbing and the overwhelming fear of the loss of everything that he had known up to that point in his life.

They stood in the doorway as Mrs. Lewis spoke. "Mr. Matthews is really a pitiful case. I hear he was a very bright and successful lawyer at one time. Did Miss Ollie say that he was in practice with your father? Anyway, his mind comes and goes now. One day he seems as normal as any healthy seventy-five-year old, and the next he'll get lost on his way to the bathroom. He stays confused most of the time now. The problem is that he is still fairly strong and can get about. We have to watch him like a hawk to keep him from wandering into other patient's rooms or even out the front door."

Ben flipped through the chart before entering the room. Other than the dementia, he saw no active problems. He spoke softly, "Mr. Matthews?"

The old lawyer whirled around and stared wide-eyed at Ben. His mouth opened and he tried to speak. He paled, his eyes rolled back in his head, and he began to crumple toward the floor.

Rushing to his side, Ben and the nurse managed to grab him before he totally collapsed. They placed him gently on the bed, laying him down flat and putting a pillow under his legs. Ben quickly examined him and determined he had suffered a simple faint. No major problems. Nurse Lewis brought a damp cloth and folded it across his forehead. Momentarily, his eyes began to flutter and open, half wide at first, and then with a terrified look when he saw Ben's face.

"Hey, it's OK, Mr. Matthews. You're fine. I'm Dr. Pike. I'm going to be your new doctor."

Matthews tried to force himself up and began to wail, "God, you're back. How can that be, Jack? You're supposed to be dead, dead. Maybe I'm the one who's dead. Dead and in hell. You're the devil, aren't you, here to claim my soul. God, forgive me, have mercy on my soul…"

His eyes rolled back and, once more, he lost consciousness.

Mrs. Lewis spoke to Ben. "He does this sometimes. He gets confused and then gets agitated and works himself into a faint. Dr. Powell used to just order a sedative and he'd be fine in an hour or so."

Ben examined the unconscious lawyer. After satisfying himself that the man was stable, he ordered lorazepam 1 mg. IM and wrote a long progress note. After finishing, he looked up at Mrs. Lewis. "He called me Jack. I guess he thinks I'm my father come back to life. Does he get confused like that often?"

"A pretty good bit," she replied. "If it happened in 1965 or 1975 sometimes he's sharp as a tack. More recent things, well…" She rolled her eyes. "He lives in the past a lot. He'll be fine. I'll keep an eye on him while you see the rest of your patients."

Miss Ollie had wheeled herself to the open door. "I heard all the hollering and commotion. Is everything all right?"

"Sure, honey, it's fine," Mrs. Lewis replied, smiling as if she could be seen. "You get on back to your room, now."

"I heard him call you 'Jack'. He sounded terrified," the blind woman said.

"You get back to your room, now, Miss Ollie," Nurse Lewis said and smiled again.

CHAPTER
NINE

THE OFFICE WAS NOT what he would have chosen for himself. But, who was Ben to argue, considering the fact it had been given to him, a gift from Dr. Powell's widow?

The building was located across the street from the hospital. Other than that, it really had little to offer, especially from an aesthetic viewpoint. Dr. Powell had designed it himself in the late 1960's—his own ersatz interpretation, perhaps, of what could best be described as a small town version of the Internationalist Style. The basic construction was concrete block faced with brick, topped by a uninspired flat roof supported by steel joints. The windows were exaggerated horizontal slits set high the walls. They provided adequate light and privacy without curtains, but gave the exam rooms the feel of a psychiatric isolation cell.

All this perched on a poured concrete floor, making renovations impossible without resorting to the use of a jack-hammer and backhoe.

The physician's private office was no better. It, too, had painted concrete block walls, but with the concession of a private bathroom and a door opening directly onto the side parking lot for quick trips to the hospital or emergency room. The lobby was adequate size but furnished with vinyl-covered chairs and settees giving it a distinctly institutional flavor. On the positive side, Dr. Powell had kept meticulous dictated notes, and he had computerized his billing and bookkeeping system two years earlier. From a professional and business standpoint, the office was up to date and well managed.

Ben had arrived on a Sunday, and the next day met with the office staff. Mrs. Powell was present to introduce him. She had kept everyone on the payroll while she made efforts to find someone to take her late husband's practice. They all seemed grateful for the chance to continue working in the same office. Excluding his wife who worked without pay, Dr. Powell had employed four office staff members. Doreen, a pert and competent twenty-two-year old, served as reception-ist, scheduler and general gatekeeper. Hilda was the transcrip-tionist. Barbara, the former full time insurance clerk, had taken over bookkeeping duties. They both shared insurance and col-lections jobs. Dr. Powell's nurse and de facto boss was Rachel Edwards, a raven-haired RN about Ben's age who ran the office like a fine-tuned machine. Ben soon discovered that she had her own daily regimen, and since it seemed to work, decided to continue it. Dr. Powell had usually arrived at nine, and she would be waiting with the most pressing telephone messages and problems, as well as a list of his day's scheduled appointments. When the morning's patients were finished, she would remind him what he needed to do while he was out of the office on his supposed lunch hour. In the afternoon when the last patient was seen, she would lay a pile of documents requiring a signature in front of him and refuse to leave until he'd signed them all.

Ben scheduled his first patient for Monday, August 1. He spent the preceding week getting to know the office staff and routine and making sure that his application for hospital staff privileges was in order so that he could start admitting patients the same day. The local hospital, Adams Memorial, was a quasi-public, 110-bed community hospital serving Walkerville and Adams County as well as five or six populous communities in neighboring counties. There were twenty-eight physicians on the staff, including three other internists, seven family practitioners, two pediatricians, three general surgeons, and two OBG's. The ER was covered by a full-time four-physician group of which Carter Steed was the senior member. By August 15 and the beginning of his third week of practice, Ben had admitted and discharged half a dozen patients and was beginning to feel comfortable with the routine.

Monday morning was uneventful, at least as Monday mornings go in the office of a small town doctor. There were the usual scheduled patients, augmented by the walk-ins and the "emergency" work-ins that often amounted to little more than colds and sprains. With effort, Ben managed to finish by the appointed time of 1 p.m. He dropped by the hospital to check on a new admission and grabbed a hamburger at a fast food drive-thru before starting on the afternoon's patients.

By five, he was finished with patients but exhausted. He dictated for half an hour and reviewed the day's mail—throwaway medical journals and drug company advertising mostly. The staff was gone by 5:30. Fifteen minutes later, Ben emerged from his private door and headed for his car. As he walked across the lot, he noted that it was empty except for a dark blue Ford sedan parked strategically near the driveway to the street. Seeing Ben, two men in dark suits got out of the car and walked deliberately toward him. Ben stopped as they approached.

"Dr. Pike?" the older of the two inquired. Both were in their mid-forties, graying at the temples.

"Yes? Can I help you?" Ben sized them up. Conservatively dressed. Salesmen, maybe, but not smiling.

Gray at the temples reached in his coat pocket and produced a black leather folder containing an ID which he opened for Ben to see. "Dr. Pike, I'm Officer Latham, and this is Officer Roble. We'd like to speak with you if possible."

"Is this about a patient? I'm on my way to the hospital and I'd really prefer to talk with you during office hours. I'm..."

The younger man spoke. "We deliberately waited until your office staff was gone for the day," he said in a slight Spanish accent. He had jet-black hair and carried a brown briefcase. "This is a matter of some importance. We wanted this to be a private conversation."

Ben took the case which Latham had continued to hold out and looked at the photo ID. At the top was printed "Department of Justice," and, under that in slightly smaller print was, "Immigration and Naturalization Service."

Latham spoke again. "We're with the INS."

"So I see. What can I do for you?"

"We'd prefer to speak with you inside," Roble pressed.

He started back toward the office door.

Ben took the hint and they followed him inside. He sat behind his desk. They took the two chairs facing him across Dr. Powell's worn teak desk.

Again, Latham spoke first. "Dr. Pike, we understand you were in the emergency room Saturday night and early Sunday morning when a man named Carlos Ortega was brought in. Is that correct?"

"Partially. I was asked to come in for a short while after midnight to help translate. The ER staff didn't have much history about what had happened to him, and the men who apparently knew him didn't speak much English. I speak a little Spanish and translated for them. I wasn't directly involved otherwise. Why are you interested?"

Roble answered. "We have reason to believe that Ortega may have been an illegal alien, and as..."

Ben was curious. "Wait a minute. You're looking for 'illegal aliens?' Half the farms and ninety-nine percent of the Mexican Restaurants around here are full of them. Why this guy?"

"Dr. Pike," Latham replied, "a man is dead, and as we understand matters, the cause of death has not been established. The INS has a responsibility to investigate such cases. Immigrants, legal or illegal, are frequently the subjects of abuse in this country. We want to be certain that no federal laws were violated."

"Why don't you talk with Dr. Steed—or the coroner, Elmo Kantt. You might even want to try Dr. Lazard. I understand Ortega was an employee on his farm?"

"We've talked with Dr. Steed, and we left Mr. Kantt's funeral home just prior to coming over here," Roble answered. "We just need two things from you."

"Which are?"

"We want to know exactly what Ortega said before he died, and we'd like you to look at some photos to see if you recognize any of the subjects as being there that night."

Roble opened his briefcase and began rummaging around inside for a folder of photographs and a spiral bound notebook, which he found and placed on the desk.

Latham continued the questioning. "Dr. Pike, tell us to the best of your memory exactly what happened."

Ben recounted what had happened from the time he received the call until the time he left shortly before 3 a.m. Roble scribbled notes in the notebook. When he came to the part about Ortega trying to write a message, Latham stopped him and had him repeat it in greater detail three times, questioning him closely as to whether or not what was written could be interpreted as any more than two letters and the part of a third.

"So, that's it? D-E-something and nothing more?"

"For the third and final time, yes!"

Roble opened the folder of photographs and handed them one by one to Ben. About half were mugshot type views. The others were evidently taken on the street with a telephoto lens. Ben noted that the photos were numbered and that care had been taken to delete any information that might reveal their source. The mugshots had been trimmed to remove the name of the jail and/or other identification under the subject's face, and some of the street scenes appeared to have been deliberately cropped to cut out background scenery. He took his time and studied them all carefully. None were familiar.

"Why are you going to such trouble? What do these men have to do with Ortega?" he asked.

Latham paused. "Doctor, we'd like to answer your question, but this is part of an ongoing investigation."

"I thought you said you were following up on a death of a man who might be an illegal alien. Now you say it's part of an ongoing investigation. I don't really understand. Are you telling me everything?" Ben demanded.

"As much as we can," Latham replied.

Ben was becoming angry. "I'm really not the person you need to spend time with. I just moved here three weeks ago. If it's that important, put the pressure on Kantt. Get the autopsy results. Better yet, do the autopsy yourself. Have them release the body to you."

"Kantt did." Roble cut him off.

Ben thought for a moment. "Well, good! Take it back to Atlanta, or where ever and..."

Roble cut him off again. "Maybe you can just look at it for us, Dr. Pike," he replied, a trace of sarcasm in his voice. He took a Zip-Loc plastic bag out of his briefcase and tossed on the desk. "Let's get your thoughts on the autopsy."

Ben looked at the bag. It contained some sort of gray granular material. "What is this?"

"That, Dr. Pike, is Señor Ortega. Or what remains of him after Mr. Kantt had him cremated last evening."

CHAPTER
TEN

"THAT'S EXACTLY RIGHT, DOCTOR," Elmo Kantt hissed
over the telephone. "It *is* none of your damned business!"

The line clicked loudly and went dead.

Latham and Roble had left. Their story was that Kantt,
in his position as coroner, had determined that Ortega's death
did not occur as a result of any known foul play, and it would
be up to the sheriff's department and district attorney to make
more out of it if they wanted to. He explained that he saw no
need to waste the valuable time and resources of the State
Crime Lab for a "dead Spic" (they quoted him), and that he had
the concurrence of the county medical examiner, Dr. Lazard.

They departed then, but not before they had given Ben a plain white business card with a number to call should any additional information come to mind. Ben jotted down their tag number as they drove out of the parking lot. As soon as they were out of sight, he immediately called Kantt—and had the phone slammed down in his ear.

Ben's next call was to Hoke Brantley at the sheriff's department. After a brief pause, the chief deputy came on the line. "Deputy Brantley."

"Hoke. This is Ben Pike. What is this about Kantt cremating that guy who died in the ER? I just had a couple of federal guys in here investigating and ...."

"Whoa, Ben, slow down a minute. Did you say federal guys? And what's all this stuff about a cremation, huh?"

"Sorry," Ben replied. "Ortega, the guy who came into the ER Saturday night, remember?"

"Sure, of course."

"Well, two men from the Immigration and Naturalization Service were just here asking me questions about what happened. I told them they needed to talk with Kantt, and they said he'd already cremated the body. Hoke, the man hadn't been dead twenty-four hours, and no autopsy was done! That whole case smelled of foul play. Is that the way you do things around here?"

"Ben, this is bad." Hoke sounded concerned. "Let me check on some things and I'll call you right back. Where are you?"

"At my office. And, Hoke, can you do me a favor? There's something that's not right about this. How about running their tag number so I can find out if these guys are really who they say they are?"

Half an hour later the private line rang. It was Hoke.

"Ben, look, I've checked things out with Kantt and I found out about the tag for you. It seems pretty clear to me that an autopsy should have been done, but there's not a hell of a lot we can do about it now. Kantt's point is that Ortega died in the hospital of an irregular heart beat, which I guess is correct. They've got some witnesses who say he was bad to drink, and by his reconstruction of things, there's nothing he needs to present to a coroner's jury. He asked me if I thought I could come up with something to present to a grand jury, and I really had to say no. Kantt did send off some toxicology, but if that's negative, then we've just got a man that died of unknown reasons. Kantt thinks he had a bad heart."

"Dammit, Hoke, Kantt's not a doctor!"

"Well, that's the other thing. Dr. Lazard is the medical examiner, and Kantt says when he checked with him, that Dr. Lazard told him he'd been treating Ortega for heart trouble ever since he hired him. Lazard said he believed that Ortega had some sort of heart seizure to cause his problems."

"Hoke, it's just not right." The frustration showed in Ben's voice.

"Oh, about the tag. The car is registered to a federal government car pool in Atlanta. It's used by multiple agencies, so there's really no way I can find out quickly who had it out on a given day, but it sounds legit. Ben, I know it's been a long time since you moved away, and in a sense of the word, you're kinda new around here. If you need anything, or if I can do anything for you, let me know."

"Thanks, Hoke. I appreciate your help."

Ben hung up and stared at the phone for a few minutes. He had always been a loner, with few close friends. With Erica gone, he was again on his own. It had been a long time since he'd seen Hoke, but it was good to know there was at least one person he could call on for help.

❧

On Tuesday morning when Ben arrived at the hospital for rounds, there was a message waiting for him at the main nurses' station. Elton Shaw, the hospital administrator, wanted to see him immediately.

He took the elevator to the ground floor and walked down the tile halls from the patient care areas to the carpeted floors and muted pastels of the administrative wing of Adams Memorial Hospital. Shaw's secretary, the stout and stern Mrs. Leggett (he decided later that she didn't have a first name) ushered him in without waiting.

"Dr. Pike. Ben. You don't mind if I call you Ben, do you?" Elton Shaw was effusive. At fifty-four years old, he was bald, five-feet-four-inches tall at most, and given to natty suits and bowties. Despite his appearance, he'd been an effective administrator, or at least this seemed to be the general agreement amongst everyone when the subject had come up.

He waved Ben to a chair. "Sit down, sit down. Coffee? Mrs. Leggett, let's get Dr. Pike some coffee. You do drink coffee don't you?" It occurred to Ben it would be served whether he drank it or not.

Mrs. Leggett appeared almost instantly with a tray bearing two mugs, a steaming carafe of coffee, stirrers and a dish containing sugar cubes, artificial creamer and a couple of chemical sweeteners in blue and pink packets.

Ben said little except good morning. He sipped his coffee black while Shaw fussed over his own mug, using a packet each of sugar and creamer, and two packets of the pink chemical. "Great bitter-sweet taste wakes you up in the morning," he explained.

Ben decided he was nervous.

"So, how's it going?" Shaw inquired.

"Great. Enjoying myself immensely," Ben replied. He strained to be cordial. "Mr. Shaw, I've got to make rounds. Did you have a reason for calling me down here? I need to see a couple of patients before I go to the office."

"Well...this is a bit embarrassing," Shaw began, "because you.... well, what I'm trying to say is that we—the hospital—didn't recruit you like we do most new doctors in this town, and I guess I don't—I didn't know you as well as I should. First of all, let me say that you're one of the most highly qualified members of the staff, and if we had a chance to recruit you as a new doctor to come here and practice in Walkerville, we would in a minute. It's just that Dr. Powell's wife was the one who contacted you—I looked at your résumé of course—and we're really glad you're here, and..."

"Mr. Shaw, just what are you trying to say?"

"What I'm trying to say is, I didn't realize that you're Troup Lazard's half brother."

"So. What has that got to do with anything? Until a few days ago, I hadn't seen or heard from Troup in more than twenty years. What concern is that of yours—or the hospital's?"

"It shouldn't be any, I suppose," Shaw blurted. "But, I'm the administrator and I'm paid to worry, so I do. The Lazard name is something close to magic here in Adams County. When I was hired here at Memorial Hospital eighteen years ago, that was one of the first things they told me. I presume you know that the 'Memorial' part of the hospital is a dedication to your father who gave the land for this building, plus a healthy start on the indigent care endowment fund? They wanted to name it Lazard Memorial, but he wouldn't let them. Haven't you read the plaque in the Main Entrance?"

"No," Ben replied, "and I don't see how that relates to me or my practice of medicine. I once was a Lazard, but my father disowned me in his will for reasons I'll never know. I have no connection and no claim to the Lazard name, or the Lazard fortune for that matter."

"I know that, but it's not you I'm concerned about. It's your half-brother. He's a major supporter of the hospital, both politically and financially. I guess you know he's the largest landowner in the county, and he gives a tremendous amount to charity, either personally or through Lazard Farms, Inc. It's embarrassing for me to say this, but I hope your presence here doesn't cause any friction." Shaw tented his hands, sat back and waited for a reply.

Ben thought for a moment before speaking. "I don't know what to say, Mr. Shaw. Mrs. Powell's offer came at a time when I was eager to make a change. Yes, I'll admit it did cross my mind that coming here might be a bit awkward, but whatever happened nearly thirty years ago is all in the past. I don't see how the events of long ago will affect me, or Troup, or our relationship. Genetically, we're half-brothers. Beyond that, nothing. I'll treat Troup like I would any other colleague, no better, no worse."

Shaw smiled and stood up. "Thanks," he chirped. "I feel a bit better. Can we just forget this conversation?" He extended his hand.

"Sure." They shook hands. "But you can do me one favor," Ben asked.

"Name it."

"How about checking on a case that came through the emergency room over the weekend. His name was Ortega, and he ended up dying. What I'm concerned about is not anything that happened in the ER—I think they did all they could—but the fact that the body was cremated in a matter of hours after death without an autopsy. Is that the policy of this hospital?"

Shaw appeared concerned. "I'll check on it," he said, hastily scribbling a note to himself. "See you at staff meeting tonight?"

"Right," Ben said.

As he left the room, he was gripped by a strange sense of uneasiness.

Medical staff meetings were held on the third Tuesday of every month in the hospital conference room beginning precisely at 7 p.m. They were preceded by a dinner served in the hospital cafeteria that began around six. An hour or so later, individual staff members would wander toward the conference room. The meeting would start whenever both the chief of staff and a quorum were present.

On a practical basis, staff meetings fell into two parts: one, the printed agenda with the usual Old Business, New Business, Committee Reports, etc., on down to the final item which was always listed as Other Business. With that, the meeting usually degenerated into a series of individual complaints and polemics on topics ranging from the poor quality of the coffee in the doctor's lounge to whether or not the hospital should construct a fitness center.

Ben had met most of the medical staff, either formally when he was visiting prior to his decision to return to Walkerville, or informally in the halls or the nurses stations. When he entered the cafeteria, Carter Steed grabbed him by the arm and made certain that he had been introduced to all the physicians. Most staff members were present, including Troup Lazard. He and Ben spoke politely and shook hands. Lazard asked how the practice was going and offered to help cover Ben's patients on an occasional weekend. Ben thanked him as Carter pulled him away to introduce him to Nick Greene, the pathologist. They ate. Ben shared a table with Carter Steed, Nelle Bradley and Jane McClarin. Nelle and Jane practiced together as Adams County Family Physicians and were probably also lovers.

This was the last meeting of the hospital's fiscal year, and the last meeting of the medical staff year. Staff officers for the coming year were elected. Jane was reelected for another year as chief, Carter Steed was voted vice chief (with the understanding that he would become chief of staff the following year), and Ben was nominated and elected secretary of the medical staff. He could not fathom how he could be elected to a medical staff office at his first staff meeting, but Carter explained that it was tradition to elect the newest physician as secretary in an effort to get them involved with staff activities and to get to know the other doctors.

After the meeting, Ben asked Carter about Ortega, and about his visit from Latham and Roble.

"Yeah, I was major-ly pissed off about that, too," Carter responded. "The agents apparently talked with me before they interviewed Kantt, and I didn't find out until this morning that the body had been cremated."

"Did they do the picture show bit with you, too?" Ben asked.

"They did, and the interesting thing is that I think I recognized one of the men in the photos. It was one of those made with a telephoto lens. I can't remember where I saw the fellow, though. I think he works as a foreman on one of the farms around here, but I'm not sure which one. He came in one night with some migrant workers that had been injured in a wreck. I could have been mistaken, and I told them that. Hate to say it but they all look alike to me."

"But what I can't understand is why Kantt cremated the body. It just goes against common sense in a case like that," Ben said.

"You're right. It does sound pretty stupid, but I don't think Kantt is stupid, and I can't imagine he'd have any ulterior motives in disposing of the body. You know what I think it is?" Carter paused. "Money."

"How so?"

"Well, about four or five years ago, Kantt built a crematorium. I remember him saying that was the wave of the future, and he'd have the only one between Macon and Augusta, so he'd be sure to pick up on all the business of folks from these small towns who wanted to be cremated. He may know his business, but I think he miscalled that one. Ain't nothing like standing around the funeral home wailing about how 'Don't Grandma look like she's just asleep?', and you can't do that when the old lady's been reduced to a pile of ashes. I know for a fact that the county's got him under contract for all the funerals that nobody else will pay for—paupers, people who die in jail and the like. He's gets a flat fee to take care of things. If he does it the usual way, he has to embalm the body, come up with a coffin and a vault, pay the grave diggers, et cetera. But if he zaps the body in his underused crematorium, *voilá*, no embalming fluid, no coffin, no grave diggers, no nothing except a little bump in his monthly bill to Georgia Natural Gas. That's what *I* think. He does it quick and cheap, sends the county a bill which they pay, and if some relatives show up, lets the county try to collect from them when they're back in Tijuana. Maybe he ain't so stupid after all."

CHAPTER
ELEVEN

THE LAST GLOW of the August twilight was fading as Ben turned off the highway onto the gravel drive that led to Dr. Powell's cabin. The road entered a mature pine forest and wound its way down a hill into a narrow valley filled with giant white oaks, tulip poplar and hickory trees. In a large clearing at the edge of a long and very narrow lake sat the cabin. It had not started out to be what it was today. According to Mrs. Powell, the main part of the structure, an ancient square-hewn log home, dated from about 1840 and had belonged to her great-great-grandfather. Shortly after marrying Dr. Powell nearly fifty years earlier, they had —with a lot of help, she stressed—disassembled it log by log and moved it here from her family's farm. The cabin was reassembled, a well was drilled and the lake created by damming a small creek running through the hardwood bottom.

As Dr. Powell's family grew, so had the cabin. The simple one-room structure now had three large bedrooms and modern plumbing in wings on either side of the large central room. Overlooking the lake was a modern kitchen and glass-enclosed dining area that opened onto a large wooden deck with a magnificent view. Mrs. Powell explained that they had just finished a complete renovation of the cabin only months before her husband's death. He had planned to retire, and they were going to move here, giving up the big house in town.

"It meant so much to us—the cabin, the lake, this place," she explained to Ben. "I just can't come out here anymore by myself now that Paul's gone. It's best you stay here. He would have liked that."

The one annoyance was the light switches, or lack thereof, Ben thought. The twelve-inch hewn logs did not lend themselves to standard wiring. So, on entering through the front door, it was necessary to blunder across the room in the dark to find the switch on a lamp, the receptacle for which had been placed in the floor as a matter of practicality.

He parked his car, sorted through his keys and unlocked the front door. Across the dark room on the table next to the lamp he could see the message light on his telephone answering machine flashing a red "1" indicating he had one message. He found the lamp switch and hit the playback button.

The machine clicked. "Ben! What the hell are you doing down here in Georgia? This is Mark Brett." Mark and his wife Becky had been close friends in medical school. He was now doing family practice in the suburbs of Atlanta. "Look," Mark's voice continued, "we hadn't talked to you in three or four months, so we decided to call you up and invite ourselves up to Nashville for the weekend. We got Erica and she says you two have split up and that you've moved out and are practicing medicine in some god-forsaken small town in Georgia that doesn't even have a mall." There was a snicker, and the voice continued: "Well, Becky and I just want to say we're sorry about all that, but Erica never was your type anyway. So, look…if we can't come see you, how's about you coming up to see us? We're free this weekend. I can get four good tickets for a concert at Chaistain Park on Sunday afternoon. We'll get you a date—there's lots of available women up here. When you come in call us at 404-636-4736. We can…"

The message cut off suddenly and an electronic voice from the machine intoned, "Tuesday. Seven-forty-six p.m."

As he reached for the phone, Ben mentally reminded himself to buy an answering machine that would accept a message more than sixty seconds in length.

The next morning Ben rose early, fixed himself some coffee, drank orange juice and ate yogurt while he sat on the deck and watched the wood ducks depart from the lake for their day of foraging. At the hospital, he made quick morning rounds, then arrived at the office shortly after nine. As always, Rachel had his day superbly organized. She announced that Barbara was out with the flu, and that he'd have to make the bank deposit on his lunch hour because the rest of the office staff had other errands to run and things to do and this task had fallen to him by default.

The morning went smoothly. At 1 p.m. Rachel thrust a blue zippered bank bag at him and told him to be sure to get the deposit retotaled and to get a proper receipt. He felt like he was back to being a first year medical student. Dr. Powell's bank, his bank now, occupied a staid brick edifice on the main street just off the city square. The sign in front of the building gave the time and temperature and announced in neat black letters that the Miller State Bank lived up to it's motto of "Courteous and Conservative." The bank was entered through a foyer protected on either end by glass doors and used to display various awards garnered by the bank over the years. The largest, Ben noted, was a bronze plaque labeled "For Service to Local Agriculture" and dated 1961. On the inside, a row of six teller windows lined one side of a huge lobby, while four small, semi-open offices, two of which were occupied by loan officers absorbed in the sports section of the daily paper, dominated the other. Beyond the small offices was a loan counter. The bank president's office, surrounded by glass windows now obscured by mini-blinds, was adjacent to the front door.

Ben approached the first teller. The sign said "Mrs. Jennings." He laid the bag in front of her as she looked up and smiled. "Hi," she said. After unzipping the bag, she looked up again and said, "You must be Dr. Pike."

"Yes. I took over Dr. Powell's practice."

"I'm Alex Jennings. Good to meet you. Dr. Powell was my doctor." She looked at him with intensely blue eyes. "I guess I need to come and see you sometime soon. I need some of my asthma medicine refilled. All these fall plants, golden rod, fennel, and so on really get to me."

Ben studied her as she totaled his deposit. Very attractive. Late 20's, maybe 30 at the most. Medium blond hair. He noticed she was not wearing a wedding ring. "Are you originally from Walkerville, Mrs. Jennings?"

She looked up and smiled again. "Yes, I am. Call me Alex." She continued to shuffle through the checks. "I've been living back here about three years now. I was working in Atlanta but moved back here after I got married."

"Is your husband in business here?"

She looked up suddenly and seemed to stare at him for a brief moment, then resumed adding the deposit. "No," she said in a distant tone. "I'm widowed. My husband died in an accident a couple of years ago."

"Oh, I'm sorry..."

"Please don't worry about it. You wouldn't have known unless you'd been living here." She pushed the bank bag with the completed deposit back to him. "I'll make an appointment to come by and see you in a few days." This time she looked him directly in the eyes and smiled.

"I'll look forward to that," Ben replied, and smiled back.

When he got back to the office he told Doreen to notify him if Mrs. Jennings called for an appointment.

The remainder of the week went quickly. Ben admitted three more patients. One of his older patients, one with a kidney stone, was discharged, and another with gallbladder problems went to surgery. On Saturday morning after rounds he signed out to Skip Malcom, one of the younger internists who'd agreed to cover his patients for him and headed north on State Route 15, then west on Interstate 20 to Atlanta. He arrived that afternoon to find that Mark and Becky had planned a full weekend for him.

"...and so we just knew that with you and Erica split, and you living down there in the country, that if we didn't get you a date with a real woman they'd catch you some night doing something totally unnatural with one of the local farm animals," Mark explained over a beer.

"So, tonight," Becky continued for him, "we're having a nice, quiet dinner at Bones on Piedmont. We've invited a friend, Dianne Price. She's cute, divorced about two months ago and really wants to meet you. She's doing great in real estate sales."

"And tomorrow," Mark took up, "We'll be taking Jessica Sheppard to the concert with us. She's twenty-five, works as a lab tech at Crawford Long and has a fantastic body." Mark rolled his eyes and lolled his tongue.

Becky gave him a grow-up look.

"Look," Ben volunteered. "You guys really don't have to fix me up. I'm fine. Really."

Mark and Becky looked hurt. Ben quickly added, "But maybe you're right. I do need to go out more."

His friends looked at each other and grinned.

The dinner was pleasant enough. Dianne Price turned out to be a bitterly divorced thirty-six year old whose chief goal in life, it seemed, was to make more money than her ex-husband so she could prove to him just how much he'd lost. Ben wasn't so sure. The concert on Sunday afternoon was more fun. Jessica was intelligent, educated, articulate and probably totally in love with someone named Miles, who she off-handedly referred to at least a dozen times during the course of the afternoon. She said she'd like to go out again, but Ben knew she was lying.

He left Atlanta about eight-thirty and arrived home after eleven.

As he entered the door of the cabin, he could see the message light on the answering machine blinking "2." He turned on the lamp, pressed the playback button and listened. The machine gave its usual click. "Dr. Pike? This is Ollie Duggan. You remember me from Golden Age Manor, I hope. If you're there Dr. Pike, please pick up. I need to talk to you." There was a pause. "I guess you're not there, so call me as soon as you come in. I really need to tell you what happened tonight—just a few minutes ago. Mr. Matthews next door was in one of his ranting spells again. At least I think he was. I know they've called someone to calm him down. Anyway, he got out of his room and came over here and was trying to tell me all this stuff about your father. He was saying something like, 'He made me do it,' and, 'I didn't know all the facts then,' and so forth, so I asked him what he was talking about, and he told me the most amazing story. It was like he was his old self back when I worked in the law office. The thing is that he..."

The message suddenly cut off and the machine announced, "Saturday. Eight-eighteen p.m."

The machine clicked again. "Dr. Pike, this is Ollie again. Your machine cut off, so I called back. You really need to hear this. Mr. Matthews was in here ranting about 'page nine' and..." She paused, and a muffled noise could be heard in the background. "Who's there?" Another pause. "Who's there? I'm blind and I can't see you. I'm on the phone right now. Maybe you can come back later."

Miss Ollie was silent for a moment, then spoke back into the telephone. "Ben, I'm afraid I've got visitors. I'll call you back soon."

The line went dead, and a dial tone could be heard before the announcement of "Saturday. Eight-twenty p.m."

Ben looked at his watch. It was nearly eleven-thirty and the messages were more than twenty-four hours old. He was tired and decided he'd simply go by the nursing home early the next morning before rounds. He flipped off the lamp and headed to bed.

At seven-fifteen on Monday morning Ben was dodging the breakfast carts as he walked down the hall at Golden Age Manor. He reached room 352, Miss Ollie's, knocked once and pushed the door open. The room was bare. The bed had been stripped, and the green plastic-covered mattress lay naked on the metal bed frame. Miss Ollie's plants, her radio, her tape player—all gone.

He went back to the door to be sure that he had the correct room. The card holder on the door still said: "Miss Ollie Duggan."

He looked for a nurse, and failing to see one, grabbed the arm of one of the kitchen workers who was unloading a tray from a large, heated stainless steel rolling cart.

"The lady in this room—Miss Duggan—did they move her?"

The kitchen worker, a middle-aged obese black woman, stared at him. "I ain't 'xactly sure, but I think she's done died. They's always doing that around here you know." She pulled out another tray. "I know that man over there, he died, 'cause my mama, she used to work for him, and she told me that at church yesterday."

"Who? What man?"

"Old Lawyer Matthews. He was mighty old and kinda crazy mean, anyhow."

Stunned, Ben walked to the nurses' station. He found the night RN sitting at the desk giving morning reports to the day shift supervisor.

"What happened to Ollie Duggan and Crawford Matthews?" he demanded. "They were both my patients, and I come in here and find out they're both dead. What happened?"

The RN looked up and sighed. "They both died Saturday night, Dr. Pike," she explained matter-of-factly. "It happened on the 3 to 11 shift and..."

"Why in hell wasn't I notified? When a doctor's patient dies..."

"You left word that you were going to out of town for the weekend," the nurse interrupted. "We did call Dr. Malcom and he said he'd tell you on Monday."

Ben was embarrassed. "I'm sorry. I guess I'm just upset. Could you just tell me what happened? Did Dr. Malcom have to come over and pronounce them?"

"Like I said, they both died Saturday night on the evening shift. What they told us in report was that Mr. Matthews went into one of his rages again, and they had to sedate him. The nurse found him dead when she checked on him a couple of hours later. I understand he had a lot of medical problems. And Miss Ollie, I don't blame you for being upset, that was so tragic."

"What do you mean, tragic?"

"Apparently she fell out of her bed sometime in the night and suffered a broken neck, at least that's what Dr. Lazard thinks. She was in pretty good shape overall, except that she was blind and in a wheelchair. She liked to go to bed early, and so we never would check on her after about eight o'clock at night. Let her sleep, you know. They found her between the bed and her bedside commode when they brought her breakfast tray Sunday morning. They took the body over to the hospital and did x-rays and found a broken neck and..."

"Wait a minute. Did I hear you say Dr. Lazard? What does he have to do with this?"

"Well, he's the medical examiner. We had to call him as

well as Dr. Malcom. Since it was an accident, we have to report it to the coroner and all, not to mention the state, the federal government and god knows who else. You wouldn't believe the paperwork for something like that."

"What did Dr. Malcom say about Mr. Matthews? What does he think happened to him?"

This time it was the nurse who looked embarrassed. "Dr. Malcom didn't see him. Dr. Lazard did."

"What...?" Ben exploded.

"I was working a double Saturday so I was here," the night nurse interjected. "I'll tell you what happened. Dr. Lazard was over here seeing another patient who was having some problems when Mr. Matthews got in one of his ranting rages. He was sitting here at this desk writing on a chart when he heard me call Dr. Malcom. He picked up the extension over there—" She pointed to a phone on the desk. "—and told Dr. Malcom that, since he was already here, he'd be glad to see Mr. Matthews. He said he knew his case because he'd help cover Dr. Powell's patients before you came. He told Dr. Malcom there was no sense in him coming out on a Saturday night and to stay home with his kids and he'd take care of everything. We then went down to see Mr. Matthews who, by that time, had gotten in Miss Ollie Duggan's room babbling away, and we got him back in bed. Dr. Lazard called for a shot—Ativan 1 mg. IM—and I went and got it. I gave the shot and came back here, and Dr. Lazard sat there for a while calming Mr. Matthews down while the shot took effect, and then he came back and said he was asleep and to call him for any more problems with Mr. Matthews that night and then he left."

"When did you find out he was dead?"

"When I was making the end of shift rounds, about ten-forty-five. I called Dr. Lazard and he came in and pronounced him and wrote a note on the chart. You want to see it?"

"No, not really," Ben replied. He paused. "Don't you think it's kind of strange that two people in rooms right next to one another die the same night?"

The nurse looked at Ben with incredulity. "Dr. Pike. This is a *nursing home*. People come here to die. That's what's *supposed* to happen. Lighten up."

CHAPTER
TWELVE

SKIP MALCOM WAS JUST GETTING OUT OF HIS CAR in the doctors' parking lot of Adams Memorial Hospital when Ben drove up. He waved and walked over. "How was your weekend? Blind dates any fun?"

Ben was not in a good mood. "It was something to do. Thanks for covering for me. Tell me about the two patients at Golden Age Manor."

Malcom was a bit taken aback by his tone. "So you heard about that already. I think Mr. Matthews just died. To be truthful, I didn't see him. Troup Lazard was already there and offered to handle the problem. He said he knew the man's case since he'd helped cover Dr. Powell's patients. I really don't know the details."

"Did he get an autopsy?" Ben fired back.

"I don't know, but Ben, look, the guy was old and in the nursing home. Those people die. I know you've been at Vanderbilt and all, but that's academic medicine. Down here this is the real world. If someone is old and not doing well and dies, just maybe it was their time. About Miss Ollie, that was really bad, but I don't know what anybody would do different-ly. I went over there when they called me, and it honestly looked like she'd fallen trying to get on the commode at night."

More calmly, Ben said, "I'm sorry, Skip. I've gotten myself all worked up about this because of a message on my answering machine from Miss Ollie. Something about what Matthews was raging about and how I needed to hear it. I guess we'll never know."

"About the autopsy, I really doubt it. Kantt's Funeral Home probably has the body. You could call over there."

"Thanks, Skip. I probably will. Again, I appreciate your help." Ben paused as Malcom started to walk away. "Skip?"

"Yeah?"

"Do you know a girl—maybe I should say a woman—named Alex Jennings? Works at the bank."

Skip smiled. "Sure do. She was my sister's best friend in high school and one of the finest people I know. Her husband John was killed in a plane crash a couple of years ago." Malcom looked at Ben for a brief moment. "Why? You inter-ested in going out with her?"

"No. I mean, I don't know. I met her at the bank the other day. She seemed nice."

"Listen, Ben. Alex is an incredible person, but she really had a hard time after John was killed. I can think of at least ten guys who've tried to get her to go out with them, but she won't. I think she keeps a lot bottled up inside her."

Malcom waved good day and headed for the emergency room entrance.

Ben made rounds and arrived at the office by nine. He looked up the number for Kantt's Funeral Home in the phone book and dialed it. A languorous female voice announced "Kantt's Mortuary. How can I help you?"

"This is Dr. Pike. I was calling about Crawford Matthews. Do you have the body?"

There was a pause. "We did, Dr. Pike. The service is this afternoon at three."

"You *did?* What do you mean by that?"

"The family requested cremation. That was done yesterday morning. We'll have his ashes in a lovely memorial urn at the service."

"I don't suppose an autopsy was done?"

"A post-mortem examination? Oh, no. I think not. No one requested one and Mr. Kantt *is* the coroner."

"Thanks," Ben said, and rang off. He picked up the chart of the morning's first patient from his desk and headed toward the exam room.

By ten-thirty, Ben had seen eight patients and was sitting at his desk taking a coffee break when the intercom on the telephone buzzed. He pressed the button to turn on the speaker and answered, "Yes?"

"Dr. Pike, Dr. Lazard on line three to speak with you. Can you take the call, or do you want me to tell him you'll call him back?"

Ben thought for a second. "I'll talk with him," he

replied and picked up the phone. "Good morning, Troup"

"Ben, I've gotten three phone calls already this morning about the Matthews case. The nurses at Golden Age called me to say you were upset, Skip Malcom called to tell me more or less the same thing, and I just got off the phone with Elmo Kantt who said you called over there demanding to know if an autopsy was done. If you have a problem and I'm part of it, why don't you just call me? I think we need to sit down and have a long talk."

"You're right, Troup, I have been upset. Maybe I should have called you. When do you want to talk?"

"We both take Wednesday afternoons off. How about my house, 7 p.m.?"

Ben hesitated. He had not set foot on Marsellaise Plantation in almost thirty years. It was where he had spent the first years of his life, but it carried many bitter memories. He knew he'd have to face it eventually so he replied, "Wednesday, see you at seven," and hung up.

On Wednesday, Ben finished with his office patients at one o'clock, ate a leisurely lunch in the hospital cafeteria, and then spent an hour in medical records catching up on his charts. He then went back to the office to review lab data and dictate letters to patients who needed follow up before their scheduled visit. By five o'clock he was tired and tense in anticipation of his meeting with his half-brother. He decided to go to the grocery store on his way home. It was something he basically detested doing, something that Erica used to do, something that reminded him of how they'd failed together.

The Piggly Wiggly was in one of the shopping centers that had sprung up along the extension of Main Street to the south of town. It was at least convenient, but he hated being the only man pushing a shopping cart among the housewives and welfare mothers with their books of food stamps. He grabbed a cart, loaded it with a generous assortment of microwave dinners, fresh fruit, juice, yogurt and a six-pack of beer and headed for the check-out line. As he rounded the end of the frozen food aisle heading for the ranks of cash registers, he saw Alex Jennings at the very moment she saw him. He smiled, she smiled, and he got in line behind her.

"Dr. Pike. It's good to see you without your coat and tie." He'd taken them off when he was hunched over paper-work at the office.

"Call me Ben, please. It's nice to see you again, Alex." He noticed that her cart held the same assortment of microwave dinners, fruit, juice and yogurt as his.

They both tried to speak at once and laughed.

Alex said, "I see you must hate grocery shopping as much as I do."

"Yeah. It's really no fun shopping for one. Not to men-tion eating alone," Ben replied.

Alex looked at him. "I would have thought you'd have a wife and family, Dr. Pike."

Ben smiled. "No. No such luck yet. Maybe one day."

"Well, we're glad to have you here in Walkerville. I still haven't made my appointment yet, but I keep hearing good things about you."

The shopper in front of her had finished checking out, and she began to pile her groceries on the conveyer belt lead-ing to the scanner. She wrote a check and watched while the food was bagged.

As she hefted up the two sacks she turned to Ben and said, "I hope we'll meet again soon," and walked out.

Ben drove home, put up the frozen and refrigerated foods and looked at the clock. It was six-fifteen. Half an hour before he'd have to leave to meet Troup. He sat on the deck in the afternoon shade and thought about Alex Jennings.

At a quarter-to-seven, Ben left the cabin and turned onto the highway north back to town. He drove through the city square, past the hospital and along the dense pine forest that marked the beginning of Marsellaise Plantation property. The Plantation lay to the north of Walkerville, bordered on the west by the Opahatchee River with its swamps and sloughs and on the east by State Route 15. Ben remembered from somewhere that the Plantation took up almost ten percent of the land area of Adams County and encompassed nearly forty square miles of forest, pasture and swamp land. The property was shaped roughly like an inverted triangle with the bottom (southern) tip cut off. The southern boundary stretched only about a mile from the State Route 15 to the river. To the east, the property line followed the highway for more than eight miles. The northern boundary was about ten miles in length from the road through gently rolling hills of planted pines to the river swamps. The serpentine western boundary was marked by the main course of the river as it meandered through a wide alluvial valley.

The entrance to the main house was about midway

along the eastern border, marked by massive iron gates set between pillars and short walls of stone and slate. On either side on top of the gateposts, large stone eagles stood guard.

Ben had avoided coming here since his return to Adams County. He'd driven by several times, but had not paid much attention to the plantation property. As he drove north now he noted that the pine forests were bounded by a chain link fence with barbed wire on top and neatly printed yellow signs every hundred yards or so that stated:

LAZARD
FARMS, INC.
NO TRESPASSING
VIOLATORS WILL BE
PROSECUTED

Ben realized that while he had always known his father's land as Marsellaise Plantation, it now appeared to be also known as Lazard Farms, Inc. He reached the stone gates and turned onto the paved drive.

The majestic entrance to Marsellaise Plantation was just as he had remembered it. The drive, absolutely straight and lined by huge maple trees set back on either side of manicured grass bordering the road, stretched for two miles over rolling countryside. It then made a forty-five degree turn to the left and climbed a gently rising hillock on the top of which sat the main house. Along the way various other small farm roads disappeared into the forest, some of them leading to huge open fields or pastures that could be seen in the distance. Some two-hundred yards in front of the mansion, the drive passed through a second set of stone and wrought iron gates with eagles that matched the ones by the road. Ben looped around the circular driveway and parked his car on the cobblestones under a giant elm.

The house seemed almost unchanged over the years. The grounds were still immaculately manicured, the white columns pristinely gleaming in the afternoon sun. It was a huge house by any standard. Six massive wood columns with intricately carved Corinthian capitals sprouted from the front of a wide "U" shaped porch. Two more columns on each side completed the sides of the "U." The porch itself was made of tightly fitted flat stones that Ben remembered were ballast stones brought more than a hundred miles by mule and wagon from Savannah to construct the foundation of the first house built in the 1830's. Twin front doors with brass hardware long polished into an ancient patina opened into a long foyer that ran the length of the house. He remembered his mother standing on this porch and sobbing as their few possessions were loaded in the moving van after his father's death.

Ben lifted one of the massive door knockers and rapped it sharply. It was exactly 7 p.m.

An old black woman dressed in a gray and white maid's uniform opened the door. Her eyes lit up the moment she saw him. "Mr. Ben!" she gushed. "How are you? Don't you remember me? You sat on my lap for a hundred Sundays when you was little."

"Pearlie Mae?" Ben had not thought of her in decades. She was old now. He wanted to embrace her but thought better of it.

"Yes, sir. I been here all these years. I'm kinda stuck with the house. I'll tell Mistuh Lazard you here. You want to wait here?"

"That'll be fine, Pearlie Mae. It's good to see you again." She disappeared through a portal.

Ben looked around. The house was the same, yet very different. There was something about the style that was more formal and stilted than he had remembered it. To his right through an ornate arched opening was the dining room with its single piece mahogany table that could seat twenty-four. In the center was a large sterling epérgne filled with cut flowers. To his left through a matching opening was a formal parlor with silk and damask-covered sofas and chairs stiffly arranged about a fireplace with a verde marble hearth. Before him on one side of the foyer an intricately carved marble topped table sat under the portrait of Augustin Lazard. Across from it was a silk-lined Chippendale breakfront displaying a set of china. He idly examined the china. It occurred to him that he knew next to nothing of his half-brother. He had no idea if Troup Lazard was married or who he now claimed as his family. Even though he'd spent the first years of his life here, he now realized that this house, this lifestyle, was no longer a part of him. He wondered why he had agreed to come here in the first place. Why not meet at a neutral spot? He thought of leaving.

"It's Chinese armorial porcelain. The coat of arms— and the motto '*Tempis omnia revelat*'—is of the d'Ayen family. It dates from about 1775."

Ben turned to see Troup Lazard standing behind him. He extended his hand. "Glad you could come, Ben. Let's go to my study to talk."

Lazard led the way through the parlor and down a short hall to a paneled study that Ben remembered had been his father's favorite hide-away. He motioned for Ben to sit down.

"Would you like a drink? Bourbon, perhaps."

"No, thanks, Troup. What did you want to talk about?"

"All business, aren't you, Ben? At least observe some social amenities. I'll have one if you won't." He poured himself two fingers of an amber liquid from a crystal decanter and sipped it neat. "Some coffee, perhaps? I can have Pearlie Mae..."

"I'm fine, Troup," Ben interrupted.

"Well, then, we'll keep this brief and to the point. I want to know why you're back here in Adams County." He took a long draw on his drink and waited for Ben to reply.

CHAPTER
THIRTEEN

THE QUESTION CAUGHT BEN completely off guard.

"Troup," he said, quickly recovering. "I came here to talk about a couple of my patients who died last weekend. Not my reason for being in Adams County."

Lazard smiled. "Look at it my way," he said smoothly. " I've lived here a long time. I'm a successful businessman and a reasonably respected physician. You've been here less than a month, and if what I'm hearing is right, you seem to do a lot of complaining about things that are not your business, and it seems like they all involve me."

Before Ben could reply, Lazard cut him off.

"Just shut up and listen for a minute. You had a lot to say to Carter Steed and Hoke Brantley and to the hospital administrator about that fellow Ortega's death. You even talked to the Feds about him, too. I suspect it was you who sent them to me."

He slowed long enough to take a sip, then continued. "And this week, I hear about the bitching at the nursing home—and to Skip Malcom and to the lady at Kantt's. Let's see, Dr. Pike, that's averaging more than two complaints a week, and you just don't stop."

He took another sip before continuing. "What I'm getting at is this—do you have some kind of an agenda? I'm pretty well connected and I haven't gotten word about you complaining about anybody else."

"Troup, of course I don't have an agenda! It's just that some things have happened that have really concerned me. Like Ortega. You just can't write him off."

"A fucking spic. I've got two dozen of 'em doing my farm labor here. One dies and there's six more waiting to take his place. You want to know why I hire 'em? You can't get the niggers to work, and they will. So what's it all to you? You had absolutely nothing to do with that whole case except that they called you in for a moment to help translate."

Lazard drained his glass and placed it on the small table by the armchair.

"But you just can't do things like that. A death is an important event that requires documentation. And part of it you've got wrong. I was concerned about Matthews and Duggan because of the message that Miss Ollie left on my answering machine Saturday night before she died."

Lazard blanched. "Message? What are you talking about?"

Ben noticed his half-brother was nervously twirling a large gold signet ring on his right hand.

"When Matthews got agitated he apparently came in her room and was reasonably rational, at least that's what she said. She told me that I needed to hear the story, but evidently was interrupted before she could finish telling it to me. She said she'd call back but never did. She was found dead the next morning."

Lazard poured himself another drink. Without looking up, he inquired, "Just how much did she tell you?"

"Not much, really. The only thing I remember is something about 'page 9,' whatever that means."

Lazard seemed to relax. "Well, Ben, I don't know about all that, but I think you and I better get some things straight. First of all, I'm a very rich and very powerful man. My family's been in this county for a long, long time. People owe me favors. Some of them respect me, maybe some of them fear me. I don't know if you've got some strange idea that just because my father slipped up in his dotage and sired you that somehow you've got a claim to all this." He gestured around the room. "Or, maybe you're going to try to cash in on the fact that I'm genetically your half-brother. You did introduce yourself as my brother to Carter Steed, remember? In case you've forgotten, let me remind you of something. It was my father—our father, unfortunately—who chose to write you and your mother out of his will. I don't think he could have made things any plainer. Their relationship, and you for that matter, were a simple mistake that he did his best to correct before he died. As far as I'm concerned, you and I have no relationship other than two physicians who just happen to practice medicine in the same town. I'm not going to give you the old 'This Town Ain't Big Enough for the Two of Us' line, but if you get in my way I'm going to step on you. Is that real clear?"

"You can't intimidate me, Troup."

"I don't want to. That was a private, civilized warning from one adult to another. As far as the public knows, we could be the best of friends." He lowered his voice. "But let me tell you, there won't be another one."

Ben rose to leave just as a squat muscular man appeared at the study door. Lazard beckoned him in. "Hector. I'm glad you could make it. Hector, I want you to meet Dr. Ben Pike. Ben, this is Hector Torrez, my farm manager. I wanted you two to meet. Hector does a great job here on the plantation, and sometimes he handles an occasional little problem for me on the side."

Hector nodded but did not smile.

"Ben," Lazard continued, pausing for emphasis. "You don't want to meet Hector late at night. You know these Latin temperaments. *¿Comprende?*" He grinned at Hector who grinned back. "But, hell, I'm really not being the gracious host. Will you join me for dinner? Pearlie Mae's got an excellent pork tenderloin she's preparing..."

"Good night, Troup. I'll find the door."

Ben strode out of the study, through the parlor and foyer and out the front door taking care to shut it quietly as he left. Lazard and Hector followed, standing on the porch and watching him as drive away.

⌣‿⌒

Ben's head was reeling with a medly of unconnected thoughts as he mechanically retraced his path back to town.

The meeting with Troup had been a mistake. He had imagined they'd sit down and discuss some problems with communication. Instead, he found himself drawn into events in his life that he thought were long past. Troup somehow seemed to believe that he had returned to Walkerville for a purpose, and nothing could be further from the truth.

The sharp honking of a horn from the car behind him reminded him that the traffic light had turned green. On impulse he turned to the right and pulled his car into a small landscaped park. He sat behind the wheel, staring blankly at the waning light, trying to think, trying to get his thoughts together. A noisy pickup with four high school kids in the front seat roared past him, breaking his reverie. For some reason he noticed the large bronze sign next to a formal fountain whose bubbling water flowed away into a landscaped pool surrounded by blooming late summer flowers. It read

---

LAZARD MEMORIAL PARK

**Dedicated to the
Honor of the Lazard Family
of Adams County, Georgia,
in Remembrance of
Their Generous Support
of Numerous Civic Projects
and Public Works**

B.J. Asher, Mayor
May 1, 1991

Still in a daze, he restarted the car and drove toward home. A memory of his mother came to his mind. It was late one night after they'd left Marsellaise Plantation. He could see her, head bent over her writing desk sobbing and swearing that she wished she'd never heard the Lazard name.

⁓

Thursday passed quietly, as did Friday morning. Ben was scheduled to work on the weekend, covering for three other internists in an informal rotation schedule. Around noon, Doreen buzzed him on the intercom. "Dr. Pike, you said you wanted to know if Mrs. Alex Jennings called. She just did and asked if she could come by on her lunch hour at about twelve-thirty to pick up a refill on her asthma medicine. I told her it was OK, but you said to tell you."

"Doreen, how about bringing me her chart?"

A few moments later Ben sat in his office, quickly scanning Alex Jennings's chart. She had seen Dr. Powell only occasionally for asthma. Two years ago she'd gotten a prescription for sedatives and sleeping pills, apparently right after her husband's death. He buzzed for Doreen.

"Yes?"

"Could you xerox a copy of Mrs. Jennings's entire chart and put it in a manila envelope? When she gets here, don't put her in an exam room, just ask her to wait in my private office and put her chart and the copy of it on my desk. OK?" He picked up the phone and called Skip Malcom.

Half an hour later, Ben returned to his office from seeing a patient to find a smiling Alex Jennings seated in front of his desk.

"I'm really sorry to bother you, Dr. Pike, but I just needed my medicine refilled before the fall pollen season. The drugstore told me I needed a new prescription." She leaned forward slightly. "It's really no big problem. I've had asthma for years and usually just a few puffs from a Proventil inhaler..."

"Alex," Ben interrupted, "I know this is strange, but I'd really prefer to refer you to another physician." He held up the folder containing copies of her records. "I've copied Dr. Powell's records for you, and I've taken the liberty of calling Dr. Skip Malcom who says he'll be happy to see you right away."

An astonished look flashed across Alex's face. Or was it hurt? "Dr. Pike, Skip's a good doctor and a great friend, but I came here to see you. Dr. Powell was my doctor, you've taken over his practice, and from what I've seen and heard of you, I think I'd be happy to have you take his place."

"Alex, I realize that, in truth, I hardly know you and that you hardly know me, but I don't really want to develop a doctor-patient relationship with you."

"I don't understand. You're a doctor. I'm a patient. And, as far as a relationship..." She stopped, suddenly realized what he meant. "Oh."

"What I'm trying to say without making a total fool of myself is that I would like the opportunity to ask you out socially which I would not feel very comfortable doing if you were my patient."

Alex stared across his desk at him. "Oh."

"I mean..." He fumbled for the right words. "I realize this may be...that I'm...Do you have any idea what I'm trying to say?"

Alex smiled. "I think you're trying to get me to go out with you."

"Uh, huh," Ben mumbled.

"Well, for all your education you're still a bit rough on

the social skills. I appreciate your sending me to Skip. That'll be fine. As for the other—I want you to know that I haven't dated since John died. I'm not even sure I want to." She rose to go. "Call me at home over the weekend. My number's in the book."

She picked up her records and walked out of the office. Ben stared at her chair, feeling like an utter dunce.

CHAPTER
FOURTEEN

BEN SPENT THE FOLLOWING WEEKEND ON CALL. He was busy, but not excessively so. On Sunday morning he stood in the hospital corridor waiting for the elevator as Troup Lazard walked up and stood beside him.

"Morning, Ben," he said. "Things going well for you?" It was as if the conversation of the preceding week had never taken place.

"Fine, Troup. And you?"

The elevator doors opened, and they both entered, riding silently to the third floor.

"Well, good to see you," Lazard said matter-of-factly

and walked off toward the nurses' station.

Amazing, Ben thought. It was like nothing had happened. He silently promised himself to be careful around Troup. From now on, he would avoid confrontations only he could lose.

On Tuesday of the following week he called Alex. They talked for a long time on the phone. She seemed cautious, he thought, getting to know him from a distance first.

The next night he called and invited her to Augusta for an early evening production of a comedy by Molière and a late dinner at a small Cajun restaurant. The evening went well.

Over the next few weeks they went out several times, always to crowded public places and then straight home. A brief goodnight. No invitation to come in. An invisible wall seemed to surround Alex. She was great fun to be with but avoided revealing anything personal. She talked about growing up in Walkerville, about living in Atlanta before her marriage to John Jennings, but nothing about her husband's death and her life since that time. They talked about the things she liked—art, the theater—and about the one thing he knew and enjoyed—medicine and his work. He told funny stories. She laughed. On the fourth week of their dating, she invited him to her house for dinner on Saturday night.

Alex lived in a small house in one of Walkerville's better neighborhoods. Built in the late 1920's, it was a squat bungalow in the pseudo-Spanish style of the day, renovated half a dozen times by the various owners over the years. She was almost apologetic as she opened the door.

"The house is really a mess," she apologized. "I haven't been much on trying to fix it up since..." She hesitated. "Since I've been living alone."

"Looks great to me," Ben replied.

It did actually. The exterior of the house gave no hint as to its interior design. The front door opened into a small marble-floored foyer, which is all that he had been able to see from the outside. To his surprise, the foyer merged into a huge open space that, at one time, had been divided up into smaller, more formal rooms. A brick fireplace and chimney stood in the middle of the space, with decorative columns providing structural support where the former walls had been removed. The floors where light oak, the walls were white. In the front, in what was probably once a formal living and dining room, an eclectic group of comfortable chairs and two small sofas faced the fireplace. An oversized dining table with twelve carved chairs was on the other side. Three large freestanding bookcases served as room dividers. In the rear, the back wall of the house had been removed and replaced with a series of French doors that opened up into a spacious walled courtyard with a small fountain in its center. A modern kitchen could be seen through an open door to the right. To the left, walls of glass surrounded a small studio with a half finished painting on an easel in its center.

Ben was impressed. "It's amazing," he said, "You'd never have a hint as to the interior looking at it from the outside."

"I hope you don't think it's too nontraditional," Alex said. "John and I bought it from the estate of the previous owner. He was an architect, and this was his dream house. Lots of open space in a very private area. We really couldn't have afforded it, but he died of AIDS, and the house stayed on the market a long time before we made an offer on it. It's silly, I know, but people must have thought the house was poisoned, or jinxed, or...." She was suddenly silent. "Let me show you the courtyard."

The summer heat had given away to the cooler days of September. They ate at a small table in the courtyard illuminated by candles and the flickering lights of flambeaux perfuming the air with the soft smell of citronella. The dinner was superb. Alex had prepared a cold pasta salad with sun-dried tomatoes, shrimp, black olives and fresh basil. A succulent pork tenderloin with an herb garnish followed as the main course, with a light tiramisu for dessert. Afterwards, they sat by the fountain, sipping sweet wine and talking.

She brought it up suddenly. They had been discussing travel, and Ben was recounting his jungle warfare training and his secret fear of flying. "You know, I've really been angry since John died," she said.

It was the first time she had said anything about the subject.

"I used to think that I had a really great life," Alex continued. "John and I were happy, money was not a problem, we were thinking about kids, and then...then the roof crashes in."

Ben thought he saw a tear form in the corner of her eye. He waited another moment, then said, "Would you like to talk about it?"

"Oh, you don't want to hear all this."

"Try me. I'm a great listener. Especially when I like the person telling the story."

Alex thought hard for a moment. "You know, Ben, it seems like I've known you a long time. At least long enough that I can talk to you about what really happened."

Ben waited.

Alex began to tell her story. She told about how she and John had met, fallen in love and gotten married. She had finished college at Agnes Scott in Atlanta with a major in Art and a minor in Business Administration. She'd gotten a job as an assistant curator for American Art at the High Museum, and had met John at a fund-raising reception. She was twenty-five. He was two years older, an engineering graduate of Georgia Tech and working for a planning-design firm that had business interests across the Southeast. They were drawn together because he had just spent two months in Walkerville, her home town, doing engineering studies preparatory for a county-wide land use ordinance that his firm had been retained to help implement. He was from Atlanta, but he had fallen in love with Walkerville. One of the local companies with a need for a planning and design engineer had offered him a job there. He was considering the offer.

"After that, one thing led to another, I guess," she continued. "He took the job and moved here. I started coming home every weekend. It was driving my parents crazy. Their daughter had left home years before, and suddenly they can't keep her away. You probably don't remember my father. He didn't get the manager's job at Marsellaise Plantation until several years after you left."

"Your father works for Lazard?"

"Did. He's retired now. Actually, I guess they fired him when they incorporated Lazard Farms, but he's pushing seventy now. I was the youngest child."

She took a sip of wine and poured some for Ben, momentarily distracted from her story. "So we got married. Not long thereafter John's father died and left him a rather large insurance settlement. He was an only child. We were able to buy this house. John wanted the airplane and I was going to open an art gallery on the square. God, we were so foolish! But we had the money, and we said we'll only be young once, and he wanted it, and...."

She faltered, stared at the candle for a moment. "It's funny how things can fall apart so quickly." Another pause. "Anyway, he'd gotten a Cessna 172 Skyhawk II that he bought used from some doctor in Macon. The plane was maybe ten years old but in tip-top shape. John was really into his flying. He had Saturdays off, and had gotten up to about thirty hours solo when..." Here, she faltered again. "...when his plane crashed."

"Alex, are you sure you want to talk about this?"

"Damn right I do. I've been angry at the world for too long. It does me good to talk."

Ben leaned back, listened.

"He was doing cross-countries, you know, flying to places like Savannah or somewhere in south Georgia, landing and then flying back to build up his time and practice his navigation. He would call an airport and get permission to do touch-and-goes and then fly there, do that all afternoon, and fly back. then one day he just didn't come home. The called it pilot error, but I just can't believe it—he was always so careful."

She explained how the exact cause of the crash had never been exactly established, but the National Transportation Safety Board hearing had ruled "probable pilot error" based on their investigation of the crash.

"But if that wasn't bad enough," she continued, "John's life insurance company refused to honor his policy because of the ruling. Things have been a bit rough since then. I appealed the denial to the insurance company, but I didn't get anywhere with them. I tried getting some help through the

State Insurance Commissioner's office, but they turned me down. I finally hired a lawyer and a private investigator, but the only thing that got me was a huge stack of legal bills and an empty savings account. I finally just gave up and decided to get on with my life. That's when I went to work at the bank. It's amazing how fast your life can change."

Ben didn't know what to say. After a moment he asked, "Is there anything I can do?"

"Nothing that you haven't already done. Thanks for listening." She paused, took a sip of wine. "But maybe there is one thing. You're a doctor, you deal with insurance companies all the time, right?" He nodded. "By state law I've got two years to appeal an insurance company's ruling on a policy benefit, and that deadline is coming up in a couple of months. How about going over the reports for me and see if you have any new ideas?"

"Alex, I don't know anything about life insurance..."

"I know. But you're a good thinker and maybe you'll have some ideas. It won't hurt to get one more opinion. It was a big policy and I could use the money."

She rose and hurried through the French doors into the house. Ben could see her extracting three bulky manila envelopes from the drawer of an antique chest. She reemerged on the patio and handed them to Ben. "Find something for me, Ben."

Ben stared at the envelopes as Alex stood over him. He looked at her again, then at the packages in his lap. "OK, I'll look at these for you, but what do you want me to look for?"

"Anything. Anything they might have missed. Any reason to make the insurance company pay. Five-hundred-thousand dollars is a lot of money, Ben."

CHAPTER FIFTEEN

IT WAS NEARLY MIDNIGHT when Ben arrived home. He brought with him a foil-wrapped package of tiramisu—for a "bedtime snack," Alex said—and the three large envelopes.

He fumbled for the lamp and laid his packages on the table. He ate a bit of the dessert, saving the rest for later, and looked at the envelopes. Despite his curiosity, he decided to wait until morning to examine them and went to bed.

The sun woke him on Sunday morning. He tried to go back to sleep, but couldn't. In the kitchen he fixed himself an indulgent high fat, high sodium breakfast of ham, grits and eggs, justifying it by the fact that it was his day off, and that he ate yogurt and juice most mornings. Pouring himself a second cup of coffee, Ben laid the three envelopes before him on the breakfast table. The thinner of the three bore the return address of Stavenger & Stavenger, a Savannah law firm. Inside were three file folders, neatly labeled in Alex's handwriting "Insurance Company-Correspondence," "Insurance Commissioner-Correspondence," and "Stavenger."

The top letter in the insurance company file was dated approximately four months after John Jennings death. In blunt and unequivocal terms, the letter stated that "per the policy amendment agreed to by the deceased, no benefits shall be payable for death related to aircraft accident if such death occurs prior to the second anniversary date of this policy if: a) the insured is the pilot of the aircraft in which death occurs, and b) there is evidence of pilot error contributory to such aircraft accident." The rest of the file contained photocopies of letters from Alex appealing this decision with repeated denials from the insurance company, Southeastern Life and Casualty. The letters back and forth to the State Insurance Commissioner's office basically advised Alex of her right to appeal denials, but at the same time advised her to take legal action if she felt she had a strong case.

The "Stavenger" folder contained copies of more than a dozen letters from the attorney to Alex and to the insurance company, plus a lengthy independent report from a private investigator named Phillip Smith. The last letter, dated some nine months after John's death, advised Alex that pursuit of her claim would "likely be denied in a court of law," but that the attorney would be willing to pursue the claim for a pre-trial retainer of ten-thousand dollars. In the back of the folder Ben found legal bills totaling nearly nine-thousand dollars, all marked "Paid" in Alex's neat script.

The other two envelopes were both imprinted with the logo of the National Transportation Safety Board and the address of the Atlanta regional office, and both were sealed with tape. The bulkier of the two was labeled in pen "John A. Jennings-Personal Items," followed by a series of numbers giving the official designation of the investigation. The other was labeled simply "John A. Jennings-Final Crash Report." He opened it first.

Inside was a thick bound folder with blue plastic covers and a computer printed stick-on label that read "National Transportation Safety Board Investigation 92-8769, Final Report of Inquiry, December 3, 1992." The first page was a table of contents, followed by a summary, the entire formal report, and about three dozen attachments consisting of investigative reports and interviews, crash scene analysis reports, autopsy and death certificate, and photographs, all neatly marked with colored index tabs. Ben flipped to the summary page. In terse wording, the Board of Inquiry attributed the cause of the crash to "presumed pilot error resulting in loss of structural integrity of the airframe," but with the caveat that, "due to the fact that the wreckage of the aircraft had been removed from its original site of impact, conclusions based on the crash site analysis are at best speculative."

Ben turned to a section labeled "Death Certificate/Autopsy Report." A copy of the death certificate, signed by Troup Lazard, MD, Medical Examiner, and Elmo Kantt, Coroner, listed the cause of death as massive trauma to the thorax and abdomen due to aviation accident. The autopsy report, and the extensive negative toxicology studies that accompanied it, confirmed this. Turning back to the full formal report, he began to read.

An hour later he closed the folder and tried to digest the details of the report. The accident had occurred on a cloudless October Saturday at approximately 4 p.m. John Jennings had taken off at about three hours earlier at 1 p.m. He had not filed a flight plan but, instead, had remarked to the airport administrator he would be flying locally only and later that afternoon practice touch and go landings at the local airport. The investigator's report referred to several people who had seen the Cessna flying in the area. Evidently the last person to observe the plane in flight before the crash was an elderly man fishing on the Opahatchee River. The investigator described his account as "being of uncertain accuracy." The aircraft apparently went down in a cattle pasture on Marsellaise Plantation. The plane was completely destroyed. Judging from the photographs, the largest piece of wreckage was a section of wing measuring about six feet in length. For reasons the report did not make clear, the pieces of the wreckage were gathered and moved by several of the local sheriff's deputies to a hay shelter in a nearby field prior to the arrival of the NTSB investigator. Examination of the engine and propeller revealed that both were functioning properly at the time of the crash, ruling out propulsive failure as a cause. The final conclusion was that the plane had broken up in mid-air, presumably due to some occult structural fault. The aircraft itself was eleven years old, and while it had a good maintenance record, the report speculated on "failure of a major structural element of the fuselage precipitated by excessive stress from aerodynamic maneuvers beyond the design capability of the airframe." In other words, the investigators assumed that through error or ignorance, the pilot of the plane who attempted some maneuver had caused the aircraft to disintegrate in mid-air.

Laying the bound report aside, Ben opened the envelope labeled "Personal Items." Inside were a thick stack of aviation charts covering most of the state of Georgia, with
detailed maps of the commercial traffic areas around Atlanta,
Augusta, Macon and Savannah. There were two paper-bound
books that belonged to the aircraft, one a simple owner's man-
ual, the other a detailed maintenance record dating back to its
manufacture in 1981. A green hard-bound ledger book labeled
"Pilot Log" was heavily stained with a dried brownish substance that could only be blood.

Ben opened the Log Book and turned to the final entry.
It was dated October 17, 1992, in the column on the left and
had letters and numbers across toward the right. In the
"Airport" column was penciled "WVL" and under "Departure"
the time "1255 hrs." The "Arrival" column was blank. In
"Comments" column was the notation "T/G MP 1505-."

Ben looked at the preceding entries. He made a men-
tal note to ask someone familiar with flight logs the meaning
of the various letters and codes. He laid the Log Book aside
and picked up the bound report, re-reading the investigator's
summary. The only person reported to have observed the John
Jennings flying in the hour before the crash was the elderly
fisherman, Willie Lee Spikes, described by the interviewer as a
"retired farm laborer." He reported seeing the plane flying
back and forth several times at a low altitude "like he was crop-
dusting." The investigator reported the statement but did not
give much weight to this witness as he felt he was unreliable.

He closed the folders and pushed them to one side.
The report was anything but definitive about the cause of the
crash. Something was not right. It seemed that Alex should at
least have some grounds for an appeal. Yet, the attorney had
advised her otherwise. On a whim, he opened the bound fold-

er and turned to the end of the Investigator's Report. It was signed by Martin Carswell. Picking up the telephone, he called directory assistance for the Atlanta area. There were no Martin Carswells, but one M. H. Carswell and one M. E. Carswell.

Ben looked at his watch. Ten a.m. on Sunday morning was as good a time as any to catch someone at home. He tried the first number. After four rings the phone clicked and a youngish female voice said, "Hi, this is Mary Helen. I can't come to the phone right now...."

He hung up without waiting to hear the rest.

M. E. Carswell answered in a gruff voice after two rings. "Carswell."

"Mr. Carswell, my name is Benjamin Pike from Walkerville, Georgia. Are you the Martin Carswell who works for the NTSB?"

"That's me. What have we got this time?" He sounded like an older man.

"I'm not calling about anything that's just happened. I wanted to ask you about an investigation you worked on a couple of years ago."

"Well, thank God for that. I'm on call this weekend for investigations, and these 'ten o'clock on Sunday morning calls are usually always the same. Some weekend flyboy with ten hours on his book goes for a spin in a rented high wing on Saturday, and they don't miss him 'till he doesn't show up for supper that night. By then it's dark. They start the search at dawn on Sunday, find the crash site after a couple of hours, call the NTSB and then the investigator on call. That's me. But, if this is about an old investigation, why can't it wait 'till Monday when I'm in the office?"

He seemed friendly enough over the phone. Ben

decided to pursue it rather than call back. "Mr. Carswell, I'm really doing this as a favor for a friend, the widow of a pilot who crashed a couple of years ago. I know it's been a long time, but the insurance company denied her husband's life insurance claim after the crash, and the statue of limits for her to appeal the denial is running out. She wanted to have one last look at the issue before it did and asked me to look over the reports. I just wanted to get your thoughts on a few things."

"Are you an attorney? I won't talk to attorneys except in the office, and on the record."

"No, nothing like that. Just a friend."

"Well, those reports are a matter of public record. You'd be surprised how many calls I get like this. Widow just can't bring herself to believe the report, gives it to a family friend. They read it and call me. You aren't recording this are you?"

"No. Promise."

"OK, shoot. I've been doing this for twenty-one years and I do thirty or forty of these investigations a year. Hope I can remember what you need."

"Do you remember a crash involving John Jennings from Walkerville? It happened in August of 1992."

"The Cessna 172? The one where they gathered up the wreckage and put it in a barn? Do I ever! That's one of the most screwed up investigations I've ever been involved in! I was almost embarrassed to sign my name to the final report. As I recall, we never did give a clear finding on that one."

"How do you mean, 'screwed up'?"

"Lemme think. As I recall, the pilot—you said his name was Jennings, right?—a bit of a hot dog, but by all reports, a good boy and a good pilot, too. A couple of other local pilots

down there who knew him said he'd set his plane down wher-
ever he could find a smooth patch of ground. But no acrobat-
ics or crap like that that I could come up with. Anyway, he
ends up on a clear Fall day with his plane strewn all over some
south Georgia cow pasture. The real hooker was this,
though—the sheriff and his men end up gathering up the
whole wreckage before they called us. Strangest thing I've
ever seen. Called themselves 'investigating' the cause. Hell,
they couldn't investigate two bumper cars running together in
a kindergarten playground from what I saw. They ended up
apologizing, but it sure messed us up. Head man was a big guy
with a funny name..."

"Hoke?"

"Yeah, that's it. Hoke Brantley. Seemed to mean well,
but not real bright."

"So, what do I tell the pilot's widow?" Ben asked.

"Tell her we did our best under the circumstances. Hey,
are you sure you're not thinking about trying to sue somebody?
Everybody wants to sue these days. Everybody's a victim. In
the end, we blamed on pilot error. Those little planes are
mighty sturdy and about the only thing that will make one
break up in mid-air like that is some hot-shot inexperienced
pilot trying something crazy. My gut feeling was that the
plane had a fatigue fracture in one of the main spars, and, once
it broke, the tumbling in the air ripped the rest of the airframe
apart. We never could tell precisely 'cause we never did find
the exact clue we needed."

"Thank you, Mr. Carswell, I appreciate your time."

"No problem. Wish I could be more helpful, or tell you
someone else to talk to. The only semi-witness was an old
black man, Willie something-or-other. But he was about half
drunk when I talked with him and wasn't very helpful as I

recall. Call me back if you need me."

They hung up. Carswell seemed like a nice enough fellow, but probably someone who had been at the job long enough to know that he couldn't find an answer for everything. So he issued a report, however flawed, and moved on to the next case.

CHAPTER
SIXTEEN

"I HATE DEER SEASON."

Carter Steed was pouring himself a cup of coffee in the doctors' lounge on Monday morning. "We had another one this weekend."

"Another what?" Ben asked.

"Another Atlanta hunter killed."

"What are you talking about—another Atlanta hunter?"

"Just wait 'till you've been here for a while, you'll see. Every September it starts and goes on through January. Were you aware that the Boone and Crockett state record whitetail was killed not five miles from where we stand at this moment?

The deer of Adams County draw hunters like flies to shit. First there's bow season. Then..." He paused to stuff a sugar covered doughnut into his mouth. "...there's gun season and the real fun begins."

He flopped down on the couch and propped his feet on the small table in front of it. "These city fellows, they spend all summer staring at the stuffed deer heads in their basement rec room walls, and by the Fall, they're just a little crazy. Come down here in their four-wheel drive pickups that they've hardly even driven off the interstate, much less on a dirt road. And then it's trauma city. You see basically three kinds of accidents: drinking accidents, stupid accidents, and accidental accidents." He inhaled another doughnut.

"That bad, eh?"

"Ben, you're an internist. I'm an ER doc. I get the messy stuff. Get these weekend warriors away from their cookie cutter subdivisions and suddenly they're Daniel Boone, hard-drinking and armed to the teeth. They get drunk and run their Four-by-Fours into trees, they stay up drinking half the night and get up at 5 a.m. to climb up in tree-stands where they immediately go back to sleep and fall out, and, worst of all, they shoot one another—arrows, rifles, buckshot, even an occasional rifled slug. The real honest-to-God accidental accidents where somebody gets hurt or killed and few and far between. Most of them are just stupid and entirely preventable."

"What happened this weekend?"

"I haven't heard the details yet, but since I'm the ER director, I've got to do the paper work. I'm on my way down there. Walk out with me?"

The emergency room was on the way to the doctors' parking, so Ben followed Carter Steed down the stairs. Carter shuffled through a stack of papers in a tray on his desk, pulling out a green folder.

"Here it is. The man was named Thomas Latham, age fifty-five, from Atlanta." He flipped over the stapled sheets. "Looks like...yeah, here it is, shot in the head." He read on: "Entry/exit wounds consistent with a high-powered rifle. No witnesses. The guy hunting with him said he heard a shot, and when he went to look for his buddy, found him by the edge of the highway, dead. Let's see, here's a photocopy of his driver's license."

He studied the grainy picture for a moment, his brow wrinkling.

"Wait a minute! Ben, what were the names of those INS agents who were following up on that patient that came in and died? Remember, that night last month when I called you in to help translate?"

"I don't remember. Wait...the younger Hispanic one was Roble. It stuck with me because it means 'oak' in Spanish. The other guy?"

"Was this him?" Steed slid the photocopy of the driver's license across the desk.

Ben examined the paper. "Sure looks like him. Any other ID?"

Steed was looking through the remaining papers. "Not according to this. Kantt signed off on it as an accidental death, and a funeral home from Atlanta picked up the body. The report says he was divorced, closest relative is a son in California."

"That's strange. Where was he hunting when he got shot?"

Carter consulted the file. "According to this, on Highway 15 on the Tooks property. That's across the road from the main gate at Marseilles Plantation."

Ben finished his last patient of the morning, walked in his office and shut the door. He'd brooded about it overnight and decided to call the insurance company before he called Alex. Not that he had any idea what he was looking for—or what he was going to say. He simply wanted to get a feel for what Southeastern Life and Casualty would say about the status of the claim.

He retrieved the manila envelope containing the correspondence to the insurance company from his briefcase and found the original letter denying the claim. It was signed by Robin Easterling, whose title was Senior Underwriter. Calling the number listed on the letterhead, he was eventually put through.

"Robin Easterling." The voice was female, middle-aged.

"Ms. Easterling, this is Benjamin Pike. I'm calling on behalf of Mrs. Alexandria Jennings..."

"Claim number, please," she cut him off abruptly.

He read it off the letter and waited as he heard the clicking of a keyboard in the background. "Oh. That's the John Jennings claim. What can I do for you, Mr. Pike? Are you Ms. Jennings's attorney?"

The NTSB investigator had mistaken him for an attorney; he decided to bluff a bit. "I'm representing Mrs. Jennings at the moment, Ms. Easterling. I'm calling to inquire about the status of her claim for the death benefits of her husband's insurance policy."

"Have you taken over for Mr. Stavenger? It's been more than a year since we last heard from him."

"For the moment, yes," he lied.

"Well, I know how busy you lawyers are, but it's very unusual when we don't receive a reply to our offer to negotiate. We replied to Mr. Stavenger's initial letter on..." She paused and the keyboard clicked. "...January 25, 1993. When we didn't hear from you, we sent you a duplicate copy of the letter by certified mail, return receipt requested three weeks later."

Thinking quickly, Ben replied, "Well, I've got to apologize, Ms. Easterling. Part of the file was misplaced here in our office and the client asked me to look into the matter. Now let me get this straight—you didn't receive a reply from Mr. Stavenger after when, now?"

With her keyboard clicking as she spoke, Robin Easterling explained that Southeastern Life and Casualty had received a single letter from Alex's attorney, Joseph Stavenger. She admitted that the underwriters' committee had felt that the company might have some exposure in denying the claim and had authorized her to begin settlement talks with the beneficiary's representative.

"Are you certain that you didn't receive any correspondence from Mr. Stavenger after that?"

"Of course I'm certain. In answer to your question, no, and frankly, I'm suprised. A potential claim of this size is assigned to an individual underwriter—in this case me—and all communication, no matter how trivial, goes through that person. We enter all contacts in our computer, together with the texts of all letters that we send and synopses of all letters that we receive. I'll move this claim back to the active file, as I take it we'll be hearing from you shortly.

"I'm sure," he said and hung up.

Opening the folder that held correspondence from Stavenger, Ben counted copies of eight letters written between December 1992 and May 1993—all addressed to Ms. Robin Easterling, Senior Underwriter, Southeastern Life and Casualty Company. There were a total of ten letters to Alex, detailing multiple phone calls, letters and face to face (unsuccessful) negotiations with the company. The last letter, dated May 18, 1993, contained news of the insurance company's final denial of the claim and the offer to proceed to litigation.

Replacing the folder in the envelope, he decided not to say anything to Alex just yet.

The Adams County Sheriff's Department was located in a squat brick building next to the municipal lock-up on a side street two blocks off the city square. Ben drove the few blocks from his office and parked in a space marked "Reserved for Prisoner's Families Only."

The officer on duty pointed him down a dingy hall where he found Hoke Brantley sitting behind his desk, feet propped up and reading the latest issue of *Peace Officer* magazine. When he saw Ben at the door he motioned for him to come in.

"How are you, Ben? What brings you down here? Want us to arrest some of your non-paying patients?" He grinned through tobacco-stained teeth.

"Thanks, but no thanks, Hoke. I'll bet I've got the same kind of record you do—all my patients pay up, and everyone you arrest is found guilty, right?"

Hoke reached in his back pocket for a pouch of chewing tobacco, explaining, "My wife finally made me give up the cigarettes. What's up?"

"Look, I need a little favor..."

"Name it."

"You remember John Jennings, got killed a couple of years ago in a plane crash."

"Yeah, real tragedy. Word is you're dating the young widow."

"Not really. We've been out a few times. Anyway, she asked me to look over the crash reports. They apparently ruled it pilot error, but from what I read, I'm not too sure. She'd like to know what really happened."

The grin left the deputy's face. "What do you mean, Ben, by 'really happened'?"

"Well, the NTSB report is kind of vague. It doesn't really say why his plane went down. Alex wants to know if there's any more to it. What do you think happened? What's the story between the lines?"

"Awful late for her to be worryin' about it now, ain't it, Ben?" He spit a dollop of sticky brown fluid in the trash can. "Why this sudden outbreak of curiosity, and what you got to do with it?"

"Hoke, I know I'm probably wasting my time and yours, but I promised Alex I'd ask. The insurance company refused to pay the claim on John's life because of the determination of pilot error. She's got two years to appeal it and the time is about up. She asked me to see what I thought about it."

"You read the report, right?" Hoke asked. Ben nodded. "It's just like it said. The plane broke up and landed all over a cow pasture out at Lazard Farms. I don't think it said it in the report, but one of the wheels came down and killed a purebred Hereford brood cow. Doc was pissed big time."

"I talked with the NTSB investigator. Why did you guys gather up the wreckage before he got here?"

"Hey, you *are* serious about this, aren't you?" Hoke didn't smile. He shifted in his chair and propped his feet back up on the desk. "Well, I'll have to admit that was a mistake, but an honest one. It was Doc Lazard who called us out there, and there wasn't any doubt the kid was dead. It was late in the afternoon as I recall, and it looked like a storm was gonna blow up, so I had my men gather up the pieces from here and there and put them under a shelter to protect them. We were calling it preserving the evidence, but the investigator, Carter or something..."

"Carswell."

"Yeah, Carswell..., he was p.o.'ed, too. I remember I ended up that weekend with everybody mad at me—Doc Lazard, Carswell, and now it looks like the widow Jennings, too."

"Like I told you, Hoke, it's about the insurance money, nothing more than that. So I don't guess you can add much more to what I already know?"

"You got it, Ben." Hoke rose and extended his hand. "Good to see you. I gotta get back to work."

"Thanks for your help."

Ben headed for the door, but turned back as Hoke called his name.

"Ben." He looked at him for a brief moment, as if trying to decide what to say. "My daddy used to tell me that you don't ask questions when the answer you gonna get is not important anyway. You may want to remember that.

CHAPTER
SEVENTEEN

ON TUESDAY MORNING Ben Pike finished his morning hospital rounds early and arrived at the office before any of the staff. He sat in his office with the door closed and stared at out the window at the parking lot. It was all too weird, he thought. Why had Alex wanted him to look at her husband's crash report? Was he being used? And the attorney—was Alex the victim of an elaborate deception, or part of it? If so, who was lying—Stavenger or the insurance company? Or Alex? What did Hoke Brantley mean about not asking questions? He glanced at his watch. Maybe he could catch Alex before she left for work.

He dialed her number. She answered on the second ring.

"Alex, this is Ben. I looked over the letters and the reports. Yesterday afternoon I dropped by to see Hoke Brantley."

"Did you find out anything? Any ideas?"

"Maybe. Looks like your attorney made a real effort. I see he's from Savannah. How did you find him?"

"I didn't. He was recommended to me. After the accident, Dr. Lazard called a number of times to check on me. Asked if there was anything that he could do. When I told him about the insurance company and the run-around I had gotten from the state insurance commissioner's office, he insisted on helping me find me a good lawyer. Why do you ask?"

"Just wondering. Another thing—why didn't you go ahead and sue the insurance company? I think the NTSB report was pretty equivocal. You might have had a chance."

"I really thought about it, but there were a couple of reasons. Mr. Stavenger didn't really encourage it, but most importantly, I couldn't afford it. Ben, John and I had a little money saved, but after the funeral and the legal bills, there wasn't much left. I thought I'd ask somebody to look at it one last time before the limit for my appeal runs out. I can't afford another lawyer. That's why I asked you."

Ben hung up the phone and stared out the window, thinking. After a moment he retrieved the NTSB crash report from the envelope and found the name of the old man who had apparently been the last one to see the John's plane before the crash.

"Willie Lee Spikes? That name sounds familiar."

Rachel Edwards looked toward the file room. "I think Dr. Powell saw him a few times several years ago when we were still keeping records the old way, before the computer. I've already looked on line, and his name is not listed. That means he didn't have an active account when we converted over two-and-a-half years ago, and that he hasn't been seen since. Of course, he could have died and we might have purged his account. I'll look in the old files first."

Ten minutes later Rachel entered holding a worn chart. "Here it is. Willie Lee Spikes. Seventy-six-years old now. Last seen by Dr. Powell in 1990." She scanned the notes. "Looks like he passed out drunk in front of a woodburning stove and got some burns on his leg. There are a lot of drunks, and a lot of old people, but not many old drunks. It's going on five years since he's been in. He's probably dead by now."

"Well, we know he was alive in the October 1992. Do you have a phone number?"

Rachel looked at him skeptically. "Are you kidding? This fellow's not going to have a phone. Unless I'm way off, he spends every penny of his Social Security and food stamps on booze, fatback and grits, probably in that order." She handed him the chart. "There's an address in there for a Route 2 box in Chappel County. That would be the road along the other side of the river. I have some friends who live out that way. Judging from the box number, that's about seven or eight miles north of the turnoff after you cross the river bridge in Walkerville. You going to try to find him?"

"Thought I might."

On Saturday morning, Ben picked up Alex at nine. When he told her he wanted to try to find the old man, she had insisted on going with him.

From her house they passed through the center of town, west down Main Street, past the warehouse district and over the Lazard Memorial Bridge to Snooksville, an informal mass of beer joints and night spots that had sprouted just over the river in Chappel County.

Ben shook his head. "I just can't get away from it," he said. "It's 'Lazard this' and 'Lazard Memorial that' every time you turn around. I don't remember all this when I lived here nearly thirty years ago."

"It's always been there, Ben. Maybe you just never noticed. Whether you want to admit it or not, the Lazard name is magic in this county. Your father—and now Dr. Lazard—have given tens-of-thousands of dollars to support just about every good thing we have here. The library, the civic center, the ..."

"I know." Ben cut her off. "I just get tired of hearing about it. That's all."

"There was a time there when I was off at school and working in Atlanta that Dr. Lazard was having some financial troubles. That was when my father was working for him and got laid off. When he incorporated Marseilles Plantation as Lazard Farms, Inc., I understand he got some refinancing and pulled himself out. I don't know the details. My father might if you're interested."

"That sounds like an invitation to meet your parents?"

Alex smiled. "Could be," she said with a sly smirk.

They turned north on State Route 63. In contrast to the swamps of the Adams County side, the land on the Chappel County side of the Opahatchee River was high and flat, usually dropping sharply from a high bluff to the river below. Except where stands of trees indicated small streams emptying into the river, the land was cultivated in huge open fields, with the deep green of mature cotton plants interspersed here and there with stands of soybeans, some of which were being harvested. The road roughly paralleled the river, passing the occasional farm and small house.

Alex was watching the box numbers.

"OK, that was box 2657. You said Willie Lee's was 2852, right?"

They rode for another two miles. The open fields stopped and the land became hilly as farmland gave way to stands of planted pine and cut-over timberland.

"2852," Alex called out. She pointed at a rusty mailbox hanging at an odd angle from a crooked post, and crudely numbered in bright blue paint. Under the number was lettered "SPIKES" with both S's drawn backwards. An overgrown dirt track led into the woods toward the river.

The road, such as it was, went straight on for a quarter mile through a stand of cut-over pines now thick with sweet-gum and scrub oak. Turning sharply right, it descended a gentle hill to a low bluff overlooking the river. A sagging unpainted shack stood in a clearing surrounded by the rusting hulks of three pickups and a 1950's vintage finned Cadillac. A mangy dog barked furiously as they drove up. To one side of the sagging porch was a woodpile with an ax fixed in a chopping block, on the other a well with its bucket swinging on a chain from a rusted hoist.

Ben got out of the car and whistled at the dog who ran tuck-tailed under the porch where he continued to growl.

Ben stood at the base of the steps and yelled, "Mr. Spikes."

No reply. He yelled again and waited. After a moment he walked back to the car and pressed the horn twice rapidly. The dog began to bark again, and now emboldened by sounds of stirring in the house, emerged from under the porch snarling.

The front door creaked open and an elderly barefooted black man with woolly white hair and a full yellow-stained white beard poked his head out and then stepped tentatively on the porch. He was dressed in a pair of bibbed overalls, ripped at the knees revealing a stained pair of long johns. He called, "What you want?"

"Mr. Spikes? Are you Willie Lee Spikes?"

"That be me." He squinted at Ben. "You the 'surance man? I don't want none, so go 'way." He turned to go back into the house.

"Mr. Spikes, I'm not selling anything. I'm a doctor. I wanted to talk with you about something."

The old man turned around. "What's that?"

"Can I come up?" Ben asked.

"Hold on. Lemme get some shoes on. Y'all have a seat in my garden." He pointed to two bench seats evidently removed from the rusted pickups and propped on concrete blocks.

Alex emerged from the car and they walked over and sat down after brushing the dust off the sun-cracked vinyl. Momentarily, the old man slouched down the steps and shuffled over, sitting down on the other bench. "What can I do for you?" he rasped.

"Mr. Spikes..."

"Call me Willie Lee. I'm seventy-six-years old and ain't no white man ever called me 'mister.' Too late to start now, too old to change." He appeared to be quite sober.

"Willie Lee, I'm Ben Pike, and this is Mrs. Alex Jennings. I'm a doctor over in Walkerville. I know you don't know us, but we came here to ask you about that plane crash that happened a couple of years ago. Do you remember?"

"Yes, I remember. I was drinkin' bad back then. Done quit now. What 'bout it?"

"It was Mrs. Jennings's husband that was killed in that crash, and we're here to find out if there's any more you can tell us about what you know."

"Lemme see now. Truth of the matter is, I don't rightly 'member that much 'bout it. I told the gov'ment man what I knowed then, which is what I knows now, I reckon."

"Would you mind telling us what you remember? Did you see the plane go down?"

"No, but I heard it. It hit right over there." He pointed to the forest across the river. "There's a big field 'bout half a mile back 'cross the swamp there, and they tells me that's where it went down." He seemed flattered that someone was asking him about anything.

"You say you heard it? Tell us what happened from start to finish," Alex asked. She was sitting forward on the bench.

"Well, I was fishing on the river that day, a Sat'day if I recollect, and there was this little red and white plane that kept buzzing down over there and then roaring his motor and then buzzin' down again. Like he was crop-dustin'. You saw them cotton fields down the road? Like they do with them."

"How long did that go on?"

"A while, not too long, and then he quit."

"Is that when the crash happened?"

"No, that was when he took up again."

"What do you mean 'took up'?"

The old man looked at them like they were a bit dense.

"I mean when he took off after he landed, like all them planes do."

"What planes?"

"Them planes that stay over there 'cross the river. They usually come at night, but sometimes they fly around during the day."

Ben was confused. "Mr. Spikes—Willie Lee, where are you talking about?"

"Where do you think I'm talking 'bout. Over there, on that big Marsey Plantation!"

Ben and Alex exchanged puzzled glances.

"Go on. What happened then?"

"Well, he takes up—I could hear the engine—and he flies over the river here and turns back toward Walkerville, and then I hears this big 'thump' and then a bunch of other thumps and then the sound stops."

"What do you mean by big thump?" Ben inquired.

Willie Lee raised his bushy white eyebrows. "For a white man, you shore axes a lot of questions." He paused, thinking. "It was like when we usta blow stumps to clear new ground for pasture. Kinda like that."

"An explosion?"

"I s'pose you could call it that."

"Willie Lee," Ben asked slowly, "did you tell all this to the investigator?"

"You mean the gov'ment man? Like I says, I was bad to drink back then, and I don't rightly recollect what I told 'im."

CHAPTER
EIGHTEEN

"WHAT DOES ALL THIS MEAN?"

Alex's sat on the passenger side of Ben's car, face flushed, her speech rapid and pressured. They were on their way back to Walkerville following their visit to Willie Spikes' place. Before driving away, Ben had given the old man a twenty and thanked him. Seeing the crisp bill in his hand, Mr. Spikes lit up and promised to call him if he had any more information.

Ben considered Alex's question carefully. "I don't know," he finally replied. "But we need to talk."

He slowed the car and pulled off the highway under

the shade of a stand of white oaks on a hillock surrounding the ruins of a chimney where an old house had stood. He turned off the motor. Fields of cotton stretched to the horizon in all directions. The only sound was the wind rustling the leaves and a crow cawing in the distance. Opening the door, he walked to the base of one of the huge oaks and sat down, his back propped against its trunk. He stared out across the endless fields. She sat down beside him.

For a long moment they sat in silence, and then he told her what he had learned from the NTSB investigator and from the insurance company underwriter. She stared at him, disbelieving.

"Alex, there's something very strange going on here. I need to know if you're part of it."

Her look shattered any misapprehensions he might have had about her involvement. "You bastard!" she hissed.

She jumped to her feet and walked to the edge of the rows of cotton, her arms folded, gazing blankly into the distance. After a moment he came and stood beside her. He could see that she'd been crying.

She glared at Ben with anger in her eyes. "Goddammit! What's happened to my life? What kind of fool have I been?" Wiping her hand across her face, she took a deep breath. "OK. Are you going to help me, or am I going to do this by myself?"

"Do what, Alex?"

"Find out why I've been lied to. Find out what really happened and why. Well, are you?"

Ben suddenly realized he wanted to kiss her. He wanted to kiss her more than he'd ever wanted to kiss a woman. But not now. Not yet.

"Yes. I'll help you," he said.

Back at her house in Walkerville, they talked. They agreed he should speak with Hoke Brantley again in light of what Willie Lee Spikes had told them. Ben asked if she knew anyone she trusted who was a pilot. She said Skip Malcom had a plane and asked why he wanted to know. He said he'd tell her after he talked with Skip.

Ben called Hoke Brantley at home the next afternoon. "Hoke, I need to talk to you right away."

"You sound mighty upset, Ben. What's up?"

"I'll tell you when I see you. Can we meet somewhere?"

"You mean now?"

"Now."

Ben heard the deputy yawn. "Tell you what," Hoke drawled, "I ain't doing nothing but watching a football game on the boob tube. Why don't you hot-foot if over to my trailer right now?"

"Right now? You sure?"

"Hell, yeah. The wife and kids are over at her ma's. I got lots of beer and popcorn. We can watch the Falcons get their ass busted again."

Half an hour later Ben drove into the yard of a faded gray double-wide. He recognized the sheriff's car parked in front next to a shiny new red Firebird. He mounted the concrete steps and knocked on the door. It opened with a creak. Hoke, clad in a sweatsuit and holding a longneck beer, invited him in.

The place was a mess. In the far corner of the living room, a big screen TV was blaring away with halftime football commentators. Hoke pointed to a chair. "Have a seat," he said, then belched.

Ben sat down. On the table next to the recliner was a table littered with empty beer bottles. A bowl of popcorn sat next to his feet. Kernels trailed across the floor.

Glad to see you, man," Hoke said. "How 'bout a beer? Can you believe this? The Falcons are whipping the shit outta Miami. You still keep up with football?"

Ben shook his head. "Watching football is one on those luxuries I gave up about the time I started medical school. Guess I never got back into it."

Hoke turned the volume down, retrieved two beers from the refrigerator and leaned back in his chair. "What's on your mind? You sounded awful suspicious on the phone."

"Hoke, I know all this is none of your concern, and I guess I've got to say I'm a little embarrassed to bother you about it. But, on the other hand, you're one of the few people around here that I feel like I know pretty well and can trust." He paused.

"Well, don't mealy-mouth, what you need?"

"It's about the John Jennings' plane crash." Ben could see Hoke's face darken. He continued: "Alex and I were following up on some things. We talked to Willie Lee Spikes— he's apparently the closest thing to a witness that there was. He told us a few things that weren't in the final crash report. I wanted to get your opinion and advice as to what to do or where to go from here."

"You talking about that drunk nigger that stays over in Chappel County off River Road?"

"I guess you could describe him like that, but he wasn't drinking when we talked with him yesterday."

"I know that fellow. He lives across the river, but he used to drink and gamble down here and over in Snooksville. I've brought him in for drunk and disorderly four or five times, and I know for a fact he's spent weeks at a time in the Chappel County lock-up." Hoke took a long drag on his beer. "I don't know if you can believe a word he says."

"You're probably right, but Alex wants to know. He was talking about John Jennings's plane landing across the river on Marsellaise Plantation land before he took off again and crashed. And he said something about other planes landing over there. Is that right? Is there some kind of airstrip over there?"

"Not that I know of. Doc's land takes up one hell of a lot of space, but I've probably walked most of it over the years. We've gotten calls about poachers, stolen equipment, and the like. There's quite a bit of pasture land, but no place for a plane to land that I know of." He scratched his stubbled face and thought a moment. "You reckon he was talking about crop-dusters? They fly low and would look like someone landing or taking off."

"Maybe. But he talked about planes at night."

"Now I know he's crazy. Ain't *nobody* gonna fly over that swamp at night. Anyway, there ain't nothing but swamp for half a mile back from the river on the Adams County side. Maybe them 'planes' was pink elephants with wings." Hoke chuckled and swigged his beer.

"Probably," Ben agreed, "but he did say one other

thing. Something about an explosion before the plane went down. He said he heard a 'thump,' like dynamite."

"Well, that could be." Hoke thought hard for a moment. "The wreckage was strewn all over a big pasture. But, then again, maybe that's what it sounds like when a plane falls apart in the air; I don't know." A long pause. "Ben, it's been more than two years. Anything else?"

"Just one more thing. Alex's attorney hired an investigator to have an independent look into the plane crash. You know with the insurance company's denial of the claim she wanted to get another opinion. What did you think of him?"

"Who? What investigator?"

"His name was Phillip Smith. His report said he interviewed you, and that you two walked over the crash site together."

"Oh, Phillip Smith, yeah. I kinda forgot about that. Well, I don't know, Ben. Seemed like he asked all the right questions. 'Course, I never saw his report and all. What more can I say?"

⌒

"Dr. Pike, there's a man out here to see you, says it's personal," Doreen said over the intercom. "Says his name is Mr. 'Robe-lay'," then to the side, "did I pronounce that right?— and that you'd remember him."

Ben picked up the phone. "Doreen, ask him what he wants." He waited.

"He says it's personal. Says to tell you that he and his associate Mr. Latham visited you a couple of months ago."

"Send him back."

The man who had identified himself as "Officer Roble" was ushered into the office by Doreen. He extended his hand. "Martin Roble, Dr. Pike. You remember our meeting before?"

"Of course. The hunter who was accidentally shot, was that your partner?"

"I'm sorry to say that it was, but we don't believe it was an accident."

"Are you saying someone deliberately shot him?"

"I'm not willing to say that at this time. Like we told you before, we were participating in an ongoing investigation."

"Why are you here to see me? I didn't hear about your partner until a couple of days after it happened."

Roble sat down. "I realize that, and as far as we're concerned, his death will remain a hunting accident for the time being. I'm here to ask you about your association with Dr. Lazard. We understand you're half-brothers and that..."

"We? Just who the hell is 'we'? The INS?" Ben leaned forward, teeth clenched. "Don't lie to me, Roble. I'm tired of people lying to me. Just who are you and what are you up to?"

Roble's face remained expressionless. "Dr. Pike, at this point, I'm doing the talking. You were observed visiting with your brother a few weeks ago. And we've had some other reports about your activity. We decided to approach you directly."

"My activity? Approach me directly about what? What the hell are you talking about?"

"About what you do or don't know, and about what you may or may not be involved in."

"Are you watching me?"

"I assure you, no. I'm here as much as anything to see the expression on your face, and I think you've answered my question."

He rose to leave, tossing a card on Ben's desk that said simply: "Martin Roble," and listed an Atlanta area number. "Call me if you need anything at all."

"Wait, hold on a second. You walk into my office, and after a thirty second conversation in which you do all the talking, you get up to leave. Just what do you want?"

"At this point, Dr. Pike, nothing from you. In fact, I'll *give* you something—a bit of advice. Keep your nose clean and watch your back."

He smiled for the first time and walked out.

CHAPTER
NINETEEN

SKIP MALCOM TOSSED the thick folder on Ben's desk.

"Interesting," he said.

"How so?"

"You wanted to know if there was anything in these notes or on John's charts that might show a landing strip on Dr. Lazard's land. Ben, I didn't say anything to you when you first asked me, but I would have told you 'no' right offhand. Now I'm not so sure. Let me show you."

Opening the envelope marked "Personal Effects," Malcom extracted the blood-stained Pilot Log and a large scale aerial navigation map titled Atlanta Sectional Aeronautical

Chart. He unfolded it and pointed to a penciled-in linear mark with the characters "MP ~1500'." written beside it.

"Look at this," he said. "I think what he was recording was a landing strip which he must have designated 'MP' for Marsellaise Plantation, and then the approximate length, fifteen-hundred feet."

Ben studied the map. It was on a scale of 1:500,000 and covered Georgia and much of the surrounding states. "Are you certain about this?"

"I wasn't until I found this." He flipped open the Pilot Log and pointed to the last entry. "Look here, under 'Comments' he's written 'T/G MP 1505-'. 'T/G' stands for 'touch and go' and I presume 'MP' stands for the airstrip that he marked on the chart. And the time is right. '1505' would be 3:05 p.m. Ben, what I think this means is that the old man you talked to was right. John was doing touch and goes at that airstrip, and then he must have landed there before his plane went down."

"But why do you suppose the NTSB investigation didn't pick up on this?"

"Why should they? From what you told me, they didn't get as much information from the old man as you did, so there was no reason for them to try to correlate what was in the log book with what John had penciled on his chart. And what would all that have to do with his plane crashing, anyway?" He paused. "But if you really want to see what's there, why don't we have a look at it from the air?"

Two hours later they were flying at low altitude over the Opahatchee toward Marsellaise Plantation. They had taken off from the airport south of town, traveled west to pick up the course of the river and were following it north. The afternoon sunlight cast long shadows across the fields and pastures below. The boundaries of the Plantation became obvious as the patchwork pattern of smaller fields and roads gave way to the dense stands of pine timber. In the distance, the main house could be seen sitting on top of a small hill, brilliantly illuminated by the sun against a green background.

"We're about there," Skip called out over the noise of the engine. He pulled back on the yoke and climbed gradually as he banked the Cessna gently to the west and then back toward the river and the Plantation beyond it. "I'm going to come in from the west with the sun behind us," he explained. "We'll cross the river right where John had marked the landing strip on his map. I'll watch my side and you watch yours."

They approached the river over a vast sea of cotton fields. Ben recognized Willie Lee Spikes's house below them. The river flashed below, then dense swampland that suddenly opened into a series of large, flat fields separated by hedgerows of trees. They flew over a series of sheds and barns, then over several fields of what appeared to be soybeans. Two men sitting on the back of a pickup truck on the edge of the field waved. The plantation house loomed in the distance ahead. Skip banked to the south to avoid flying over it.

"See anything?" he asked.

"I can't make an airstrip out of anything down there. You?"

"No. There are several fields big enough and smooth enough to land in, but nothing obvious. We'll make another pass."

They did and saw nothing more.

Back at the airport Ben thanked Skip and swore him to silence.

Two days later Rachel greeted Ben's arrival at the office with a matter of fact, "Looks like you got there just in time."

"What are you talking about?"

"This," she said, thrusting a copy of the Chappel Courier at him. The headline screamed, "ACCIDENTAL FIRE CLAIMS LIFE OF ELDERLY MAN."

Ben grabbed the paper and quickly scanned the article. The body of Willie Lee Spikes, aged 77, of the River Road section of Chappel County had been found in the smoldering ruins of his house one day earlier. Preliminary investigation by state and local officials indicated that the cause of the fire was accidental, probably as a result a spark from a wood-fired cooking stove. Preliminary autopsy results indicated that the deceased was alive at the time of his death based on the finding of inhaled smoke particulates in the lungs, and that he was intoxicated, based on a very high level of blood alcohol.

"Damn!" Ben thundered. "Rachel, you don't suppose that it wasn't an accident, do you?"

"Dr. Pike, what are you talking about? Who would want to hurt an old man? You know he didn't have anything worth stealing. Remember what I said about old drunks?"

"You're right. Did you tell anyone that Alex and I went to see Willie Lee?"

She looked perplexed. "No, why should I?"

Picking up the telephone, he dialed the Miller State Bank and asked to speak to Alex Jennings. She came on the line after a brief delay.

"Alex, did you tell anyone that we went to visit Willie Spikes last week?"

"No." She caught herself, then said, "Yes, I did. I asked my dad if he knew anything about an airstrip at Marsellaise Plantation."

"Anybody else? It's important—think carefully."

"No, no one else, I'm sure. Why do you want to know?"

"He's dead. I just found out. According to the paper he was drinking and was burned up in an accidental house fire."

"Are you trying to say it wasn't an accident?" Her voice was shaking.

"Not yet. I'll call you back later. I've got one more call to make."

The dispatcher at the sheriff's department put him through quickly to Hoke Brantley. "Ben, you almost missed me. I was just on my way out the door. What's up?"

"After we talked the other day, did you tell anyone that Alex and I had been over to see Willie Lee Spikes?"

"No. No reason to. Why?"

"He's dead, Hoke."

"What!" Ben sensed true surprise in his voice. "How? What happened?"

"The Chappel County paper says it was an accidental house fire. The article said that he was drinking again. That's all I know."

"Well, damn." The tension had gone from his voice. "Sorry to hear that. Those things happen. Look, I've got to serve some papers on a fellow before he skips town. We'll talk later."

"Sure," Ben said and hung up.

⌒

"Ben, there's one common theme in this whole thing," Alex said. They were at his cabin, sitting on the deck overlooking the lake. "Lazard. He's got to be involved somehow. I've been thinking about it. All the unanswered questions are somehow connected to him. Think about it. John's plane crashes on his land and the wreckage is moved before the investigators arrive. He knows I'm thinking about hiring a lawyer and investigator and he finds one for me. John's charts point out an airstrip on his land and there's no mention made of it when he was interviewed by the crash investigator. But why? What's the reason?"

"I don't know. Is he hiding something? Can't be money. God knows he has enough of that."

"Maybe. Let me tell you about something that happened when I first went to work at the bank."

CHAPTER
TWENTY

"DR. LAZARD ARRANGED FOR ME to get the job at the bank," Alex explained. "He apparently owns part of it. I thought at the time he was being helpful, but now I don't know. After I had told the lawyer I couldn't afford going to trial to appeal the denial of John's insurance claim, he called me up and said he'd heard I might be having some difficulty and offered to help me out. I told him no, but then he offered to help me find a job until I could decide what I wanted to do. He told me to see the bank president and they hired me on the spot. The pay's not great but I needed it at the time. I've been getting by." She paused and looked out across the lake.

"This is the strange part, though," she continued. "When you mentioned money, it reminded me of something. At the bank, after you do your basic teller training, you're assigned to another teller to work under her direct supervision for about a month while you learn on the job. I was assigned to Susan, whose window was right next to mine. Most of what you do is pretty simple, but there are always little things, and she was right there for me to ask if I had a question or needed help. Susan was twenty-five, single, and loved to party. When I started working at the bank, she'd been going out for a couple of months with this guy named Greg Coleman. She'd met him at the bank. I was new there and really lonely after John died, and she sort of took me under her wing. All she could talk about was Greg. The way she told it, he was an accountant that had been brought in to help straighten out things at Lazard Farms, Inc. Now that's something I haven't quite figured out. When my dad worked for Dr. Lazard, basically all of the business was done in his personal name. But by the time I went to work at the bank, everything—the cattle operation, the timber company, even his medical practice income—went through one account or another of Lazard Farms, Inc.

"Greg was a lot of fun. He was about thirty, wore his hair in one of those short Steven Segal ponytails, and loved music—especially old stuff from the '60's. Susan was head over heels for the guy. And you couldn't help but like him. The three of us went out two or three times. She couldn't take her eyes off him, and couldn't stop talking about him when we were together. She was determined to marry him, but I kinda got the impression he wasn't that committed. Greg would come in every Friday morning to make a deposit. One thing I remember very distinctly is Susan was talking about all the cash she had to count."

She hesitated. "May I have a glass of water? I guess I'm getting too worked up about all this."

Ben went to the kitchen and poured her a glass of ice water from the fridge. She drank deeply from the glass before starting again. "It didn't really hit me at that time—I was new and didn't know what was usual or unusual—but I realize now that, except for grocery stores, almost nobody brings in big cash deposits. Essentially every large transaction is made up of checks, or wire transfers, or even credit card deposits. One day after Greg had been in, I noticed that she was rechecking his deposit, and there was a lot of cash, like, stacks of hundreds and fifties and twenties. Maybe I shouldn't have said anything, but I asked her about it—curiosity, you know—and she got a little defensive. She said it was mostly from Dr. Lazard's medical practice, and..."

"Wait a minute. From his medical practice? Are you sure?"

"Yes. It didn't really click at the time, but the reason I remember it was that the cash was more than ten-thousand dollars, and I was thinking she was going to fill out a C.T.R. and I wanted to see how it was done."

"What is a C.T.R.?"

"A special IRS form, Form 4789, called a Currency Transaction Report. You're supposed to fill out one of these forms for all cash transactions for deposits ten-thousand dollars or more. They harp on it when you're getting your teller's training, and give you all this grief about how, if you don't do it and the bank gets audited, you can be liable for prison time and all that. Anyway, I asked her about it, and she said that since Dr. Lazard was one of the bank directors, the rule didn't apply to him, and that since most of the deposits of Lazard Farms were more than that amount anyway, filing the form every week would have been silly. So that was that, and I didn't think much more about it until just now."

She paused and drank more water.

"Alex, take my word for it, *no* doctor is going to be hauling in lots of cash from his medical practice. Some big checks maybe, but not hundred-dollar bills. But how do you tie this in with John's death."

"I don't know, dammit!" Her voice was firm, full of frustration. "What I'm trying to tell you is that *something* is going on. I don't know what it is, but Dr. Lazard is part of it, and it's all got to be connected somehow. Let me finish."

"Keep talking."

"I'm not really sure what happened, but Susan and Greg had some sort of a fight. She wouldn't talk about it, but she was really mad at him, and said something about getting even. And then they eloped—or that was the story. She just didn't come to work one Monday morning. She lived alone in an apartment—her parents were divorced and she didn't have any family here. She had packed up and moved out, or at least that's what Mr. Miller, the bank president, explained to us. I came into work that morning and Mr. Miller and Mr. Ewing, the vice president of the bank, were at her window going over some figures. I asked if she was sick, and they said she wouldn't be coming back to work. For a couple of days all kinds of rumors were flying around. Then on Wednesday afternoon after the bank had closed, Mr. Miller and Mr. Ewing called everybody into the conference room to explain that Susan and Greg had apparently decided to run off and get married. Mr. Miller said she'd left a note resigning from her job, and that they had been worried about some 'irregularities,' as he put it in her daily tapes, but that they'd checked things out and everything was fine. He said he'd talked with the folks at

Lazard Farms, and Greg had done more or less the same thing, and that he wished them well, and all that.

"That was the end of it until Mr. Miller came out one day several weeks later with a postcard he said was from them. Somewhere in the Caribbean, the Cayman Islands, I think. I remember he passed it around, and that it was apparently written and signed by Greg, but I wouldn't know. I wouldn't have recognized his writing."

"So?"

"I'm almost done." Alex cleared her throat, continued. "After that, Dr. Lazard started making his own deposits. In fact, he still does. Every Friday afternoon he comes in with a bag, and now Mr. Miller does it himself. They go in his office, pull the blinds and stay in there for about twenty minutes."

"Isn't that a little strange for a bank president to be taking deposits?"

"Probably. But this is a small town, and some people are real peculiar about their money, especially a few old people who lived through the Depression. They basically don't trust banks. He keeps a teller drawer in his safe for those types."

"So, he takes Dr. Lazard's deposit every week—which means, I presume, that no one but him sees it."

"Right! Probably because he doesn't want anyone to see it." She watched a pair of wood ducks settle in on the water across the lake. "Ben, if we want to find out what's happening, we have to follow the money—Lazard's money. And I think I know how to do it."

Douglas Christopher Ewing, senior vice president and comptroller of the Miller State Bank, was snoring loudly. She had been listening to him for ten minutes now. She wasn't sure that the contents of the four Xanax tablets she had dissolved in his drink would be enough.

She shook him gently. He continued to snore.

Slowly, Alex eased herself off of the bed and padded softly to the chair where he had tossed his pants. Fortunately, he hadn't gotten hers off despite his best efforts. The keys were in the right-hand pocket.

Silently, she crept out of the bedroom and down the hall to his private study. Moving slowly in the dim light of the street lamp streaming through the window, she switched on a desk lamp illuminating the paneled room. She knew the records were here somewhere. The desk drawers contained nothing of interest. The cabinets under the bookshelves held only an assortment of books and papers. Inside a closet she found a locked filing cabinet. The top tow drawers were labeled "Lazard-Personal," and the bottom two, "Lazard Farms, Inc."

Fumbling with the accountant's key chain in the semi-darkness, she found the right key and turned the lock. The top drawer slid open with ease, revealing neatly labeled files arranged in hanging folders. Grabbing a file folder designated "Troup Lazard-Personal Financial Statements," she shut the drawer and opened the next which appeared to contain copies of tax returns.

The third drawer—Lazard Farms, Inc.—was tightly stuffed with computer printouts bound in bulky folders. Lifting out one labeled "Accounts," she found a pen and paper on the desk and began to copy down names.

Down the hall a toilet flushed. She laid the papers on the desk and quickly flipped off the lights. Sprinting down the hall, she leaned against the bedroom door frame and smiled. "You fell asleep," she said in a soft voice. "Just when things were getting interesting."

"Sorry," the accountant said in a slurred voice. "God, I feel like I'm drugged."

"You're just tired, Chris. I'll get you another drink," she said, reaching for her pocketbook.

"You did what?" Ben exploded over the phone.

Alex said, "Calm down, Ben, and listen." Ben had never heard a woman speak so decisively. "I don't know everything that is going on, but I know this much. The one man I married is dead. I've been swindled. I've been lied to. God knows what else has happened behind my back. But I can tell you this: I intend to find out some answers and put my life back together. You can help me, Ben, or you can get out of my way. Either way, this game is over. I'll call you when I've had a chance to go over all this."

The phone clicked dead.

CHAPTER
TWENTY-ONE

"THE BASTARD HAS BEEN HITTING ON ME ever since I came to work at the bank. It's the sort of thing you just ignore, usually. You wouldn't understand it. You're a man."

Ben grunted acknowledgment.

"He was at it again this week," she continued. "His usual accountant's smirk under his coke bottle glasses and slicked-back hair casually mentioning that his wife and kids were going to her mother's for the week and, gee, wouldn't it be nice if I could drop by for a drink, *et cetera*. Normally, I just ignore him, but he is Lazard's accountant and..."

"Alex, you didn't."

She gave him a sharp look. "I'm not crazy. I had a few sedative pills that Dr. Powell had given me after John's death. I told him I did a great strawberry daiquiri if he would pick up the fixings. I figured that would cover the taste of Xanax. After what happened last night, he called me into his office this morning and spent fifteen minutes apologizing for getting drunk and passing out. I acted shocked and insulted, and basically told him that his wife wouldn't find out, and I wouldn't press sexual harassment charges provided he never speaks to me again other than in a totally professional manner. I don't know when or if he'll miss these files, but I doubt if he'll run to the police—or Lazard for that matter. I've spent several hours going over these papers. Let me show you what I've found."

Opening a folder, Alex removed a sheaf of documents and spread them out on a table. "What I have here are Dr. Troup Lazard's personal financial statements going back to 1983. These are the sort of listing of assets and liabilities that he'd have to file with any bank he borrows money from in the course of business. Just looking at these numbers by themselves is not going to tell you a lot, but you have to assume they are correct and verifiable. Bank auditors do that sometimes—pick out an asset the bank is holding as collateral and ask to see it. The interesting thing is the pattern in Lazard's finances that emerges when you look at what's happened over the last ten years."

She picked out two documents from the stack on the table. "Look, if we take these two years, 1984 and 1985, as a baseline, it looks like Dr. Lazard is a very wealthy man. Basically, a financial statement has three parts: a listing of assets, a listing of liabilities, and a section on current income. Now remember, we're assuming that what is listed is basically true. In those years, he recorded as his major asset approximately..." She paused to consult the paper. "...24,350 acres of land in Adams County known as Marsellaise Plantation. He's assigned that a value of ten-and-a-half-million dollars, which seems about right for the time. Other major assets include roughly one-million-dollars in liquid securities—he's attached a list here—and about four-hundred-thousand dollars in cash. On the liability side he lists about a hundred-and-fifty-thousand dollars owed to Miller State Bank, which he's labeled as a line of credit for his timber and farming operation. For income, he lists a net of a hundred-and-ten-thousand dollars from his medical practice, and a net total of two-hundred-and-forty-eight-thousand dollars from the plantation."

She looked up at Ben from the papers. "Not bad, huh? The 'bottom line'—I hate that phrase—of assets minus liabilities is a net worth of roughly twelve-million dollars, with total debts of a bit more that one percent of his assets. He's rich, no doubt about it."

Picking up another document she continued, "Now, moving on to 1987, the whole picture changes. It looks like Dr. Lazard decided to gamble, and gamble big, on an investment. He still lists Marsellaise Plantation as his major asset, but now the other big asset is an eighty percent interest in something called Pelican Island Development Partners, a limited partnership in which he is listed as the General Partner. He's got his interest in that valued as eleven-point-five-million dollars. Also, it looks like he sold most of the securities, and his cash reserves are down to about fifty-thousand. Meanwhile, on the liability side, he's acquired a mortgage on Marsellaise Plantation from the Miller Bank for five million, and a mortgage on the Pelican Island property from a bank in Jacksonville for another five million. Apparently he bought into the Pelican Island deal for about ten percent cash down, and borrowed against that and his other assets for the rest."

"What is Pelican Island?" Ben asked.

"I have no idea. That's what I want you to find out for me. I think it was some kind of development down on the coast. What makes me believe something is going on is what happened after he bought it. Look at these."

She held up several more documents. "Dr. Lazard files his financial statements shortly after the first of every year. Pelican Island shows up first in 1987, so he must have bought it in 1986. Now, if you look at the statements for 1988 through 1991, the only thing that really changes is the amount of money he owes the Miller State bank, which goes from five million to just above six million. Think about it—his cash income, according to these statements, is four or five-hundred-thousand dollars at best, and he would have had to owe at least a million dollars in interest alone each year on the ten million he'd borrowed from the local bank and the one in Jacksonville. Despite the fact that it looks like he sunk everything he could into this Pelican Island thing, he reports no income from it. I asked my Dad about all this. He was working for Lazard at the time, but he didn't know anything about his finances. What he did know was that the cash flow to run the plantation, which had been very good at one time, just about dried up. He was telling me that Doc—he always calls him 'Doc'—had cut back on everything from fertilizer to equipment maintenance. In fact, he thought the farm might go under because Dr. Lazard kept drawing money out of the farm accounts to pay for something else. Retrospectively, it seems he was probably trying to make payments on the Pelican Island loan. By pulling money out of the farm accounts he could make up some of the difference, but he still had to borrow more from the local bank to at least keep current with the interest and avoid foreclosure.

"The real clinchers are these, though." Alex laid a small sheaf of letters in front of Ben. "These were in the folder for the 1992 financial statement. There are letters from both Miller State Bank and First National Bank Jacksonville threatening foreclosure on the Pelican Island property. Listen to this from one letter dated September 2, 1991:

> *Because recent events have made it clear that the value of the collateral used to secure this loan has dramatically decreased, it is the position of this bank that if we do not receive a substantial payment on the principle of this note by September 30, 1991, we will have no choice but to begin foreclosure proceedings. A minimal acceptable payment amount will be one million dollars."*

Ben's head was spinning. "So, where's all this going?" he asked.

"Look at the 1991 statement and compare it with the 1992 and 1993 statements." She handed the three documents to him. "In early 1991 when he filed that statement, Lazard owed more than eleven-million dollars. Of course, he had some assets on paper to cover him, but apparently the Pelican Island property was not worth anywhere what he paid for it, or what he lists it as being worth. In fact, I imagine if any of his creditors had decided to go through with a foreclosure, he would have been forced into bankruptcy. On the 1992 statement, things change. He no longer lists the Pelican Island property as an asset, and his debt to the First National Bank in Jacksonville is also gone. But look…" She pointed at the column of figures. "…the amount owed Miller State Bank has increased by approximately another million dollars, with the Marsellaise Plantation property used as collateral. It looks like he must have sold his interest in the Pelican Island deal for about half what he paid for it and paid off the Jacksonville bank with it."

She lay the papers back on the coffee table and leaned back on the sofa. "In the end, he lost about six-million dollars on the deal. If you study the numbers, I don't think there's any way he could have paid it without selling some property. Now, look at the 1993 financial statement, which would cover transactions that took place in 1992. Suddenly everything changes. Dr. Lazard's major asset is listed as a fifty percent interest in Lazard Farms, Inc., for an estimated value of some six-million dollars. There's a note here that says the chief asset of Lazard Farms, Inc., is some 24,350 acres—in other words, Marsellaise Plantation. And, on the other side of the balance sheet, his debt to the Miller State Bank has disappeared."

Ben perked up. "So he sold half interest in his land to pay his debts. That's not illegal."

"But look at this. He also acquires a twenty-five percent interest in Miller State Bank, and apparently gets appointed to the board of directors."

"Alex, again, where is all this going? Dr. Lazard made some business deals. He gets himself out of debt. He invests in a bank. So what?"

"Look at the 1994 statement—the income part. For years, he has been reporting an average income from his medical practice of just over a hundred-thousand, and income from his property of a quarter-million to three-hundred-thousand. In 1992, he sells half interest in his property, and suddenly, for the next calendar year, his net income triples to nearly eight-hundred-thousand dollars from the plantation, and his medical practice income is more than two-hundred-thousand dollars. Ben, he sold half his assets and more than doubled his income!

Something is going on and it doesn't make sense."

"Alex, what is all this going to tell us about John's death?"

"I don't know, but we're going to find out," Alex replied grimly. "Your assignment is Pelican Island. I've got some more digging to do on these." She pointed to a list of names written on a sheet of paper. "This a payroll list for Lazard Farms, Inc."

CHAPTER
TWENTY-TWO

IT WAS ALL A BIT CRAZY, Ben thought. Maybe too crazy. Alex was beautiful, fascinating and lots of fun to be with, but her new-found obsession with Troup Lazard was beginning to drag him into—into what? Something he did not want to deal with? Or something he was afraid of?

Troup was already suspicious of him, had already warned him. Or was it a threat? Ben wasn't quite sure which. He made up his mind he'd find some way to extricate himself from this mess, even if it meant not seeing Alex again.

Maybe something was going on. But what business was it of his? Lazard's finances were a private matter. There was nothing he or Skip Malcom had seen from the air to suggest a secret landing strip.

"I don't need all this. I don't want all this," he said aloud to no one.

He could at least call about the Pelican Island thing. Alex had asked him to do it, but after that? Who did he know from that part of the state? He'd gone to high school in Savannah. There must be someone...

He suddenly remembered. Of course, his friend Mike Brett was from somewhere on the coast. He might know.

"Yeah, I grew up on St. Simons Island, Ben," Mike Brett said into the phone. He sounded pleased to hear Ben's voice. "I'm glad you decided to call. We haven't heard from you since that weekend. Look, I'm sorry if the girls...."

"I'm not calling about that, Mike. Ever heard of a development on the coast called Pelican Island."

"Of course, who doesn't? We had a hell of a time stopping it."

"Who is we?"

"Well, the whole eco-community. The Sierra Club, Nature Conversancy, Friends of the Georgia Coast, you name it. What's it to you?"

"The name came up. I was curious."

"Pelican Island was—and, as of the moment, still is—the last undeveloped barrier island on the Georgia coast. It's just north of all the resorts at St. Simons, Sea Island and Jekyll Island, about an hour or less by car from Savannah, Hilton Head, and Jacksonville. I should say that it would be an hour or less by car if there were a road to it, but there's not, and that's the crux of the story. If I remember correctly, Pelican Island had been owned since the 1920's by a privately held timber company. The title ended up in the estate of an elderly widow who died in the mid-1980's, and the property came on the market. The place is beautiful, Ben! Virgin sea island pine and live oak, about three miles of unspoiled beach. Any developer would give his right hand for it. The problem was, to get to it, you had to cross about fifteen miles of marsh and small islands, essentially all of which were unspoiled wetlands.

"Looking at it strictly from a business point of view, whoever got title to Pelican Island should have made a fortune. I don't know the exact sequence of events, but it was announced that this group—Pelican Island Development Partners—had won out in the bidding, and that the state was willing to build a causeway from I-95 to the island funded by development bonds and tolls. A bill was even introduced in the general assembly to allow casino gambling on Pelican Island once it was opened up for development. The justification was that the state would make a whole lot of money on gaming taxes and fees. It would have been the only site of legalized casino gambling within hundreds of miles, and just off the main route from the Northeast to Florida. A great stopover for the snowbirds and a veritable gold mine for the developers, right?"

"I guess so," Ben replied.

"Wrong. The developers had miscalculated the politics of the project. No sooner had the plans been announced than a huge coalition of groups opposing it launched a campaign to stop it. That's how I got involved through The Nature Conversancy. You had the environmentalists who wanted to stop the development of an unspoiled coastal island and the causeway across the marshes, you had every religious organization in three states railing about the evils of gambling, and you had stiff opposition from the mayors of Savannah and Jacksonville, as well as the resort owners who all thought they might lose tourism business from the competition. By 1990, when I was familiar with the situation, things were looking bad for the developers. Then a new governor was elected, which totally killed the deal. As I understood it at the time, the state called off the causeway project out of 'environmental concerns' but the real reason was that the governor had cut a deal with various opposition groups not to vigorously oppose his plans for a statewide lottery. You see, he wanted the lottery for the income to fund various education projects, and needed the support of the groups opposing the Pelican Island development. The religious groups got a promise of no casino gambling, the mayors and the resort owners had their potential competition scuttled, and the environmentalists were happy that the land was undevelopable, since there was no easy access. The owners eventually sold the property to the Sierra Club because nobody else wanted it at that point."

"The Pelican Island Development Partners. Do you know who they were—their names?"

"No, but the attorney who worked with us will. I'll try to find out for you. But, Ben, I do know one thing about them."

"Which is?"

"When it came to making any money on the deal, they really got screwed."

⁓

They talked for a while and hung up. Ben thought about calling Alex immediately, but decided to hold off until tomorrow. He'd invite her to lunch, tell her what Mike Brett had to say, find a nice way to tell her he was bailing out.

Yes, he had promised he'd help find out some things, but this was more than he'd bargained for. I don't want to hurt her, he told himself, but she'll just have to understand.

CHAPTER
TWENTY-THREE

SOMETIMES FATE takes sardonic pleasure in the whimsical manipulation of a man's life.

The emergency department of Adams Memorial Hospital served a semi-rural population from Adams and surrounding counties. It was unusually busy for an emergency room of its size. This fact was easily explained by the geographically diverse population, many of whom had no local doctors, and by the regional economy with its farming and timber operations, and its clay mining, all of which produced horrific injuries on a too-frequent basis. The nearby freeway provided a unhealthy allotment of motor vehicle accidents, and the poor and uninsured filled in the remaining time with their secure knowledge that in the emergency room, they would always be seen and treated by a physician, regardless of their ability to pay.

Physician coverage of the emergency department was provided by Walkerville Emergency Medical Associates, PC, a four-physician emergency medicine group headed by Carter Steed, MD. The physicians worked twelve-hour shifts, changing at 7 a.m. and 7 p.m. The assignment schedule was made up months in advance, and generally provided each physician at least fours days in a row off every three weeks, as well as liberal vacation and educational leave time. The emergency room physicians did not take care of patients after the initial consultation and treatment; if they required admission to the hospital, they were referred to a physician of the appropriate specialty.

Coordinated with this, the admitting physicians on the staff of Adams Memorial provided back-up coverage for "unassigned" patients—those needing admission but who had no local personal physician or surgeon. On a practical basis, such patients were rare, and most physicians were given an "unassigned" patient only every month or two. As it usually worked out, however, such patients were almost never insured and almost always acutely ill, a fact that was considered one of the less desirable requirements of having admitting privileges at Adams Memorial Hospital.

On Saturday, November 5th at precisely 11:47 a.m., Dr. Earle Cooper, the attending ER physician, noted an incredibly severe pain in his right mid-abdomen and flank . He was sitting at the counter in the emergency room at the time, and doubled over with pain, gripping his side. Flo Prosser was the RN on duty, and became aware of Dr. Cooper's plight when she saw him bent over, very pale with rivulets of sweat running down his face. She was alarmed.

"Dr. Cooper, are you all right?"

"No, I don't think so." He grimaced. "I think I'm having another kidney stone."

"Can I get you anything?" She noted he was doubled over in the chair.

He grimaced again. "No, not right this minute." He paused, holding his side. "I've had these before, I'll just sit..." He interrupted his own sentence by vomiting on the desk.

Flo Prosser grabbed a wet cloth and began to wipe his face. "Dr. Cooper, I think we need to call the urologist."

Earle Cooper looked up. "Flo, I'll be fine. Like I said, I've had kidney stones before and I know..." at which time he fainted.

Ten minutes later the telephone rang at the home of Mr. and Mrs. Kenneth Webster in north Atlanta, in-laws of Dr. Carter Steed. It was Flo Prosser calling Dr. Steed.

After a brief delay, Carter Steed answered the phone, "Flo, what's up?"

"Dr. Steed, I'm sorry to bother you, but Dr. Cooper is having another kidney stone and he's really too sick to work. We need somebody to cover the ER. I tried calling your other partners, but I can't reach either one of them."

"Damn! I'm sorry, Flo. Is Earle OK?"

"Puking his guts out and writhing in pain, but otherwise fine. Dr. Evans is down here with him now, and I'm sure he'll want to admit him."

"The reason you couldn't find anybody else in the group is that Jim Tine is at a medical meeting in Orlando, and he won't be back until Monday. Bill Kendall and his wife are on vacation in St. Croix, and I don't expect them back until the end of next week. I'm here at my in-laws, and it's going to take me at least two-and-a-half hours to get there if we leave right away. I was scheduled to go on at seven tonight, but I'll leave right now and get there as soon as I can. We need some coverage, though—who's on back-up call for Primary Care?"

"Dr. Lazard. I've already checked."

"Good. Call him and tell him he's got to cover until I can get there. Any problems at the moment?"

"No, not really. A mother with a couple of kids who've had colds for a week. I can tell her to come back later this afternoon. I don't think she'll mind. No emergency at the moment."

"OK." Carter Steed looked at his watch. "It's twelve-fifteen now. I'll try to be there by a quarter-to-three. Hold it down if you can, and if not, have Dr. Lazard come in and take care of things." He hung up.

Everta Mimbs was black, thirty-two years old, and the mother of five children ranging in age from eighteen months to seventeen years. She had been married to the same man for twelve years. She thought about that a lot. Sometimes she wanted to say that she was a single parent charged with the care of six children ranging in age from eighteen months to thirty-seven years, one of whom was the father of at least three of the others. His name was Larry, and she didn't really hate him, but she certainly didn't love him. Oh, she had at one time when she was twenty and he was twenty-five and he could talk to her like no man ever had before. And when they made love, it was like she'd heard it was supposed to be. He made her feel so special, and she wanted to be with him all the time and be the mother of his children. And now, twelve years later, she had to work two jobs to make ends meet while he sat around with his friends all day, drinking, sometimes doing an odd job here or there, never helping, always complaining. But for all that and despite her mother's urgings, she could never leave him.

Larry had not come home on Friday night. That was not unusual, she thought; he frequently got drunk and slept over at the house of one of his drinking buddies—or so he said. Maybe he had another woman, but she doubted that. The whiskey and the beer had left him pretty much unable to perform at home, so she doubted he would do any better with someone else. He was not there when she'd come in at eleven-thirty from her evening job at Hardee's and was not there when she awoke to tend to the baby the next morning at seven. Around noon she heard him at the door.

"Hey, baby, I'm home," he called.

"And just where have you been?"

"Oh, I was over at George's," he lied. "We got to playing cards and next thing you know, it was three-o'clock. He let me sleep on his sofa."

He smelled of stale beer, but she couldn't detect the crack cocaine in his blood.

She looked at him. He'd been losing lots of weight lately and had been acting strangely. "Honey, you ain't into something bad, are you?"

"What you mean, girl?" He eyed her suspiciously.

"Larry, I been sticking by you all this time, but you acting different lately. You more jumpy, and you losing weight. You ain't into no dope, are you?"

"Baby, you know I wouldn't do that." He was sweating. "I drink a little, that's all."

He collapsed hard on the floor.

Everta screamed and bent over him. Satisfying herself that he was breathing, she reached for the phone and dialed 911.

⁓

Twenty-five minutes later, Pearlie Mae answered the telephone at Marsellaise Plantation.

"Dr. Lazard's residence." After a brief pause, she continued, "He's eating his dinner right now, but if you want me to get him, I will."

Flo Prosser waited on the phone. Lazard finally answered, and she began by apologizing. "Dr. Lazard, I know I told you I wouldn't call unless we needed you, but we've got Larry Mimbs down here with chest pain, and maybe you should come down and check him out. I think he's OK, but..."

"Flo, who is Larry Mimbs? You sound like you know him."

"Oh, god, I do. We all do. He's a drunk, and he's in here twice a week at least. If he's not dead drunk, he's been beat up, or has a cold, you name it. Nothing very serious."

"I don't know him."

"Well, you probably wouldn't. He's black, thirty-seven years old, unemployed and supported by his hardworking wife and food stamps, which he trades for beer whenever he can. A real loser."

"What's wrong with him now?"

"Apparently, he had a syncopal episode at home. His wife says he just 'fell out' and she called the EMS. By the time the ambulance got there he was coming around, but he's been complaining of some chest pain since he got here."

"How old did you say he was? Thirty-seven? A little young for coronary disease. Is he drinking?"

"Reeks of it!"

"Hell, give him some Mylanta and call me in fifteen minutes if he's not better. I'll be damned if I'm going to interrupt my lunch for some drunk nigger. I'll come down and see him when I get through eating."

Flo Prosser walked back into the treatment room. She spoke to the patient and his wife. "I'm really sorry our regular ER doctor got sick. I called Dr. Lazard, and he said to give you this medicine." She handed him a small plastic cup filled with a thick, white liquid. "He's going to come down and see you just as soon as he finishes his lunch."

Everta Mimbs leaped from the chair. "Nurse, you look here! My husband says he's hurting and I want him to see a doctor—now! He could have something bad wrong with him. That's why I brought him here."

"Mrs. Mimbs, Dr. Lazard is coming just as soon as he can, and he's ordered some medicine for your husband. I'll go call him again."

"You better. And, you just tell that doctor to get his ass down here right now! Jes' cause we be poor folks..."

"OK, OK." Nurse Prosser backed out of the room.

She called Marsellaise Plantation again and, after a moment, Dr. Lazard came on the line. "Dr. Lazard, I hate to keep bothering you, but this man's wife is adamant that you come down here right now to see him."

Troup Lazard was sitting at his dining table talking on

a portable phone. He took a sip of iced tea and wiped his lips. "How does he look, Flo? Is he critically ill?"

"To be honest, no. He's got a little chest pain, he says, but he looks like he always does. Bad hangover and smelling like a brewery."

"Fine! Tell his wife to cool her heels, and I'll be there when I get there. You might better get an EKG, though, just to be sure." He hung up and called for Pearlie Mae to bring him some pecan pie with a scoop of ice cream on top.

Five minutes later the EKG tech wheeled the machine into the treatment room. She busied herself attaching stick-on pads for the leads, one on each extremity, six across the chest. As she typed his name into the keyboard, she noted that the patient was a youngish, black male who was sweating profusely and holding his chest. She cautioned him to lie very still and pressed the "AUTO" button on the instrument, waiting while the internal computer recorded and analyzed the results. When the display blinked "DATA ACQUIRED, " she began to remove the leads, legs first, then arms. She started to remove the chest leads carefully, noting that the sticky jell might pull the hair on the patient's chest, causing pain. As she removed the first one, she glanced up to be certain it was not hurting him and noted that he seemed to be staring blankly at the ceiling. An instant later she realized he was not breathing and that the now finished EKG emerging from the instrument read:

INTERPRETATION: *** Acute Anterior Myocardial Infarction ***
*** Multiform Ventricular Ectopy ***
*** Ventricular Fibrillation on Rhythm Strip ***

She pressed the "Code Blue" button next to the stretcher and screamed for the nurse.

Chapter
Twenty-Four

HE HAD EVERY INTENTION of telling her. He had really meant to do it, Ben thought to himself. He had planned the whole scene in infinite detail—the conversation, her response, his response. He had called and invited her to lunch. She had countered with an offer of dinner. He'd hesitated, then accepted.

It was Sunday night. They lay in the bed in each other's arms. The room was dark, and they hadn't spoken in at least half an hour. Ben thought she was asleep, but dared not move for fear of waking her. The remains of the half-eaten dinner were on the table. Empty wine glasses on the bedside table reflected the red light from her clock. He looked at the time. Eleven ten. "Alex, are you awake?"

"Dreaming, I think." She stretched and snuggled up against him.

"I really hate to wake you up, but I need to get home. I've got an upper endoscopy scheduled at 7 a.m. tomorrow."

"Don't go. I want you to stay."

"I'd like to—I really want to, but I need to get back home. I'll stay all night another time, I promise. I really hadn't planned...." His voice trailed off.

"Neither had I. But I don't want you to leave. We didn't finish our conversation."

"I think we got distracted."

She sat up and switched on the light, her long hair falling over her breasts. She kissed him on the cheek. "Ben, I... I want to say so many things. I just don't know where to start."

He touched her face. "Later." For the first time in a long while, he felt truly guilty.

She put on a silk dressing gown while he fumbled to unsort his clothes from the pile on the floor at the foot of the bed. She watched him as he dressed, and observed, "You know, we didn't mention Dr. Lazard all evening."

"Yes, I know. That reminds me. I got a call from Carter Steed this afternoon. Something happened in the ER yesterday that had to do with Lazard. Jane McClarin—she's the chief of staff—has called an emergency Medical Staff Executive Committee meeting for 5 p.m. tomorrow. I'm not really sure what it's about but I think it has to do with that."

"Who's the Executive Committee, and why are you on it? You just started practicing here a few months ago."

"That was my question, but apparently it's the local custom to vote the newest member of the medical staff into the office of secretary. The Executive Committee is made up of the chief of staff, that's Jane, the vice chief, Carter Steed, and the secretary, in this case, me."

"So what's the emergency meeting about? Sounds serious."

"I have no idea. Probably some bureaucratic bullshit. I'll go because I have to."

Mrs. Leggett, his ever faithful secretary, was waiting for Elbert Shaw at 9 a.m. as he pulled his late model Cadillac into the space designated ADMINISTRATOR at Adams Memorial Hospital. He was puzzled to see her; why was she standing in the parking lot? He grabbed his briefcase, opened the door, and said, "Good morning, Mrs. Leggett. What are you doing out here?"

"Thank god you're here, Mr. Shaw! You must have come in by the back drive."

"I did, but why...?"

"Then you don't know? You haven't seen them?"

"Seen who?"

"The protesters. They're picketing by the main entrance and in front of the emergency room."

"Protesters? What are you talking about?"

She led him across the employees' parking lot to the corner of the building where he could get a clear view of the front of the hospital and the emergency room entrance. From his vantage point he could see about two-dozen figures carrying placards pacing back and forth slowly between the main and emergency entrances. Faintly he could hear them singing, and caught the phrase, "...we shall overcome someday...." He squinted to read the signs—he could make out two: ADAMS MEMORIAL KILLS POOR AFRICAN-AMERICANS and JIM CROW LIVES WHILE INNOCENT BLACKS DIE. He turned to Mrs. Leggett. "Just what the hell is going on?"

She wrung her hands. "I don't know, Mr. Shaw. They just started about fifteen minutes ago. I tried to call you at home but your wife said you'd already left for work. I tried to talk with them, but they demanded to see you."

"Did you call the police?" She shook her head negatively. "Well, let me drop off my papers in the office and I'll go talk with them."

Ten minutes later a smiling Elbert Shaw, breath fresh with peppermint and silk tie gleaming in the morning sun, emerged from the main entrance to face the protesters. He smiled and called loudly over the singing, "Good morning. I'm Mr. Shaw, the hospital administrator. How can I be of help to you people?"

The pacing and singing stopped and a woolly-faced black man dressed in coveralls emerged from the group. "You Elbert?"

"That's right. What can I do for you?"

"You can stop the killing of innocent African-Americans, and we gonna shut you down 'till you do!"

"Mister..., er, what is your name?"

"William Turner. I'm the Bishop of the Third World Evangelical Holiness Church, and I'm the President of the Adams County Black Coalition. You can call me Mr. Turner, Elbert.

"Mr. Turner, I assure you I want to be of help..."

"Well where were you Saturday when Brother Larry Mimbs lay unattended and died of a heart attack in your emergency room while one of your rich white doctors finished his dinner?" The crowd echoed a chorus of Amens. "And where were you when his suffering wife pleaded with your lily white nurse to get the doctor to see him?" He pointed now to Everta Mimbs who was carrying a sign that had an eight-by-ten photo of her, Larry and the five children pasted to the middle of it. "Where were you, huh?"

"Mr. Turner, I'm familiar with what happened, and I assure you that the matter is being addressed. The autopsy results will be available today. There's a medical staff Executive Committee meeting scheduled for this afternoon, and..."

"Elbert, you can 'dress the matter' all you want," Turner interrupted him, "but we gonna be right here 'till justice is done. You got that?"

"I got it." Elbert Shaw smiled his best bureaucratic smile and turned to reenter the hospital.

⌒

The clock on the conference room wall read seven-thirty-five. The meeting had lasted more than two-and-one - half very intense hours, and they all were exhausted. Jane McClarin opened the door and Elbert Shaw, Troup Lazard and Mrs. Leggett, who was serving as recording secretary, filed back into the room. Troup Lazard took his seat at one end of the long table. Opposite him at the other end sat the medical staff Executive Committee, Jane McClarin in the middle facing Dr. Lazard, Carter Steed on her right and Ben Pike on her left. Mr. Shaw and Mrs. Leggett assumed neutral positions midway down the table on either side.

Jane McClarin was all business. "Dr. Lazard, the Executive Committee has considered this situation in detail. We've interviewed you, Mrs. Flo Prosser and the other emergency room personnel on duty, we've studied all the ER notes, the EKG's and the autopsy report, including the toxicology. I want to make it very clear that we have tried to be as thorough as possible, so let me review the facts with you as we see them. I want to stress the word *facts* because that's what's important here, not justifications or rationalizations."

Putting on her half-frame reading glasses, McClarin consulted a yellow legal pad in front of her. "Two days ago, a thirty-seven-year old black male named Larry Mimbs arrived at the emergency room by ambulance. He had been brought in in response to a 911 call from his wife, who said that he suffered a syncopal episode at home. Mr. Mimbs was well known to the emergency room staff, and it seems well established that he's an alcoholic, but with no known history of drug abuse. You were called approximately fifteen minutes after he arrived and advised that he was there and complaining of chest pain. You ordered no labs, no EKG, no IV, no cardiac monitoring; instead you gave the patient some antacid. You told Mrs. Prosser, and I quote," she consulted her legal pad again, "'I'll be damned if I'm going to interrupt my lunch for some drunk nigger.'"

"Jane, that's not..." Lazard interjected.

"Dr. Lazard," she cut him off, "you'll have your time to speak in a moment. Let me finish."

"You were called a second time, and again refused to come in, but you did order an EKG which clearly documented that the patient was having an acute myocardial infarction. The rhythm strip done just after the EKG documents the onset of ventricular fibrillation, which in this case proved fatal despite vigorous CPR. The preliminary autopsy and toxicology reports..." She held up a thin folder, "indicate that the patient died of an acute occlusion of the left anterior descending coronary artery, but in the absence of significant atherosclerotic disease. In view of the high blood and urine levels of cocaine, it can be assumed that this event was drug induced."

"Jane, Elmo Kantt, the coroner, has ruled that this was a drug-related death. How was I to know..."

"Dr. Lazard. I'm not going to ask you again to let me finish." She paused to let her words sink in. "Now, the Executive Committee has carefully considered all the facts, including your testimony and explanations. We all are aware of the serious nature of this unfortunate event, and the uproar that it has apparently caused among certain members of the community." She looked at Elbert Shaw, making silent reference to the protesters who had spent the entire day picketing the hospital.

"Accordingly, it is our recommendation that your hospital admitting privileges be suspended on an emergency basis, pending resolution of this matter. This type of action is within the power of the Executive Committee as specified in the Medical Staff By-Laws, and of course you will be afforded a formal hearing and due process before any final action is..."

"Goddammit, McClarin! This is a set up!" Troup Lazard was on his feet now, red-faced and screaming. "Your punk little committee can't get away with this. I'm no fool and I know exactly what went on in your private star chamber deliberations. You've got Ben Pike here who wants to damage me in any way he can. He's a loser who's still trying to fight a battle he lost thirty years ago. This will not stand!"

Slamming his fist on the table, Lazard strode to the

other end, bending close to Jane McClarin's face. There was rage in his eyes. "You," he yelled, pointing his finger at Jane, Carter and then Elbert Shaw, "will hear from my lawyer. And you!" he turned to glare at Ben Pike, "You pluperfect son of a bitch, you...." He didn't finish the sentence. Lazard slammed his fist on the table once again and stormed out of the room.

CHAPTER
TWENTY-FIVE

"DID HE THREATEN YOU?" Alex wanted to know.

It was Tuesday night, twenty-four hours later. They were sitting in front of a cracking fire Ben had built to ward off the early November chill.

"I think so, but I'm not sure. I'm not really worried, if that's what you mean." He drew a deep sigh. "There really wasn't a lot else the committee could do. Lazard really did screw up. All he had to do was drive five minutes to the ER and examine the guy. And calling him 'a drunk nigger' didn't help anybody."

He shifted uncomfortably. "Turner and his buddies are

still picketing the hospital. They tell me he's a real parasite. He doesn't work, and supports himself through *contributions* to his church and his salary as *bishop*. This issue is very legitimate, but he's using it for his own gain as much as anything. This has gotten to be a real mess."

"Lazard frightens me, Ben." Alex stared at the fire for a moment. "I don't know what he is capable of doing, but the more I know, the more it scares me. When do you have to meet with him again?"

"According to the medical staff by-laws, we have to hold a formal hearing within sixty days at which time each side has the right to be represented by counsel. That's between the executive committee on one side and Dr. Lazard and whatever witnesses he calls on the other. From what they tell me, most problems get worked out at that point, and both sides agree on a settlement or some course of action—for example, putting Lazard on supervised probation for three months or the like. If we don't reach a settlement, then the whole thing goes before the hospital authority which hears evidence and sits as a jury. Their word is final, but it can then be appealed through the courts if either side disagrees with their findings. In truth, I don't know what's going to happen."

"Sounds really serious for him."

"It is serious. I got a call from Jane McClarin today. Lazard wants to meet informally with the executive committee on Friday. We're going to meet with him, but as far as it's gone, we can't take any action without a formal hearing. Oh, almost forgot. He's bringing his attorney, the distinguished Mr. Stavenger."

"The lying bastard!"

Joseph Stavenger was slick. That much Ben could tell right off the bat.

Lazard's attorney was a bit short, about five-eight or five-nine. He was nattily dressed in a tweed suit with matching vest and ornate bow-tie. He was the epitome of civility. He sat to the right of Troup Lazard, this time across the conference table from the three members of the executive committee, with Elton Shaw at one end, and the faithful Mrs. Leggett at the other to take notes.

It was shortly after one p.m. on Friday afternoon. Everyone had been pleasant, if reserved. Mrs. Leggett had served coffee, and they all exchanged a few banalities.

Stavenger took the lead. "Let's get this underway. I know how busy you all are, and I'm here on behalf of Dr. Lazard to see if we can't get this matter settled as quickly and painlessly as possible. I've read the summary of your meeting this past Monday, and I've reviewed the information you had available to you in reaching your decision. We all must agree this was an unfortunate incident that should not have happened, and my client, Dr. Lazard, has been most humbled by it all."

Stavanger glanced over at Lazard who sat expressionless.

Stavenger continued. "I've also reviewed your medical staff by-laws. It would appear that you have acted within the bounds of the authority granted you, and that, thus far, my client has been afforded due process. Dr. McClarin, we are in receipt of your letter formally notifying Dr. Lazard of the executive committee's action and of our need to respond to you within twenty days to schedule a hearing on the facts in the presence of counsel. We also understand our rights of appeal, and so forth." He smiled. "But, let me say that all this formality may not be necessary. We're here today to discuss the options and to make a settlement proposal that will get Dr. Lazard back to the very important job of caring for sick patients. We think this proposal will be beneficial to all parties concerned. Let me outline it for you."

Jane McClarin spoke. "Mr. Stavenger, I don't need to tell you that the next step is a formal hearing on the record, and you can make your proposals at that time."

"Ms. McClarin..." Stavenger caught himself. "I'm sorry, Dr. McClarin. I'm well aware of that, and we fully intend to participate in the hearing. It is our hope, however, that that proceeding can be one whose purpose is simply to ratify a compromise that we've worked out in advance. We are here to give you a bit of time to consider our proposal, as well as the alternatives to pursuing your actions on an adversarial basis. Do you understand that?"

She nodded.

"Let me give you a brief summary." He extracted a single sheet from his crocodile skin briefcase. "First of all, my client is willing to accept a period of supervised probation for all of his admissions for a period not to exceed one month. Secondly, he is willing to make a contribution of fifty-thousand dollars to be used for the upgrading and/or augmentation of services in the emergency department. Thirdly, and I might add after some preliminary discussions with Bishop Turner, we will be making a significant contribution to Mr. Mimbs's widow and family, as well as to the Third World Evangelical Holiness Church in Mr. Mimbs's memory. We feel these proposals will solve the whole problem."

He slid the sheet across the table to Jane McClarin.

She read the sheet through her half-glasses and passed it to Carter Steed and Ben Pike. She then slid it back across the table to Stavenger.

"Mr. Stavenger," she said, "formally make your proposal in writing, and we'll consider it. But let me tell you right now, the Lazard money is not going to buy your way out of this matter that easily."

Stavenger smiled, mechanically. "Doctor, we're not trying to buy our way out of anything. But we hope you will consider this proposal—or one similar to it—favorably, because the alternatives are not nearly so pleasant."

"Is that a threat, Mr. Stavenger?" Carter Steed asked.

"Don't be silly. Certainly not at this point. But think about it. You three physicians in closed session have made a decision that could ruin the professional career of my client. It's only natural that one questions your motivations. For example, you, Dr. Steed, are the head of a group of physicians contracted to provide twenty-four hour a day coverage in the emergency room. Through lack of adequate planning you did not. A young man with a long life and large earning potential before him, not to mention a wife and five children, is dead. You are wide open for millions of dollars in losses in from both medical malpractice as well as civil litigation. You'd be ruined."

He turned to Elton Shaw. "And, of course, Mr. Shaw, I don't need to remind you that such litigation would no doubt be directed against Adams Memorial as well. I hear the hospital is self-insured, by the way. I hope you have adequate reserves.

"And Dr. McClarin." He paused. "What can I say? Do you have a personal antipathy toward Dr. Lazard because he's a male physician? I'm sure that your living arrangements and your relationship with your friend—what do you people call them, 'life partner?'—will no doubt be explored in open court."

Jane McClarin turned suddenly pale.

"And most importantly, Dr. Pike." He paused again for

effect. "Trying to fight old battles under the guise of authority. That opens you up to all sorts of civil litigation. Still angry because you and your mother were disinherited by Dr. Lazard's father? Want to get even? You're new in town and want to build up your practice by heaping professional ruin on one of this community's finest physicians. We'll be able build a strong case against you, I feel certain. Oh, I might add, that our preliminary investigation would indicate that any action we might bring against you or any other conspirators would entail issues that would best be addressed in Federal Court, which means treble damages when we prevail."

They all sat in silence as Mrs. Leggett furiously scribbled on her steno pad.

Stavenger spoke again. "Well, enough said, perhaps. Jane—I can call you Jane?—you'll be hearing from us with a request for a hearing date. We would like to hope that the hearing will be a mere formality, but if not, well....You have our settlement offer. In the meantime, we'll be researching your individual personal motivations for whatever actions you may have taken under the guise of your *Committee*."

Rising, Stavenger and Lazard walked deliberately toward the door of the conference room. As they started to exit, Lazard whispered in Stavenger's ear. The lawyer nodded and turned to Elton Shaw.

"Mr. Shaw," Stavenger stated, "my client has reminded me that the laws of this state require you to report to the State Board of Medical Examiners any *adverse action* taken against him that results in a diminution of his hospital privileges. We would like to advise you not to take such an action, as we feel that such a move on your part might draw undue attention to my client, when, in fact, there are others in this whole matter who may be at greater fault through conspiracy and the like.

Your notification of the State Board could be construed as a furtherance of this conspiracy, and, of course, make you an individual party to all the litigation that will certainly be directed toward the conspirators. Do I make myself clear?"

Lazard and his attorney left the room, closing the door more firmly than necessary.

Except for Mrs. Leggett, who continued to scribble away, there was silence in the conference room. Finally, Carter Steed stood up and quietly said, "Damn. They play hardball, don't they?"

Everyone nodded their heads except Elton Shaw, who stared straight ahead blankly.

"Elton, what do you think?" Steed asked.

"I think maybe I shouldn't have called the State Board last Tuesday morning."

CHAPTER TWENTY-SIX

"MAYBE I SHOULD just pick up and leave town."

Ben Pike paced back and forth across the cabin floor as Alex sat on the sofa and watched him. He had told her everything that had happened that afternoon in the meeting with Lazard and Stavenger. She'd questioned him closely, asking every detail. In the end, he'd paced for half-an-hour while she sat and listened.

"I mean, what else can I do? For most of my life I've been running from who I am—or should I say, who I was at one time. I've been back in this godforsaken town for less than six months and it's all blown up in my face."

He turned to Alex, half expecting a reply. She stared, not speaking.

He began to pace again. "Did I ever tell you that my mother said she never wanted to hear the name Lazard mentioned in her presence again? And that we never, ever talked about our life before we left Marsellaise Plantation? It was like being reborn at age six without a childhood, with poisonous memories that you were told to forget. It was learning to try to hate a father you secretly loved, and hate him only because you were told in the end that he hated you. Hated you so much that he had you thrown out of your home and left you to make your way in the world. I didn't understand it then; I don't understand it now, and I don't know if I want to face it all again. I feel like I've suffered enough at the hands of one Lazard, and I'll be damned if I want to give another one the chance to inflict the same pain."

After a moment, Alex asked, "Are you finished?"

Ben did not reply.

"You can't leave. Not now. You can't run away from something all of your life. If it was fate or destiny that brought you back here, you've got to see this out. You've done nothing wrong, and you don't deserve all this. You've got to stay and do what's right. Leaving town is not going to solve anything for you. It's not an option."

She paused. "And there's one other very important thing."

He looked at her. "What's that?"

"Me."

She rose and embraced him. "I'm here for you, and I need you here for me."

After a moment she said, "Why don't we go talk with my father? Maybe he'll have some insight. You've been wanting to meet him. Now's the time."

"You can't be serious. Under these circumstances? Come on, think about it. Do you want the first new guy you've brought home to meet your parents coming across like a psychological wimp, wanting to run from his first real confrontation? Don't you think we should wait until later when things are on a more even keel?"

"Not really. You remember what you told me a few days ago? You said you'd help me when you had no real obligation to do anything. It was *my* problem, then, *my* fight. Well, now he's taken *you* on, and it's *our* problem, *our* fight. My father is the one man who really knows Troup Lazard. He worked for him for more than twenty years. He can tell us what we're up against."

"How much have you told your father about your suspicions? Does he have any idea that you think Lazard is involved in something shady, or that somehow he has something to do with John's death?"

"I've told him basically nothing. He knows I've been asking some very pointed questions about the good doctor, but also knows I'll tell him why in my own time."

～～～

Margie and James Wren lived in a modest but spacious brick ranch house in one of Walkerville's older subdivisions. It was a neighborhood built by parents with young children now transformed by time into a community of grandparents eagerly awaiting the next visit of their grandchildren.

Margie Wren greeted them warmly at the back door. "So, we finally get to meet Ben Pike!" she said as she shook his hand. "You must be a pretty good guy, doctor. I haven't seen

Alex this happy in a long time. My husband's in the den, reading as usual. Come meet him."

Jim Wren rose with some difficulty from his overstuffed green leather reading chair. Hobbling across the room supported by a cane, he took Ben's hand in a crushing grip. He was a tall and handsome man, at least six-two by Ben's estimate, and all the more striking for his full head of shocking white hair. "Ben, it's good to finally meet you. We've heard a lot about you from Alex. I apologize for my limp. I've got a bad hip, and it keeps me down sometimes. Have a seat. Let's get acquainted."

They sat down, Ben and Alex on a couch, Margie and Jim in their reading chairs. They exchanged pleasantries as Ben studied the room. It was not at all what he would have expected for the den of a man who had spent his entire working life as a farm manager and timber logger. It was a large room paneled in exquisitely grained longleaf pine. The chairs and sofa were illuminated by strategically placed brass reading lamps. A huge stone fireplace dominated one end of the room. The outer wall was made up of a series of French doors opening to what Ben assumed was a yard beyond in the November darkness. On the opposite wall a doorway led off into the rest of the house, but, otherwise, the wall was completely covered by shelves filled and overflowing with books. From his vantage point he could see a wide assortment of topics ranging from architecture to theology. The most striking thing was the absence of a television. Jim Wren noted his curiosity.

"I guess you've figured out that I like to read. It's something I got from my mother. When I was growing up we lived on a farm. Being the oldest, after my father died, I had to drop out of school to help run things. I got a bit shortchanged on my education, but two of my younger brothers went on to college and medical school. They practice up north now in Pennsylvania and New York. I guess I felt a little inadequate, so I always tried to keep up with them through my own self-education. After a while the accumulation of knowledge becomes a habit. And with the kids gone..." He paused. "But enough of that. Alex said when she called that you wanted to know a bit about your half-brother. What's all this about?"

Ben thought a moment before speaking. "Mr. Wren, I know this sounds strange, but I hardly know Troup Lazard. I suppose you're familiar with the circumstances under which my mother and I left Marsellaise Plantation."

"Of course. No one in town could understand old man Jack cutting off his wife and child like that. After a while, though, folks here figured he must have had his reasons, and the talk kinda died down. So when your mother married and y'all left town everybody just forgot it. That was a number of years before I went to work out there."

"Well, as you might imagine, after that the Lazard name was never brought up in our presence. Troup was off in school when I was there, so I hardly even saw him. The reason I want to talk with you is that something has come up at the hospital. It's a professional matter, and I don't really think I'm at liberty to discuss the details."

"You mean the Mimbs's fellow's death?"

"You know?"

"Who doesn't? This is a small town, remember, and bad news travels fast."

"It does involve that, but my main concern is that Dr. Lazard has threatened to sue me for all sorts of things if we don't sweep the whole thing under the rug. He more or less promised my professional and financial ruin. Is he capable of all that?"

Jim Wren ran his fingers through his thick white mane and seemed to be considering what to say. After a moment he said, "Maybe an example would be appropriate. Did you know about Dr. Lazard's marriage, and what happened?"

"No. I never knew he ever had a wife."

"Her name was Katie, and she was a fine woman. They'd been married for about two years when the previous farm manager, Bo Larson, had his heart attack and Doc hired me to take his place. I got to know her pretty well over the next three or four years. They never had any kids—I heard he accused her of not being able to have children—but they generally seemed as happily married as most young couples. One day, something happened. I don't know what it was, but from what little she told me, it was nothing really important. The main thing was, she had disagreed with him. He decided right then and there he wanted a divorce. No compromises, no apologies. He told her to get out, and when she refused he started building his case against her. Accused her of all sorts of things, and I think he was willing to bring any number of witnesses to back up his claims. He cut her money off, then hired fancy lawyers to serve her summons while they were living under the same roof. He made her life a living hell. Finally, she couldn't take it anymore and moved out. They found her body a week later in a hotel room in Atlanta along with a suicide note. But Doc never missed a lick. Kept on seeing patients, going to the hospital, running the farm just like it never happened.

The old man slowed down, took a deep breath. "Let me tell you, Ben. There are two Dr. Lazards. The world knows one of them, and some of us have caught glimpses of the other one. The Lazard family has always owned a big chunk of this county, and a lot of people owe them something one way or the other. You know what all your father did over the years, giving his money and support for the good of the community. Troup's been like that, too. He's funded scholarships, given his time and his dollars for good works, and generally has been a positive force around here. If we were to go down to the corner store this very minute and ask the first person we see to give us his opinion of Dr. Troup Lazard, you'll hear that's he's rich, intelligent, gives of himself and his means for others, and is generally a good doctor. But lurking behind all that is a man who's driven to play a role, and whose real personality only God understands. I think the only thing I can say is that if things are going his way, and they usually do, then he's a true gentleman. If not, then gird your loins, because he'll stop at nothing to have his way."

Alex spoke this time, "But what really motivates him? It can't be money—or power. He's got all of those he needs. Why does a man with all his wealth work, especially as a physician? It's not the income or the recognition. Why?"

"Here's what I think," her father replied. "He does it because he believes that he's supposed to do it, just that simple. Sometimes I used to think it was almost like Doc was an actor playing the role of Southern Gentleman Farmer. It would be unseemly for him not to do something, a violation of the traditional work ethic. Maybe a lot of people wouldn't understand that, but most people wouldn't ask the question to begin with."

He paused and turned to Ben. "So you're about to feel the wrath of Troup Lazard? I wish I could help you, but I can't. The only advice I can give you is to prepare for battle and watch your back."

They rode back to Alex's house without speaking. She could sense Ben's frustration, his uncertainty. As he walked her to the door she said, "I got into the computer at the bank today, Ben. Something's going on, I swear it! Don't give up now, I can't do this without you."

"Why didn't you tell me all this? he asked.

"You've been so upset about what happened with the lawyer today I thought you needed more of my listening than anything. I'll tell you all about it tomorrow, I promise."

She kissed him good night, closing the door and locking it behind her.

Ben drove back to the cabin. He searched for the door lock in the half light of a rising moon, then stumbled half-blind across the darkness of the room to find the lamp switch guided by the red light on his answering machine. As he turned on the light, he noticed the white card with Martin Roble's phone number where he had tossed it weeks before. He glanced at his watch, picked up the phone and dialed the number. After six rings, a neutral female voice answered the phone, "Dr. Pike?"

"Uh, yes." They knew who was calling? "I want to speak with Mr. Roble."

"Just a moment."

After a series of clicks and an indeterminate silence, Martin Roble came on the phone. "Ben?"

"Yes. How did you know it was me calling?"

"The miracles of modern science. How can I help you?"

"You said to call you if..."

"Now is not a good time to talk," Roble interjected. "I'll be in touch with you soon."

The line clicked again and Ben heard a dial tone.

CHAPTER TWENTY-SEVEN

THE PLANE WAS LATE.

Again.

Hector Torrez sat in the semi-warmth of the truck, the engine off and the windows open to listen for the sound of a distant motor. Periodically, the radio snapped and hissed, but no signal yet.

He looked across the field, now faintly illuminated by the moon above the tree-line. A thin layer of ground fog gave it the appearance of a giant cloud-filled lake.

He'd been here—how long?—two-and-a-half years now. At an average of one flight a week, he'd unloaded more than a hundred loads. How many planes, he wondered? Thirty? Forty? The cartel rarely used a plane for more than three flights, and even then never the same route twice.

Not that many pilots, though. Maybe fifteen or eighteen at most. The last three loads had been flown by the rough-looking one who wore those ridiculous boots and called himself Cowboy. It could be him again, maybe not. Hector didn't know and didn't want to know. In this business, the less you knew, the longer you were likely to live to enjoy your pay—*if* you made it to "retirement."

Then again, he'd done a good job managing the farm and had learned a lot in the process. After all, he did have a degree in agricultural economics from the Universidad Autónoma de Barranquilla. Maybe in a year or two he could buy a few dozen hectares in one of the mountain valleys near Cali and live like the Doctor, or....

The radio snapped, and a voice with a distinct southern drawl whispered, "One, two."

Hector picked up the microphone and replied, "Three, four," while reaching to flip on the transponder beacon.

In the distance he could hear the faint hum of a twin-engined airplane.

She'd refused to talk about it until they had finished dinner on Saturday night.

"We need to calm down and get our lives back to as normal as possible," she'd told Ben, so they'd talked about nothing in particular while she prepared the meal and they ate.

Afterwards they sat in front of her fire and drank hot mint tea.

"Ben, I know this is all crazy. When you back off and look at all this you've got to ask yourself how we got into all this—me poking through confidential records, and you wondering about your professional future and talking about leaving town if the hospital thing blows up? But we're in it, and we've got to see it through."

Ben shrugged. She could tell by his expression he probably wanted to avoid the whole subject.

"There's one thing I do know, though. I lost the one man I loved—and now I'm afraid I might lose another I care a lot about. Maybe it's all coincidence, but there's no doubt Dr. Troup Lazard is somehow connected with both situations. I can't change what happened before, but I swear I won't let it happen again."

Ben started to speak, but she cut him off.

"Just listen to me for a few minutes," she said, "and let me tell you what I found out yesterday. Remember my friend Mr. Ewing who was so kind as to provide me with some of Dr. Lazard's financial statements? He keeps his password to the bank's computer taped under the blotter of his desk."

"Alex! Not again?"

She grinned—and went on to explain in detail how the computerized ledger system of Miller State Bank had multiple levels of access. That meant if she wanted to get anything more than the most basic information, she needed a password that provided complete access at all levels. She'd managed to slip into the vice-president's office and borrow his.

"It looks like Dr. Lazard is depositing tens-of-thousands of dollars every month," she continued, "probably two-thirds in cash."

"Where does it come from?" Ben asked.

Alex shook her head. "I couldn't really find out without looking at the hard copies of the deposit slips in bookkeeping, and that would have aroused too much suspicion. What I did find out, though, is that just as soon as it's deposited in the Lazard Farm accounts, a lot of it goes right back out by direct transfer to other accounts. It's a complicated system, but when you look at the whole picture, a pattern seems to emerge. You remember my telling you about Greg Coleman, the accountant who worked for Dr. Lazard and who ran off with Susan, the other teller? Before I came to work for the bank, he was the one who opened all the new accounts, set up all the automatic wire transfers, direct deposits for employees and so on. That made it a little bit easier to figure everything out. Since most of the new accounts were opened at one time, their account numbers are all sequential. I could just call up one and move right on to the others. Now this is the interesting part. In the computer a check drawn on an account is simply shown by the date, check number and amount, but a direct deposit or wire transfer also shows the number of the account that received the money. So it was pretty easy for me to get a list of accounts that get regularly scheduled transfers or deposits. About half of them seem to be employee paychecks, but even then something's not right."

Alex extracted a scrap of notepaper from her purse and laid it in front of Ben. "Here's a list of about a dozen accounts that appear to be employees getting direct deposit. Some of the names I recognize—here's Jennifer Black, and Lois Ingram—they both work in Dr. Lazard's medical office. But there are others—look at these four accounts, for example. They're listed as personal checking accounts that apparently belong to employees of Lazard Farms. They were all opened on the same day, and as far as I can tell, the bimonthly deposit for each one of them has been exactly the same since about a week after they were opened. But when you start looking at those accounts individually, you find that about once a month, most of the balance is transferred by wire to another bank, there are never any checks written. I tried to find a pattern there, but I can't. Two of the banks are in Macon, one in Augusta, and one in Atlanta."

Ben studied the paper. "Do you recognize any of the names?" He read the list, "William Sheers, Brian Epstein, M. W. Edison, Richard Starkey. Are any of them in the phone book?"

"No, I looked. I have no idea who they are, but they're well-paid. Between the four of them they get a total of about eighteen-thousand dollars a month. But that's not all." She pointed at other names on the list. "There are transfers every month from the main Lazard Farm account to Walter Miller, the bank president, and to Douglas Ewing, the vice president. By the way, I found out also he came to work right after Dr. Lazard bought into the bank. I don't know what that means, either, but it connects him to all this."

"Well, OK, so Lazard is up to something," Ben ventured. "It looks like he's running too much money through his accounts—a lot of it in cash, has well-paid employees who may not exist, and is paying off the bank president and vice - president. Where does this get us? Where is it all going? How is it going to help you find out about what happened to John and get me out of the jam I find myself in at the hospital?"

"I don't know," she said simply.

They had pushed the airplane under the shed that served to shield it from the eyes any casual airborne observer might have that was equipped with night vision gear. A waste of time, Torrez thought. Here, in the middle of nowhere on a moonlit November night—who's gonna ever know? But, the Partners had insisted after what had happened before.

The men were quick tonight. The twin-engine Cessna with auxiliary wing tanks was swiftly unloaded. Torrez counted the tightly-wrapped plastic packages as they were laid in the back of the pickup. The southern drawl on the radio had indeed belonged to Cowboy, who now leaned against a support post taking short swigs from a bottle of Meyer's Rum.

Eleven minutes on the ground. Cowboy was back in the plane, and the men were now pushing it back to the end of the runway. Torrez flipped the switch illuminating the low power lamps they had laid out on the ground along the grassy strip. With both engines roaring, Cowboy jerked the Cessna into the air, clearing the trees at the end of the runway by a few meters. The men were already rolling up the wires and packing the landing lights in a metal drum to be stored for the next time.

Torrez looked at his watch. Fifteen minutes total ground time.

They were good.

On Monday afternoon at four Ben walked back to his private office after seeing a patient to find Martin Roble sitting in the chair in front of his desk. He rose and offered his hand.

"How did you get in here?" Ben asked.

"Your receptionist remembered me. I told her you'd asked me to come by, so she showed me back. Actually, I was about ten miles from here Friday night when you called. The operator patched you through to my cellular phone, but I was busy at the time and couldn't talk." He paused. "Perhaps I should apologize for my attitude at our last meeting. We know more now than we did then."

"Is my phone tapped?"

Roble laughed. "No, not by us anyway. You're wondering how we knew it was you, right? Simple. The number you called is in a basement office in Atlanta. With routine Caller ID, your number appears on a screen in front of the operator, and meanwhile, is matched with a name from a database that we establish for each investigation. If the computer gives the operator a name that's of interest to us, we answer it. If not, the phone just rings and rings. I wouldn't be surprised if someone was listening to your conversations, though. You need to be careful what you say."

"Are you kidding?"

"No." Roble didn't smile this time. "You called. How can I be of help?"

"I won't beat around the bush. Are you investigating Troup Lazard or anyone at Lazard Farms?"

"Dr. Pike, I'm really not at liberty to discuss anything that we do, but don't take that as a positive or negative answer, just a statement of fact. Why do you want to know?"

"I don't suppose you've heard about Dr. Lazard and the incident in the emergency room last weekend? You seem to know everything else."

"We're aware of it, but what does that have to do with your calling me?"

"Lazard—or I should say his attorney—threatened me, threatened all the physicians on the committee that lifted his hospital privileges."

"So you got to meet Mr. Stavenger? Nice guy. So why did you call me?"

"Because you seem to know what's going on, and I don't have any idea what I'm getting into. I need some help. I..."

Roble stood up. "Dr. Pike. That's your problem. Be very careful in what you say or do. I can't help you, but call me again if you have any information that you think might be of help to me."

"Help to you how? I don't even know what you do. How can I..."

"Good day, Dr. Pike," Roble said as he walked out of the door.

CHAPTER
TWENTY-EIGHT

"THAT GODDAMN SON-OF-A-BITCH!"

Carter Steed was nearly screaming into the telephone.

Ben held the receiver back from his ear. "Carter, calm down. Who are you talking about?"

"Lazard!"

"Why am I not surprised. What's my dear half-brother done now?"

"He didn't do it, his fucking lawyer did!"

"Did what?"

"Had somebody call my ex-wife. Asked her if she wanted the opportunity to get even with me."

"I didn't even know that you had an ex-wife," Ben replied.

Carter Steed took a deep breath. "Let me calm down a minute and I'll explain it to you." He paused, took another deep breath. "Jill—my second wife—and I have been married eight years. Before that, I was married about three years to Donna. She was a nurse. We'd worked together when I was doing my residency, and we ended up getting married. I'll leave out the details—let's just say it didn't work. We didn't have any kids, and it should have been a simple divorce, but it wasn't. She hired an asshole lawyer who promised her she could get big bucks out of me if he made it ugly enough. Sure enough, it ended up being pretty nasty. Wound up in court with her asking for something like a two-hundred-thousand dollar property settlement and five-thousand dollars a month in permanent alimony. She got up on the stand and lied through her teeth. Said some really bad things to about me— all untrue, mind you. Fortunately, the jury saw through it all. They awarded me the divorce and gave her one dollar in prop- erty settlement and not a penny in alimony. Talk about bitter! Her attorney must have cost her a year's salary. Anyway, time heals a lot of wounds. We're not good friends, but we are pleasant when we run into each other. She even called me before I got married to Jill and apologized for everything, but as far as everyone else knows, she still hates me."

"What did Stavenger do?"

"Had somebody who described himself as an 'investiga- tor' call Donna. Said his name was Philip Smith, and he was gathering background for a possible legal action. Asked her if she knew anything about me that would reflect on my person- ality or personal habits—dirt, basically. She hung up on him and called me about it a few minutes ago."

"God, Carter, what are they doing?"

"I have no idea, but I know if they're after me, they're after you."

⌒

"Philip Smith," also known as Terry Phillips, or Randall White, or any one of a dozen other names, carefully set out the fluorescent orange rubber traffic cones around the white van he had parked by the edge of the highway. For this role he liked to use the name Randy Townsend, lineman-employee of Tri-State Line Management Services, a name boldly emblazoned on the sides of the windowless van by an easily removable magnetic sign. He was wearing a bright blue jumpsuit and carrying a set of lineman's equipment in a worn leather tool belt draped around his waist. If you were going to do this kind of work, he reasoned, you might as well make yourself as obvious as possible. The deregulation of the telephone system had made this part of his job immensely easier; if ever questioned, he could produce an authentic looking work order from Bell South requesting local line monitoring services. And he could hold his own in any technical discussion up to a point, after which the 9mm Glock in his right jumpsuit pocket could definitively settle any difference of opinion.

Carrying a small plastic case, he approached the green and orange Bell South box by the edge of the right of way. This was a relatively rural area, so finding the right line pair for the doctor should be simple. He cut the seal on the box, and began looking for the line by attaching the alligator clips to the junctions that connected the wires to the main underground table. Not that it mattered to him—they were paying him very well—but he couldn't understand why they were paying so much attention to this guy. For the other two, the ER doc and the dyke, the orders had been very simple: Dig up as much dirt as you can. Girlfriends, boyfriends, dope, booze, funny money, the usual. Anything for private leverage—Stavenger never let his cases get to court. He could always manage to find *something*, the revelation of which was sufficiently painful to cause the other side to give in.

But with the third doctor, Pike, they wanted more, lots more. Townsend sometimes compared his services to a menu in a Chinese restaurant. You get one from Column A, one from Column B, and so on. With Pike, they wanted the full spread from won-ton soup to Peking duck. Dig deep for the dirt, sift through his financial records, tap his phone, and—most importantly—try a little physical intimidation. Not too much—he left the heavy stuff for the guys they flew in from Miami—just enough to let him know you care.

Having found the line, Townsend opened the plastic case and removed a nondescript black plastic box with a waterproof eight pin connector. It was about the size of two cigarette packs laid end to end, and a marvel of miniaturization. Most of the sealed case contained a long-life lithium battery that would be good for up to a year with average use. The rest of it was a solid state voice activated recorder with integral compression software and a high-speed modem for burst transmission of digitally compressed recorded data to a special receiving device which he had previously installed at the Lazard mansion.

The concept was simple. A call was made or received, and box-recorded every word, minus any pauses over three seconds. Three minutes after the doctor hung up, the device would temporarily remove his line connection and call in to the programmed number at Lazard Farms. The entire conversation could be transmitted as compressed digital data in fifteen seconds or less. It could record up to thirty minutes of conversation. If the doctor tried to use his telephone while the compressed data was being transmitted, he would simply have a dead line for a few seconds before he heard a dial tone.

Besides the battery and the electronics, the sealed box contained something else—two ounces of plastic explosive which would detonate if anyone followed the instructions printed on the outside of the case stating "Open Here" with arrows pointing to two obvious screws.

With a small trowel, he dug a superficial pit just behind the telephone box and laid the device in it, intermingling the wires with those emerging from the underground cable. He carefully covered the hole and rearranged the grass so that it would be noticed by only the most determined observer. By connecting the line pair from the doctor's phone to the input of the buried box and by connecting its output back to the main cable, he ensured that all calls placed to or from that number would be monitored.

Ben Pike was not looking forward to the Tuesday night staff meeting. Since the meeting on Friday, he almost felt like he didn't want to get out of bed in the morning, much less attend a boring staff meeting. Alex had been incredibly supportive, but her father's words—and now Carter's warning— made him almost paranoid. He forced himself to think about his past—what he might have done they could dig up and use in an attempt to embarrass him. Nothing. Zilch. His life had had its ups and downs like everyone else's, but he had nothing to hide—at least, nothing he could think of at the moment.

The meeting went surprisingly well. Troup Lazard's absence was acknowledged by the pointed avoidance of conversation about it at the dinner that proceeded the meeting. Jane McClarin, looking strained, made a brief announcement about the suspension, but there was no discussion. Her companion and medical practice partner, Nelle Bradley, did not come to the meeting. Afterwards, Elton Shaw told the members of the executive committee privately he had not heard from Dr. Lazard or his attorney.

It was long after dark when Ben drove back down the tree-lined drive to the cabin. He unlocked the front door cautiously, stepped inside. Everything was quiet. Across the room he could see the red indicator light on the answering machine; he usually used it as a guide to find the lamp switch in the darkness.

Closing the door, he detected a faint smell. He sniffed, tried to identify the strange odor. Best he could tell, it was like a smell from the emergency room that made him think of trauma cases—blood? Hearing nothing, he walked cautiously through the dark toward the lamp table. His right foot caught on something, and he pitched headlong onto the floor and found himself laying on top of something—a body?—coated with a sticky substance. Instinctively, he knew it was blood.

In terror he fumbled for the light, found the switch and flipped it on. Nothing. Running his hands over the top of the lamp, he realized that the bulb and been removed. Now, almost disoriented in the darkness, he lunged toward where he thought the sofa should be, trying to find the lamp on the end table. He found the switch, he flipped it on, and the room was bathed in light.

Despite all of his years of dealing with gore and trauma in his medical training, he was not prepared for what he saw. The body of a large deer had been dragged to the middle of the room and butchered on the carpet. The severed head was now propped on the end of the sofa, staring at him through glazed eyes, and wearing draped around its neck a blood-stained white consultation coat with the name, "Benjamin Pike, MD" embroidered above the right pocket. Despite himself, he screamed.

"Look, Ben, if you want to know what I really think, it's a bunch of kids doing this kind of thing," Hoke Brantley opined. They were standing in the middle of the blood-soaked room, the deer's carcass now on it's way to the county landfill. "I hate to say it, but the high school here is full of vandals. They do stuff like this for gang initiations, pranks, you name it. And this is a pretty easy house to hit. You're off the road so no one can see what's going on, and there's nothing to stop them from pulling right down your driveway in a pickup, unloading the deer, cutting it up and leaving. They could have been in and out in ten minutes. You sure nothing's missing?"

"Not as far as I can tell," Ben replied. He was still shaken—even with the armed deputy looming next to him. "Hoke, this has got to be more than just some kids having fun. There's no sign of forced entry, and they had to know about my habits."

"What do you mean by that?"

"Two things. First, they had to know I would be gone tonight for at least two hours for the staff meeting. Second, they took the bulb out of the lamp I always turn on first when I come in—this damned cabin doesn't have a switch by the door so I've got to walk across the room to get some light in here. The deer was fixed so I'd be sure to trip over it."

"Doc," Hoke grinned, "I ain't no psychiatrist, but you sound a little paranoid to me. I'm telling you it was probably some kids night hunting and joy riding. They killed a deer and were afraid to take it home and pulled down this little road to dump it. They saw your house, got the bright idea right then and there. And you probably just forgot to lock one of the doors. I know it's a mess, but I promise we'll do our best to find out who did this. And when I catch 'em, I promise I'm gonna make 'em pay you back for what it costs to clean up this mess."

He slapped Ben on the back.

⌒

It wasn't exactly original but it had worked.

"Randy Townsend" had listened to the frantic call to the sheriff's office from Dr. Pike. Scared shitless, he thought. He'd seen the Godfather movies a dozen times. The old horse's-head-in-the-bed trick. Sometimes he'd used the family dog.

Shooting the deer was spur of the moment improvisation, but it did produce the right effect, and that was what they paid him for.

⌒

"You can just stay over here until this whole thing blows over if you want," Alex said.

They were drinking tea in the kitchen.

"I can't do that."

"Yes you can—and you will."

Ben swallowed hard. "Okay. But just until I get the cabin cleaned up. It's a real mess."

Alex refilled their cups with tea. "Do you really think Lazard is behind it?"

"I do," Ben replied, "but I may be the only one. Hoke Brantley thinks it was a bunch of kids."

"What does Hoke know," Alex retorted. She took a sip of tea. "You know, I was thinking about what you told me Friday night—about the meeting with Lazard and his lawyer. You said Lazard didn't say anything the whole time until they got up to leave, and then the only thing he was concerned about was that the state authorities not be notified about the committee's actions, right?"

"Right, but I'm not sure what that means, if anything."

"Well, it means he was concerned about it, and if you think about it, why would he be concerned about that?"

"I don't know. Now that you mention it, that would seem to be among the least of his worries in this situation. He's still potentially very liable for a big malpractice suit from the patient's family; loss of his hospital privileges would mean very likely the loss of much of his practice; I could think of other things."

"That's true. But notification of the state is the one thing that would draw governmental attention toward him. Anything else would involve private attorneys and the like, right?"

"I guess so."

"I may be the conspiracy queen, but whatever he's doing is illegal. He doesn't want anybody from any government agency poking around his affairs."

Ben brought the cup of tea to his lips, stopped. "Alex, I'm beginning to think you're right."

"Of course I'm right." She punched him playfully on the arm. "I'm always right. You should know that by now."

CHAPTER
TWENTY-NINE

"RANDY TOWNSEND" lay prone on the embankment over-looking the highway. He had been there since before dawn, silently observing the intersection some forty feet below him and a hundred yards distant. He was dressed in camouflage, his face and hands streaked with green, black and gray grease-paint to match the random pattern of his clothing. His blue jumpsuit was in the now unmarked white van parked deep in the woods more than a mile away on an abandoned logging road. The Glock was still in his pocket, but now he also held in front of him a specially modified sniper's rifle, a .223 caliber with a twenty-power scope and a padded folding stock. The muzzle was strangely deformed by a matte black cylinder screwed on the threaded end of the barrel to suppress the sound as well as the flash when he fired.

It was Friday morning. Last night was the first that the doctor had spent at the cabin since— he laughed to himself— the deer incident. It was time for a little more pressure.

The eastern sky was now bright pink, with a few wisps of clouds reflecting the sun just below the horizon. It shouldn't be long he thought, looking at his watch. According to what they'd told him, Dr. Pike usually drove by here every morning at about seven-fifteen. He'd picked this spot for several reasons. First, and most obviously, it would be necessary for his target to stop at the intersection before pulling onto the main highway north into town. Secondly, if the target was on time, the sun should be rising just over the treeline behind him and shining right in the young doctor's eyes. Finally, the area was owned by a timber company, and hence there were no houses around to provide possible witnesses. Townsend looked at his watch again, the steam from his breath fogging the crystal in the cool morning air.

The rising sun began to paint the fall landscape with a palate of yellows and golds. In the distance he heard a car, raising his rifle as the recognized the faded blue Taurus. As it slowed for the stop sign, he laid the crosshairs of the telescopic sight squarely on the driver's side rear quarter panel, tracking his aimpoint with a slow, easy swing of the barrel.

Just as the Taurus stopped, he squeezed the trigger and was jolted back by the recoil. Resuming his aim quickly, he fired a second round, again taking care to miss the tire and fuel tank.

He moved the sight to the driver now, watching him closely. Pike was looking over his shoulder toward the rear of the car. Suddenly he accelerated into the highway and sped off toward town.

Folding the stock on his rifle, Townsend loped off through the woods toward the van, thinking that he was remarkably well paid for the little work that he actually had to do.

⌒

"Ben, I know you don't want to hear me say this again, but I swear I think it was an accident."

Hoke Brantley scuffed the side of his shoe on the pavement of the parking lot outside Adams Memorial Hospital.

"Somebody shot at me, Hoke."

"Come on, Doc, think about it. Why on earth would anybody wanna shoot at you, huh?"

"Maybe the same ones who put the dead deer in my house."

"I figured that's what you were gonna say," Hoke replied. He rubbed his chin. "Tell you what we're gonna do, Ben. We're gonna check this thing out through and through, leave no stone unturned 'til we get to the bottom of it."

"Can I count on it?"

"'Course you can count on it, Ben. I give you my word."

"But, why do you keep saying it's some hunter shooting at a deer? Maybe one bullet hole—but two?"

"I know, I know."

"I swear to you, Hoke, somebody's trying to intimidate me. Both of those holes were within two inches of each other. One bullet hole is an accident. The second one was a warning. Whoever it is is trying to tell me he had me in his sights but decided to let it pass this time." Ben kicked the tire and stared at the holes.

"I think you been watching too many old Baretta movies, Ben," the deputy drawled. He leaned down, fingered some fragments from the spent projectiles recovered near the trunk of the Taurus. "Judging from these, it looks like he was using hunting rounds. Like I said, we'll follow it up."

～

Alex Jennings stood in front of the counter in the Clerk of Superior Court's office in the Adams County Courthouse, surrounded by shelf upon shelf of bound public records dating back more than a hundred years. The file clerk fumbled unfamiliarly with the computer keyboard, asking, "What did you say the name of that company was again?"

"Lazard Farms, Incorporated. I called the Secretary of State's office in Atlanta, and they told me the names of the officers and the registered agents of all active Georgia corporations are available on-line at the Clerk of Court's office."

The clerk scowled. "Well, you're about the first one who's wanted to find out that." The woman was obese, and her hair was in need of a good washing. "Give me a few minutes." She typed sporadically, muttering under her breath.

Finally, she said, "You wanted Lazard Farms, Incorporated, right? Let's see, they're right here in Walkerville, but according to this the registered agent is in Savannah, somebody named Sta...Sta-ven... something."

"Stavenger?"

"Yeah, that sounds about right. You want me to print

this out?"

"Please."

The clerk pressed a few keys, and the printer next to the terminal chattered as a sheet of paper was printed. She tore it off and handed it to Alex.

Alex quickly scanned the printout, her eyes wide with amazement.

~

"Ben you've got to stay here," Alex said. "The cabin isn't safe. I know Lazard or Stavenger had something to do with what happened this morning. This place may not be the safest place either, but around here our neighbors look out for one another."

Ben looked both anxious and dejected. "OK, but only for a while. I just can't live the rest of my life thinking that somebody's out to get me. This has got to come to an end, or I've got to...."

He didn't finish the sentence.

"Ben, don't leave. Please." After a moment she spoke. "Look, we can't just sit here and let this thing roll over us. We're got to fight it—we've got to do something. Let me tell you what I found out today at the clerk's office, and then let's plan what we're going to do next."

Ben looked at her. "That's just it, we can't do anything. I feel like I'm being moved around like a pawn in someone's chess match. I get all of the action, but I make none of the decisions." He saw her expression. "We'll try. What did you find out?"

"I'm not sure, but the cast of characters gets bigger and bigger. Lazard Farms, Inc. has three officers. As you'd expect, Troup Lazard is president. The surprising thing is who the other two are. The vice-president is Walter Miller, and the secretary-treasurer is Douglas Ewing."

"The president and vice-president of the bank?"

"Right, and of course Joseph Stavenger is the registered agent."

"What about the others?" Ben asked. "Who are the stockholders? Doesn't a corporation have to have directors or something like that?"

"I asked all that. This is a privately held corporation, so the stockholders are not listed, and the clerk couldn't tell me about any directors."

"So we don't know who owns the other half of Lazard Farms?"

"No. Lazard does. Maybe we should ask him."

"Alex, don't be foolish."

⌒

He left at dawn. They had made love until past midnight, seeking comfort and release in each other's bodies. Afterwards, she had fallen into a sound sleep only to be awakened an hour later by Ben tossing about in the bed.

At two-thirty she'd heard him get up and go into the kitchen. He returned an hour later explaining that he couldn't sleep. He had crawled out of bed again, this time just before dawn. When Alex stumbled half-asleep into the kitchen, she had found him drinking coffee and reading the newspaper. He had said he just needed to do some thinking, that he needed to go by the cabin to pick up some clothes. He also said he might drive over to Augusta to do some shopping, but pointedly did not invite Alex to go along.

Alex looked at the clock. Nine-fifteen. He'd been gone nearly two hours. She stared out through the French doors at the leaf-covered patio. The radio was playing oldies, the station doing it's usual Sixties Saturday format. She half-listened while the Beatles sang an old tune.

> *"...but I thought you might like to know / that the singer's going to sing a song / and he wants you all to sing along. / So may I introduce to you / the one and only Billy Sheers. / Sergeant Pepper's Lonely Hearts Club Band."*

Alex sat bolt upright. Billy Sheers—*William Sheers!* Ringo Starr—*Richard Starkey!* It couldn't be...? Of course it could! Greg Coleman was wild about the Beatles!

She fumbled in her pocketbook for the notepaper. Who were the others? M. W. Edison? Something about *"Maxwell Edison, majoring in medicine...."*

And Brian Epstein, he was somebody—she couldn't remember. It was all a joke, Greg's joke, and maybe they found him out. She didn't want to think about it. She needed to call Ben, she had to.

The ringing phone jolted her thoughts. Grabbing for the receiver, she said, "Ben?"

"No, sorry, it's Mike Brett. I was looking for Ben. They gave me this number at the hospital. I take it he's not there?"

"No, I'm sorry. This is Alex Jennings. Ben's been staying over here for a few days. You're his friend from Atlanta, right?"

"Yeah. He'd asked me to find out the names of the owners of Pelican Island Development Partners. Can I give you the information and let you pass it on to Ben?"

"Yes, just a minute," she reached for a pencil. "Okay, I'm ready."

"According to our attorney, there were three of them— all from Walkerville, by the way. A doctor, Troup Lazard, owned most of it, and the rest was owned equally by a Walter Miller and some guy named Elmo Kantt. What a name! You know them?"

The phone clicked dead in his ear.

Alex rapidly dialed Ben's number at the cabin. Three minutes later the intercept receiver at Marsellaise Plantation began beeping to alert the attendant to the fact that there was a recorded message obtained from one of the phone taps.

~

Ben had driven aimlessly all morning. He'd ended up in the hamlet of Gibson, and spent an hour in the local restaurant drinking coffee and swapping stories with the regulars. He needed to get his mind off things. He'd thought about calling Alex, but decided against it. He needed to apologize and get his act together. She was right.

By eleven he'd returned to the cabin, now looking deserted by the lake. When he opened the door he could see the message number "1" blinking on the answering machine. He pressed the button.

"Ben, it's Alex. I hope you get this message. I found out who the other owners were—besides Lazard, Walter Miller and Elmo Kantt each owned a ten per cent share of Pelican Island. And the other thing I realized is that those names on the bank accounts, they all have to do with the Beatles. Richard Starkey is Ringo Starr's real name—I'll tell you all about it when I see you." She paused. "Ben, I think we need to call for some help—the police, the FBI, or somebody. This is getting too big for us. Maybe I'll call. Lazard has no idea that there's any connection between me and you. I'll see you tonight." She paused again, longer this time. "Ben. I really care about you."

The machine clicked and the electronic voice announced, "Saturday, nine-twenty three a.m."

That's the only solution, he thought. If something illegal is going on, just get out of the way and let the authorities take it from here.

He gathered up some clean clothes and headed back toward town and Alex's house.

He pulled in the drive and parked behind her Camry. Gathering up his clothes he rang the front bell. When there was no response he knocked loudly.

With a sense of dread, he tossed the clothes on the porch and sprinted to the rear of the house. One of the French doors stood open, the glass smashed and the wood splintered by blunt force. He called Alex's name with no reply. The easel in the studio lay on the floor. Two chairs were turned over and a lamp was shattered on the hardwood floor. Alex's purse sat undisturbed on the kitchen table.

Ben felt a wave of panic sweep over his body. With trembling hands, he fumbled through his wallet, searching for Martin Roble's card. Finding it, he hurriedly punched in the number. After eight rings the same neutral female voice answered, "Yes?"

"This is Ben Pike. I've got to speak to Mr. Roble. It's an emergency!"

"Just a moment." The line was silent.

After what seemed like an eternity, the operator returned to the line. "I'm sorry, but Mr. Roble cannot be reached at the moment. We expect him to call in shortly, though. Do you want to leave a message?"

"Yes, please try to find him—it's very important! Tell him that Alex is missing. She found out that Lazard is up to something illegal. I think she might have been kidnapped. I know she's in danger and I'm going to try to find her—I'm going to Lazard's place now. Tell him I need help, please. Do you understand?"

"We have your message recorded. I'll play it back to Mr. Roble when he calls in. Thank you, Dr. Pike."

CHAPTER
THIRTY

DRIVING FRANTICALLY, Ben rushed through town, passing cars and running yellow lights. Reaching the chain link fence that now marked the southern boundary of the plantation, he glanced at his watch. Eleven-twenty. It had been less than two hours since she'd called, so he must have just missed whoever had taken her. He thought of stopping to call Hoke Brantley, but what could he tell him? He couldn't accuse Lazard, not to Hoke. He would dismiss Ben's fears as more paranoia. Roble would certainly call the sheriff's office or the FBI or somebody, anyway.

Reaching the stone and iron gates he swerved in, barely missing one of the farm workers standing just inside the entrance. The Taurus raced down the tree-lined drive. The maples stood golden in their autumn colors. The manicured lawn on either side still glistened fresh and green.

The main house loomed straight ahead, unchanged as ever, its tall, stately columns glaringly white in the morning sun. Lazard's Mercedes was parked in front on the circular drive. Ben stopped his car next to the Mercedes and bounded up the steps. He grabbed the massive knocker on the front door and banged. What seemed like an eternity later, he heard footsteps approaching inside.

Troup Lazard swung the door. He was wearing a starched white shirt and dark trousers. "Ben," he intoned in mock surprise. "What a surprise."

He motioned him through the door. They stood face to face, brother squared off against brother. Ben suddenly became aware of the grin spreading across Lazard's smooth, handsome face.

"Actually," Lazard said, "we were rather expecting you."

Ben felt a hard object poked in his back. He looked around and saw Hector Torrez. Torrez's thick lips were curled back in a cruel grin. In his large, beefy hands was a large caliber automatic pistol.

"You remember Hector," Lazard continued. "We'd like to invite you to join our party in the cellar."

Lazard turned and started walking through the black and white marble foyer. A firm thrust of the gun in his ribs urged Ben to follow.

"Troup, where is Alex?" Ben said suddenly.

Lazard looked over his shoulder, smiling. "In the cellar. Entertaining the boys with her stories."

Ben struggled to control his words. "If you've laid a

hand on her, I'll..."

Lazard whirled around. "You'll what, you silly bastard?" His eyes flashed with what Ben took to be pure evil. "I'll tell you what you'll do," Lazard said, softening. "You'll do exactly as I say."

He slapped Ben across the face. Instinctively, Ben drew back to return the blow—but before he could react, Torrez brought the butt of the pistol crashing down on his shoulder, sending him spinning to the floor in pain.

"Get up," Torrez commanded, "and don't say a word."

Lazard led the way through the dayroom and into the massive kitchen, now deserted with its racks of copper pans gleaming in the late afternoon sun streaming in through the windows. "I gave Pearlie Mae the day off," he explained.

He opened a door on the far side of the kitchen, half-shoving his prisoner first down the dimly lighted stairs toward the cellar. It had been years, but Ben remembered that the cellar was huge, extending under the entire first floor of the mansion. As his eyes adjusted to the darkness he could see Alex on the far side, bathed in a pool of light. He could see her hands and feet bound to a chair and guarded by two men standing over her. He recognized them as Garcia and Fuentes whom he had met in the emergency room the night Ortega had died.

Torrez goaded him toward the group. The cellar was cool, and smelled like old potatoes. As they moved forward, Ben was conscious of their footsteps echoing harshly across the cold stone floor. At regular intervals massive stone pillars rose up to support the broad, hand-hewn timbers that served as floor joists for the mansion above.

"Alex, are you all right?" Ben asked.

In the dim light he could see a bruise under her left eye and a rivulet of blood drying at the edge of her lips. Her blouse was ripped in front, half exposing her breasts. Turning to Lazard, he shouted, "What have you done to her?"

"I'm fine, Ben," Alex said weakly. "These people seem to think I have some idea about what's going on here at Lazard Farms. I told Dr. Lazard..."

Lazard raised his hand to hit her, and she instinctively flinched. "You're a lying bitch," he cracked. "We know you know more." He calmed down, straightened the collar on his expensive shirt. "As I was saying before your boyfriend here so rudely interrupted us, you cooperate and we'll make it easy on you."

"She's not my girlfriend," Ben fired back. It was a lie—but it was the only thing Ben could think to say at the moment.

Lazard whirled on him. "Please," he sneered, "spare me any more of your bullshit lies—brother dearest." He pressed his face within inches of Ben's. "You want to hear a recording of her phone call to you this morning? We can make it real hard on you, and for starters, we'll let you watch us have fun with your girl. *¿Comprende?*"

Torrez, Fuentes and Garcia laughed.

"But let's get serious about this," Lazard continued. "*Amigos,* pull Dr. Pike up a chair and make sure he's comfortable."

Garcia placed a wooden straightback chair behind Ben. Torrez shoved him down and held him while Garcia tied his hands behind his back.

"Troup, let Alex go. You have no quarrel with her."

"True." Lazard stroked his chin and seemed pensive for a moment. "But there are a couple of problems. One is that she knows too much. The other is that I sort of promised her to the boys here when we've finished our conversation. Kind of a little reward for a job well done. Anyway, let's get on with things. Why don't I bring you up to date?"

Lazard settled down in a chair facing his captives. His eyes gleamed dark and manic. For the first time, Ben saw the true evil in his brother. He suddenly felt very afraid—not so much for himself as for Alex.

"I really do need to compliment your girl here on her inquisitiveness," Lazard continued. "She's really quite talented. Too bad she found out so much, however." He smiled. "Oh, we heard all about it—everything she told you on the phone, plus, what she's been kind enough to tell us. Seems like she's been doing a lot of snooping around in my own private records. A few years ago, we had a similar problem with a couple of snoopers. Sad thing was, one of them was my employee. He made his girlfriend angry—she worked with you at the bank didn't she, Alex?—and she ended up knowing too much. The boys here really enjoyed her company before we fed them both to the 'gators in the swamp." He waved his hands and continued, "Ah, but that's a whole 'nother story. What really gets me about you, Alex, is your ungrateful nature. I tried to help you after your husband died—I got you a job in my bank, I helped you find a good lawyer..."

"You bastard!" she hissed.

Lazard smacked his lips. "Now, Alex. Look at it from my position. You got a job; I got to keep an eye on you. And the lawyer and private investigator, well, if somebody is going to be poking around, better the devil you know." He drew a long sigh. "Tell you what I'm going to do. First, Ben, I'll get Victor here to go and move your car. Bet you didn't realize that your visit at Marsellaise Plantation would feature valet parking. We really don't want inquiring eyes to ever know you've been here."

Lazard nodded his head and Garcia headed for the stairs.

"Forget it, Troup. You know you're not going to get away with this."

Lazard seemed to think about Ben's comment for a moment. "So far my track record is pretty well intact," he replied. "But, hey, in the spirit of brotherly love, let's not dwell on the morbid, shall we?" He looked at Alex. "Ms. Jennings here seems to have a real streak of curiosity in her. Do you suppose that she got it from sleeping with her husband?"

He got up, strolled across the room, then came back. "Let me shed some light, help you figure out what's going on around here. Where should I start? How about with the late John Jennings? I guess you realize by now that the terrible accident which befell him was not exactly an accident. Consider it merely an example of how curiosity can get you in trouble."

"You killed him, didn't you?" Alex screeched.

"In a manner of speaking. He just decided to drop in out of a clear blue sky because he saw a plane on the ground he wasn't supposed to see. I guess he figured if one plane could land there, so could he. For some god-awful reason he want-ed to practice his take offs and landings on our little grass strip over by the river. We were pleasant enough—we're always good hosts, as you can see—and we even gave him a little going away present when he stopped by to thank us after his last landing. Unfortunately for him, though, it turned out to be a surprise package and his little plane just couldn't stand the excitement of a few ounces of *plastique*. I had really considered the matter closed—and I guess it will be once and for all after today."

He sat back down, faced Alex squarely. "Now, the other thing. Alex, you've been exceptionally inquisitive about the owners of Pelican Island and Lazard Farms. Perhaps I'm casting pearls before swine, but since we've gone this far, I'll tell you the whole story."

He stood up again, ran his fingers down one of the massive posts. In Ben's mind, Lazard had become an actor reviewing his lines before the performance of his life.

"I presume it's hard for some of us to admit we've made mistakes," he began. "But I did. Even in retrospect it seemed like the right thing to do and even now, if the circumstances were the same, I might do it again. Looking back on it, though, after these several years have passed, I realize that the Pelican Island purchase was the folly that started me on the road I've chosen. I can't blame anyone but myself, but in truth, it was my partners Walter Miller and Elmo Kantt who brought the idea to me. You know the details—I scarcely think I have to spell them out for you. A beautiful unspoiled island, the potential for vast wealth. The old woman who owned it was a client of the bank, and when she died, Kantt did the funeral. They thought they had an inside track to buying the island, but they didn't have the money. I did. It was that simple. We did our homework well—we had commitments from the governor and a promise to get the legislation we needed pushed through the legislature. After we'd laid all the groundwork, some problems arose. I won't belabor the point, but in the end we had to bid against some other groups and ended up paying a lot more than we'd planned. Still, we thought we'd gotten it at a steal, and we went for it. I had the assets, or at least I thought I did, but poor Walter and Elmo had to borrow on everything they owned even to get their ten percent."

Lazard paused to be certain his audience was watching and then continued. "Alex, you know the rest. The protests, the double-crosses, the denials. We ended up with a millstone around our necks and were forced to sell it for less than half what we paid for it. We were all facing financial ruin. I'd mortgaged the plantation, Miller had mortgaged his stock in the bank, Kantt his funeral home."

He hesitated another moment, then looked at Ben. "It's a shame you were not a Lazard, Ben. Oh, I realize my father sired you, but you're not one of us and never were. Do you realize the history that surrounds you here?" He gestured toward the dark stone walls. "Are you aware that this very cellar was dug by slaves more than a hundred-and-sixty years ago? Or, that right where you sit at this moment is the exact spot where the Confederate Congress met in secret session for the last time as it fled before Sherman's army of barbarians? Or how the Lazard fortune and this house as it now stands was rebuilt from the ashes of defeat? Do you have any idea of the magnificent history of this family and of this place? Do you?"

He was shouting without realizing it. His words echoed from one corner of the darkened chamber to the next. "I doubt it," he said softly after a moment. "I doubt you have the slightest comprehension about the history and legacy of this place."

For the briefest of moments Lazard seemed lost in time and space—as if he were in the past, reliving some glorious moment in history. "So what was I to do?" he went on. "Let some bank take over this hallowed ground for a country club? Turn my timberland into a hunting preserve for jaded Atlanta executives and my pastures into trailer parks for the scum of Adams County? Of course not! You'd have done the same thing."

He stared at Ben.

"Like the good Dr. Faust, Ben, you would have bargained with Mephistopheles. You would have negotiated back and forth. Give an inch here, take an inch there. But, in the end, you would have preserved it at any cost, like I did."

Ben realized that, for whatever reason, Lazard was trying to justify all he had done to "save" the plantation. To buy time, Ben said, "If I had your insight, Troup, I might have felt the same way you did. There are still some things I don't understand, though—such as how did you do it? How did you get involved with these people?"

Lazard smiled, pleased at Ben's sudden interest. "I was approached," he said, "by a group of businessmen. They wanted to make some investments in the local economy and had been looking around for some land to purchase, and a business with good cash flow in which they could invest. Marsellaise Plantation was perfect, they said, and offered to buy it outright. They knew I was having some difficulty, so they were sure that purchasing all this—everything—would be a simple matter. They were persistent, very persistent, and I was about to lose everything. So we sat down and talked, honestly, openly. I told them what I wanted. They told me what they needed. You see, they wanted to do some importing, to bring in a few things that might not pass muster via the usual channels. They wanted to fly their products in from south of here and needed a very special piece of property. Marsellaise Plantation was the ideal spot. They needed to be able to land a plane, offload a few packages, then be on their way without being seen. Think about where we are, Ben. Halfway between Atlanta and Savannah. Halfway between Macon and Augusta. An ideal distribution spot for the urban sales of their products. The problem is, all of those cities have commercial airports and controlled air space. But here, at the plantation, we have a vast amount of land and we're off everyone's radar screens. They pointed out to me how easy it would be to file a fight plan over this area and make an unscheduled stop with no one the wiser.

"Ben, I agonized about it. I really did, and I didn't believe I could pull it off all by myself. In the end, though, we incorporated the farm with their buying one-half interest and my keeping the other half. Arrangements were made—perfectly legitimately, I would add—to be certain Miller and Kantt also had their debts taken care of. I paid what I owed and bought into the bank so I could have some oversight of the finances of the whole operation. We brought in some management people and set ourselves up in business. One problem we could help them with was cash flow. They had too much of it, so between the three of us, we've been able to funnel a good little bit of it thorough our businesses. We agreed to do this for five years. After that I would have the right to repurchase the other half of the stock, and they would move their game elsewhere. Ben, it's been working, at least up until now, and the five years will be up very soon."

He was smiling, earnestly, as if telling a patient that his cancer had been cured by a miracle drug.

"The other half," Ben said, "you haven't told us who owns the other half."

"True. And if your girlfriend here had picked away long enough she would have found only that the rest of the stock of Lazard Farms, Inc. is owned by a corporation, which itself is owned by other corporations, who are owned by other corporations, and so on *ad infinitum*. Suffice it to say the other owners are international businessmen."

Lazard stared at them. The silence was suddenly broken by Alex's laughter. "Dr. Lazard, you are such an idiotic fool! Do you really believe your self-serving justifications? Does saving the good Lazard name extend to murder? Does..."

He shut her up with a violent slap.

"You fool!" he roared. "You're just like the others, Greg

Coleman and his silly little girlfriend from the bank. He did-n't believe my motivations. He laughed at me, too. Even now he's laughing at me from Hell because I didn't realize he'd put some of my accounts in the names of musical characters from the '60's."

Ben noticed the dangerous change that had come over Lazard. Once again, his eyes seemed to flash with a maniacal gleam that struck Ben as blackest evil. He prayed that Alex would just keep her mouth shut.

Lazard was about to speak again when Garcia bounded down the stairs. He spoke softly and rapidly with Lazard, who then spoke to the others. "Looks like we will have to defer this for a while. It appears we have other unexpected visitors. Hector, you and Victor come with me. César, stay here and guard our guests. I don't know how long we'll be."

The three of them rushed up the stairs.

César Fuentes eyed them silently for a moment before speaking to Ben, "Your Spanish is excellent, Doctor." He paused. "And your girlfriend is *muy linda*. It's going to be such a waste."

He reached out and rubbed his hand softly across her cheek, slowly lowering it to caress her neck and below to her breast. Ben saw the look of helpless terror in Alex's eyes and knew he had to do something. Had to do something now.

CHAPTER
THIRTY-ONE

BEN WATCHED FUENTES'S eyes. They were fixed on Alex. His mouth was parted and he was about to say something when Ben struck. They had tied his hands and lashed his upper body to the chair, but had not tied his feet.

Launching himself like a fullback, he held his head low and rammed the full weight of his body into the guard. Seeing the motion out of the corner of his eye, Fuentes reached for the pistol in his belt but was hit and knocked back against the wall before he could gain a firm grip on its handle. His head struck the stone with a sharp thud, and he sank dazed to the floor. The pistol skidded off into the darkness of the cellar.

Ben found himself lying on the floor, the rope-tied appendage of his chair making any motion to right himself difficult. He managed to flip over on his knees and then stand awkwardly. Still bent sharply at the waist, he stood over Fuentes who lay on his back but was beginning to stir. Raising his right foot, he brought it sharply down on the man's larynx, crushing it with a sickening snap. Fuentes made soft, gaspy, wheezing sounds as he rapidly turned blue.

Alex watched in shock. Maneuvering behind Alex, he studied the knots that tied her to the chair. In a calm voice, he said, "I'm going to sit down and untie you. Then I want you to untie me. I don't think we made much noise, but we may not have long before they return."

"Ben..." There was pure terror in her voice.

"Alex, there's no time. This is our only chance."

He struggled with the knots. Seconds later, she broke loose, reaching down to untie her ankles and then Ben's hands. She stood in one place, shaking, while Ben searched for the pistol. Fuentes' body shuddered and his attempts at breathing stopped.

Ben found the pistol. It was a Smith & Wesson Model 59. The clip was full—fourteen rounds. He eased back the slide and saw an additional round in the chamber. Fifteen shots, how many enemy? They needed more—another gun, something.

Turning to Alex, he asked, "When they brought you down here, did you see any other guns, anything we can use for a weapon?"

She shook her head but pointed toward the steps. "There're some doors over by the stairs that look like they may lead to some more rooms."

Ben found the doors. There were two of them, both

closed with hasps and staples and secured by large padlocks. He found a large screwdriver on a workbench behind him and attacked the first door, wedging the tool under the hasp and forcing it out of the wood. With a splintering crack the hasp sprang loose and the door swung open. Inside the room was a large closet. Ben searched for a light, feeling about for a switch, a pull cord—anything, but to no avail. In the semi-darkness he could see stacks of small wooden crates. He couldn't see what was written on the outside, so he carried one back to the pool of light. The crate was painted gray and labeled "DANGER-EXPLOSIVES" with the designation "M-33" followed by a series of numbers stenciled on the end.

"I hope this is what I think it is," he said aloud as he pried the top open.

Inside the crate were two-dozen olive drab baseball-sized objects packed carefully in foam padding.

"What are they?" Alex asked.

"Hand grenades. Standard US military issue M-33 fragmentation grenades." He stuffed two in each trouser pocket.

"Why?" she began.

He cut her off. "We'll ask all the 'whys' later. Right now we've got to get out of here."

Taking her hand, Ben led her to the base of the stairs and signaled for her to remain silent. Carefully, he eased up steps, trying to avoid the inevitable creaks. He silently turned the door handle and eased it open a millimeter. In the kitchen he could see one of the farm workers he didn't recognize searching the refrigerator.

He returned to the bottom of the stairs and whispered for Alex to go back and sit in the chair as if she were still tied to it. Once she was in place, he called out, "*¡Hola! ¡Amigo! Venga aqui,*" hoping that his accent wouldn't raise suspicions.

The man in the kitchen opened the door and peered into the basement. Wary, he had begun to walk down the steps when Ben reached from under the stairs to grab his right leg and send him crashing to the stone floor. Ben was on top of him in an instant and broke the man's neck with a sharp twist of his head.

"Ben, you killed him..."

"What did you want me to do—sing him to sleep with a lullaby?" he asked.

Ben grabbed her hand again and led her up the stairs and into the kitchen. The huge house was silent. A hand-held transceiver radio crackled on the counter, startling them both. Ben picked it up, turned the volume down and told Alex to hang onto it. They peered into the dayroom. Nothing. Crossing it, they could see the foyer, also empty.

"I think we're alone," Ben whispered.

Through the sidelights beside the front door they could see the drive. His car was gone, but Lazard's Mercedes had not moved.

"What do you think?" he whispered.

"Let's go," Alex replied.

"I just hope the keys are in it."

"Where will we go?" Alex asked. "The highway? It's more than two miles."

"Where else?"

Peering out the windows to be sure that they could see no one else in the yard, they eased open the front door and sprinted for the Mercedes. Ben took the driver's seat and reached for the key. It was missing! Frantically, they opened the ashtray, lifted up the floor mats and emptied the glove box looking for a hidden spare. When Alex folded down her sun visor a single black plastic-capped key fell in her lap. Ben

inserted it in the ignition and turned it. The car started immediately.

Alex screamed and pointed to the set of gates nearest
the mansion where a pickup truck crammed with several men
was entering the main driveway.

"Damn!" Ben blurted. "Do you know any other way out?"

"No, but this place is covered with a maze of farm roads
and logging trails. Maybe we can lose them."

Ben jammed the car in gear and turned off the circular
drive toward the carriage houses in the rear of the mansion. A
well-maintained dirt track led in the direction of the river.
Without hesitating, Ben followed it.

"Turn on the radio we grabbed and let's see if they spotted us," he told Alex. She did, and in the rapid-fire Spanish he
managed to pick up a few phrases: "...have escaped..." and
"...kill on sight...."

"What are they saying?" she asked.

"We aren't out of the woods yet," he replied.

"Look!" she shrieked. "Behind us!"

In the rear view mirror he could see the pickup closing
rapidly on them, now only fifty yards behind in their dust.

They heard a loud "thump," then another. The rear
glass exploded in a thousand pieces as they realized their pursuers were shooting at them.

"Get down!" Ben ordered. "All the way, on the floor."

The road was now wending its way through a thick forest of pines, temporarily shielding them from the guns in the
pickup. Suddenly, they burst into a pasture with a herd of
brownish-red polled Hereford whiteface cattle. Swerving off
the road, Ben maneuvered to place the herd between them and
the men in the pickup. He slammed on brakes and reached in
his pocket.

"What are you doing?" Alex asked.

"Buying time, I hope," Ben said, as he pulled the safety pin and tossed the grenade in the direction of the herd.

As he hoped, the explosion panicked the cattle, sending them running en masse toward the pickup that had just emerged from the woods into the field. He gunned the motor and followed the dirt road toward the river.

On the far side of the field, the road dipped into a stand of hardwoods surrounding a narrow gully at the bottom of which a small creek flowed. A rickety wooden bridge spanned the gap. Stopping the Mercedes just past the bridge, Ben pulled the pins on two grenades, one in each hand. Holding the grenades with their safety levers in place, he instructed Alex to steer while he tossed them both through the now-shattered back window and hit the gas at the same time. The pickup was just entering the hardwood stand when the small bridge exploded into splinters.

They emerged into another huge pasture, this time with no cattle, but with a group of barns and equipment sheds in the far distance. Beyond the barns lay the river swamp.

"They'll be on foot now. If we can get far enough into the swamp before they catch up with us, I think we can lose them."

He accelerated toward the group of buildings when the car suddenly sputtered once, twice, then stopped. Ben glanced at the fuel gauge which registered below empty.

"They must have hit the gas tank," Ben surmised. "Let's run for it."

They were two-thirds of the way to the nearest barn when geysers of dirt began to rise randomly around them, followed by the distant report of gunshots. Ben looked over his shoulder to see three men in pursuit. They all appeared to have pistols in their hands.

They reached the first structure. It was a semi-open equipment shed, empty except for a wagon, a few rusting harrows and a half-dozen, fifty-five-gallon drums which appeared empty. Twenty yards away stood an enclosed barn, across a courtyard from another more carefully constructed building with an attached shed under which was parked two large tractors and a motorized harvester. It was some type of field office, Ben assumed. Beyond the barn were several smaller storehouses and sheds. The tree-line that marked the edge of the swamp was still hundreds of yards away.

"We can't stay here, it's too open," Ben shouted. "There're three of them and they'll surround us. Let's try to get into that barn."

Leaving the cover of the shelter, they ran to the barn, entering through the main door which stood half-open. It appeared to be a repair shop and storehouse. A tractor with it's engine suspended from a chain attached to a hydraulic hoist was undergoing some sort of transmission repair. On the side nearest their pursuers, tools and shop equipment were neatly laid out as if they had been in use only seconds before they barged in. On the other side, beyond the repair area, were stacks of fertilizer and drums of pesticide.

Ben peeked through a crack in the wooden siding. The three men had taken cover under the open shed, hiding behind the empty drums. They fired blindly at the barn, and Ben shot back twice, moving after each round to avoid providing a steady target. The transceiver crackled in Alex's hand as Ben listened and translated.

"They're calling for reinforcements," he told Alex. "They plan to keep us pinned down here until they can get some more men." He looked around, frantic for a way to escape. "We've got to do something quick! I've got one grenade. Can you shoot a pistol?"

"Hell, yes. I grew up in Walkerville, remember?"

Ben smiled at Alex's burst of enthusiasm. "Good. Watch them through one of these cracks. If they try to move, shoot. It doesn't matter if you miss, I just want to keep them pinned down."

He handed Alex the pistol and disappeared toward the other side of the shop.

Ben did not know what he was searching for. Anything to create a distraction—anything to give them an advantage. He found a set of welding tools with cylinders of oxygen and acetylene, but couldn't think of a way to project their potential explosive force without risking their own lives. He looked at the pesticide drums—none of them with compounds rapidly toxic to humans. He looked at the stacks of fertilizer. That was it—*fertilizer!*

He found a five-gallon bucket being used to soak engine parts and emptied its contents on the floor. Grabbing a fifty-pound bag of fertilizer, he dumped it into the bucket, then hauled it to a steel drum with a hand pump on top and marked in crude letters "DIESEL FUEL." Cranking the pump, he placed the nozzle over the bucket of fertilizer and let the foul-smelling fluid flow. When it was full, he found a shovel and used the handle to stir the thick mixture.

Alex screamed, "Ben!" and fired twice.

He looked up. Alex made a signal with her hand that all was fine for the moment. Searching frantically, he found a roll of baling twine. He set the fertilizer-diesel fuel mixture on the workbench next to a vice. Carefully, he anchored his remaining grenade in the vice, taking care to leave room for the safety lever to spring loose when the pin was pulled. He tied one end of the baling twine to the safety ring and set the rest of the roll to which it was attached by the door. He ran over and crouched beside Alex.

"Are you all right?" he asked.

She nodded. "One of them tried to get around back. I think they're waiting on some help."

"OK, this is the plan. We've got to get them in this barn while we get out."

"Are you crazy? This is the only place we can hide without being seen. They'll pick us off if we try to make it to one of the other sheds."

"I know, but once they get in this barn, they'll never get out."

He took the pistol and fired a shot at one of the men crouching behind a harrow. The shot missed, but the man pulled his head down again. Grabbing Alex's hand, he pulled her to the large barn doors.

"Now listen," he instructed. "When I start shooting I want you to run for the farthest shed over there, understand?"

"Yes, but..."

"Just do it!"

He turned and squeezed off a round at the three men. Alex dashed across the barnyard for the shed. One of the men raised to shoot at her but thought better of it as one of Ben's bullets whizzed past his head. When he was satisfied that she was safe, Ben threaded a loop of wire through the roll of baling twine that he had left by the door. Holding the twine in one hand and the pistol in the other, he sprinted after Alex, firing twice blindly at the other shed while playing out the twine behind him.

Alex was lying on the ground behind a concrete cattle trough. He threw himself to the ground beside her and waited.

Peeking around the edge of the trough, he could just see the shed and the barn without exposing himself as a target. The men in the shed did not move. After a long while, one of them cautiously crept toward the barn that their prey had just abandoned. Carefully, raising his head, Ben watched without moving. Running rapidly, the man covered the twenty yards and ducked into the main barn door. Shortly the other two followed.

Ben gave the twine a sharp jerk.

CHAPTER
THIRTY-TWO

FOR AN ETERNITY, nothing happened. The twine had tensed, then suddenly relaxed. Had it broken? Had they found it and cut it? Or was the release simply the pin pulling out of the grenade?

Ben tried to remember his military training. How long was the delay? Four seconds? Five seconds? Was this one a dud?

The barn erupted in a ball of flame with an explosive force that he felt rather than heard. The power of the blast peeled back the roof of the shed under which they were hiding, and hurled flaming debris all around them. Shielded from the force by the concrete trough, they were unhurt.

Ben looked at Alex. He eyes were closed tightly, and she held her hands over her ears as if such a position would have protected her.

He shook her gently. "I think we did it."

"My god," she exclaimed, "what did you do?"

"I tried to remember what they taught me in the military—to improvise, to use what's available."

Slowly they got up. The barn was now a jagged heap of flaming debris, and all the buildings in the compound displayed varying degrees of destruction. The building that Ben had assumed was an office of some sort had lost most of it's roof, and the wall that faced the ruins of the barn had been imploded as if kicked by a gigantic foot. One of the tractors was on it's side, a blaze fed by its leaking fuel now licking up one of the walls. He noticed that the room suddenly exposed by the blast was full of what appeared from a distance to be laboratory equipment.

"We've got to get out of here, but I need to see what's in that building," he said. "Stay here and tell me if you hear anything on the radio."

He sprinted quickly to the half-ruined building. The exposed room appeared to be some sort of a lab. Three counter-top electronic scales had been tossed at crazy angles against the far wall. Four industrial-sized microwave ovens stared at him through the shattered glass of their doors. In part of the room that must have been used for storage, blue plastic drums labeled "Bicarbonate of Soda, USP—$NaHCO_3$" lay on their side, their contents spilling onto the vinyl tiled floor. A vault room of some kind, protected by solid concrete blocks and a steel door, had stood against the wall adjacent to the destroyed barn. One of the welding gas cylinders had been hurled into it like a battering ram, smashing a six-foot opening in the blocks. Peering inside, Ben could see plastic wrapped packages laid in neat stacks. Several nearest the breech were smashed open to reveal fine white powder which now sifted down to the floor. Over the roar of the now advancing flames he heard Alex calling to him.

He ran back to the ruined shed.

"They're calling on the radio. I don't know what they're saying," she said.

Ben listened. It sounded like whoever was calling was trying to raise their three now dead pursuers. The Spanish was rapid and idiomatic. He grasped that they had apparently heard the explosion and were on the way. The words "diez minutos"—ten minutes—were repeated several times.

Ben checked the pistol. Six rounds left. "Let's go. We don't have much time and we've got a long way to go."

Even running, Ben knew they'd do well to make the swamp in ten minutes. Grabbing her hand, he led Alex at a steady jog toward the distant woodline and the relative safety of the swamp. As they neared the massive evergreen oaks that marked the edge of the pasture, a jeep with two men in it appeared out of a road that apparently led to another part of the plantation. The driver spotted the fugitives and, for a moment, veered in their direction. Apparently changing his mind, he swerved the jeep back toward the blazing complex of buildings.

Ben and Alex reached the treeline and plunged deep into the forest. The land fell rapidly toward the swamp, now semi-dry with the annual fall drought. The blazing sun of the open field had given way to a shadow world of green and damp. Because of the spring and summer floods, the forest floor was fairly open, a dense canopy of giant evergreen oak and beech trees robbing the sunlight from any undergrowth that might take root. They slogged through mud and occasional patch of waist-high brush, finally coming to a small dry hillock covered with mountain laurel. Exhausted, they collapsed in the relative protection of the dense foliage.

They were both breathing too heavily to speak. Finally, Ben said, "Now, I know his secret."

"What are you talking about?"

"Lazard. What he's doing. International businessmen—bullshit!"

Alex puffed. "I don't understand."

"Cocaine. He's flying in cocaine. I'm not totally sure, but I believe that building back there served as the laboratory where they converted cocaine powder to crack. No wonder he was talking about 'urban markets' and money laundering. What an incredible racket! Talk about cutting out the middlemen. Buy your own airstrip, your own bank, run your own distribution system."

The radio hissed and they heard a voice, this time in English and familiar. "This is Doc. What's the status?"

After a brief delay, a Spanish-accented voice replied, "The tractor barns are in flame. It looks like all has been destroyed."

Lazard's voice was terse. "Repeat that."

"I repeat, there has been an explosion and fire. The products are being destroyed as we speak."

"Where are the men who followed the couple?"

There was a pause. "It would appear that they have also been destroyed."

"And the couple?"

"We saw them going into the swamp near the complex. We were unable to reach them before they got away."

"The swamp there is narrow. You should be able to trail

them without problems. I want them brought back to me. We have a visitor here and I cannot leave. I'll send help if I can, but don't delay. Find them!"

"¡Si, *patron!*" the Spanish voice replied. The radio went silent.

Ben looked out across the swamp toward the direction from which they had come. Their footprints in the muddy ground were obvious. Lazard was right. They would be easy to track. Maybe they could find a creek to cover their tracks. But he'd said the swamp was narrow. That might mean that they were trapped.

"Let's go," Ben suddenly said.

They were on their feet in a hurry, scrambling deeper into the swamp. Lazard's reason for characterizing the swamp as "narrow" soon became obvious. A hundred yards beyond the laurel covered rise a huge beaver pond stretched into the distance and extended back to their right side. Judging from the trees growing in it, it was only a few feet deep. The muck and hidden logs in the water would make it too dangerous to try to cross. That left two choices: to their left, or back where they had come from.

Ben looked at the sky. The dense leaves blocked the sun, making it useless for navigation. He glanced at his watch. Just past two in the afternoon. There were at least four hours of good light, four hours for their hunters to catch their prey. *Got to think,* he told himself. *Remember Panama. Remember Jungle Warfare School. What would the instructor have told you to do?*

They set out along the edge of the pond.

The radio spoke again, this time in Spanish. Two men were talking, one Raul, the other...Tat?—a nickname? Ben didn't quite catch it. Raul was saying he was following the trail, and the other one said he would be *"al lado del lago de castor."* Ben tried to remember, *"castor"*—something to do with *castigo*—punishment? It had been years since he'd spoken Spanish regularly. *Castor?* Beaver? Maybe. Alongside the beaver pond. Now, it made sense.

He grabbed Alex, and they huddled down between the buttress-like roots of a giant cypress tree near the edge of the water.

"I'm not completely sure, but I think they've split up. They seem to figure that we don't have many directions to go because of this beaver pond, so one of them is going to follow our tracks in, and the other one is going to be waiting for us on what must be our only way out. Our best hope is to take them out one at a time. I want you to stay here and hide."

He handed her the pistol. "Here. We can't risk a shot, because they'd know for sure where we are. I'm going to try to take the first one out quietly." He paused. "You've got six shots left. If I don't come back, use them."

For an instant he wondered how she would interpret that.

They had been following the edge of the beaver pond for several hundred yards. Wading into the pond to cover his tracks, Ben eased back some distance to a large live oak tree standing in a foot of water and some ten feet from where they had walked. Grasping a sturdy vine, he hauled himself up into the tree and crawled out on a huge limb that extended over the trail.

He did not have long to wait. Raul—he hoped it was Raul—was intently following their tracks through the mud, moving rapidly, his eyes to the ground, but stopping every few minutes to listen. The swamp was silent except for the distant drumming of a pileated woodpecker. As he came closer to the oak, Ben saw with alarm he was armed with a military issue rifle. Alex's pistol would be useless against the guy's powerful rifle. Ben knew he couldn't let him make it that far. Raul seemed to pause under the tree limb—but, the second Ben was about to leap, walked away from the edge of the water and began fumbling with his pants. What a time to take a piss, Ben thought! It was going to be a long leap, but he might not have another chance. He launched himself into the air.

Raul was holding the rifle in the crook of his left arm as he relieved himself. Ben's feet struck him squarely on the back of his shoulders. The rifle flew into the murky water as the gunman went down. Landing in the mud, he was stunned only momentarily and came up flailing, searching for the gun. He swung at Ben and missed. Ben swung back and he ducked, only to deliver a smashing blow in return. Raul lunged at Ben and they grappled with one another, falling in the slimy mud and rolling into the dark water.

Ben fought like he had never fought before, with a strength fueled by his pent-up anger for all that was happening. Grabbing Raul's head in a hammer lock, he held him under the water until his struggling turned into a flailing, and then to a shudder, and then ceased. He held the man's under water several seconds longer to make sure.

Releasing the limp body in the water, he searched for the rifle. He wasn't sure where it had landed, so gave up after rummaging around in the mud for a couple of minutes. He heard a sound from the bank. Raul's radio had fallen on dry ground and Tat was calling. He dared not answer. After several attempts to get a response, Tat announced he was going to work his way toward him along the edge of the lake. Ben didn't know where he was. Alex couldn't understand what was being said, so she didn't know to move away and hide. It was impossible to tell who was closer to her. If he could get there first, he might be able to surprise and overcome the man.

They had originally followed the edge of the lake before Ben had backtracked. This time, he headed about fifty yards inland and paralleled the edge of the water in Alex's direction. He estimated it would take him ten minutes to reach her, but by approaching from another direction, his chances of being spotted first by the gunman would be lessened.

As he neared the ancient cypress where she had been standing, he saw Alex at almost exactly the same moment that she saw him. She stood, and signaled all was okay. He was still twenty yards away from her when the bark of the tree just above her head exploded, followed by the booming report of a high velocity rifle. She whirled, and while he could not see the shooter, Ben realized it must be the other gunman.

Alex raised her hands above her head and stepped out from behind the tree. She yelled, "Don't shoot. I'll surrender. The bastard has left me here."

Ben realized in an instant the gunman had not seen him. Crawling on his belly now, he slithered ahead to see a swarthy man holding an assault rifle and approaching Alex rapidly. The man cocked the rifle, aimed it Alex's head.

CHAPTER
THIRTY-THREE

ALEX INCHED SLOWLY toward the gunman. The gunman, in turn, walked steadily toward her, assault rifle raised and pointed straight at her head. Any second Ben half-expected the gunman to pull the trigger. For one horrific moment, he visualized what it would be like to see Alex's head blown off her shoulders.

As the armed gunman approached Alex, his eyes kept darting from side to side, suspicious of a trap. Ben noted that as Alex moved, she also moved toward the water, thus drawing attention away from where he lay hidden in the underbrush. She was talking constantly. "Look, you've got to let me go.

I really don't know anything about...."

When he was about ten yards away, Tat snarled, "Shut up!"

Approaching her even more cautiously now, weapon at the ready, the bearded gunman demanded, "Where is the other one—the man?"

"I don't know—I swear it. We were running and I fell behind. I couldn't keep up. He said he couldn't let me hold him back. I think he went back toward the pasture. I...I didn't know what to do. The bastard just left me here."

Still suspicious, Tat kept the rifle trained on Alex while he surveyed the surrounding swamp. Ben lowered his head, silently praying that his mud drenched clothes would provide sufficient camouflage. He heard Alex speaking again and cautiously looked up.

"You've got to believe me," he heard her saying. "I promise you I'll never tell anyone. I'll do anything to prove it to you."

Tat stared at her.

"Please," she said, and slowly began unbuttoning her blouse. "I'll show you. I'll do *anything* you want if you'll let me go." Her shirt now unbuttoned, she unhooked her bra in front, exposing her breasts.

Ben watched as Tat began to lower the rifle.

"Anything," Alex continued, her voice low and seductive. She began to unbuckle her belt.

Tat laid his rifle on the ground as Alex began to slip out of her mud-stained jeans. Ben could see him tugging at his belt as he approached her. Alex's eyes were fixed on his, capturing and holding his gaze as she slowly undressed. "Anything you want..."

He was two feet away when Ben hit him with a flying tackle, propelling them both onto the roots of a enormous oak.

The gunman was half-again as large as Ben, and what he lacked in strength and fighting skill, he made up in brute force. They rolled back and forth, grappling like two dogs. Now they were on their feet, swinging at each other. Tat's size advantage was becoming evident. With a powerful cuff of his fist, he sent Ben crashing into a cypress knee, striking him on the head and stunning him momentarily. He watched, helplessly, while Tat scooped up the rifle and started walking toward him.

"I think I will only bring one of you back alive," Tat grinned and raised the gun.

Ben could do nothing—only wait for the big man to pull the trigger. He was thinking of Alex, what would happen to her now, when, suddenly, the big man's face exploded in a red mist of blood and brains. The rifle dropped as he fell, revealing Alex, half-naked and holding the pistol in both hands.

She stared at the body, shaking.

Ben took her in his arms. "It's all right. We're OK."

"But I just killed a man."

"You did what you had to do."

Saying nothing, she began to pick up her clothes.

After she was dressed, Ben looked up at the sky and said, "There's a lot of daylight left. These guys were in a jeep. Let's follow this one's trail back to the field." He rolled Tat's body over and extracted a set of keys from his pocket.

Silently, they set off through the swamp, following in reverse the muddy footprints left by the gunman. Ben carried the assault rifle, Alex stuffed the pistol in her jeans. The trail led along the edge of the beaver pond for half-a-mile to a spot where the ground was trampled and several cigarette butts had been ground out in the moist earth. Turning sharply, it headed back across the swamp.

"He must have waited here. The jeep should be in that direction," Ben observed.

They followed the footprints for several hundred more yards before the terrain began to rise, the hardwood forest giving way to drier piney woods. In the distance, they could see light through the trees, indicating the open ground of the pasture.

Ben motioned for Alex to say still. "I think we should be careful before we get out in the open. Lazard may have sent more of them."

Slowly and cautiously, he approached the open pasture, moving from the cover of one tree to the next, pausing to be certain he was not being watched. He had checked to be sure the rifle had a full clip, and had set the selector for burst firing. Finding a small gully, he crawled the last fifty yards before raising his head to peer out across the expanse of grass. The jeep sat unattended near the edge of the woods. In the distance, he could see drifting in the wind wisps of smoke from the still-burning barn complex. Satisfying himself no one was near, he jogged back to where Alex was crouched behind a fallen tree.

"I don't see anybody. If these keys fit the jeep, I think we should head toward the river. Assuming they don't see us this time, I think we've got a good head start. We can swim across the river, or grab a log and float downstream toward Walkerville. Sound OK?"

Alex nodded. Cautiously, they emerged into the unprotected openness of the pasture and climbed in the jeep. It started instantly with Tat's keys. Ben glanced at the sun, now lower in the southwestern sky, and steered toward the west and the river.

They had been driving only a minute when Alex tapped Ben's shoulder and pointed across the pasture toward the smoldering barns. A vehicle was approaching rapidly, raising behind it a cloud of dust. They looked at one another as Ben stepped on the gas.

The distance between the jeep and the faster pursuing vehicle closed quickly. Reaching the edge of the pasture, Ben steered onto a small farm road that crossed a neck of the swamp via a raised earth causeway. They emerged into a long smooth narrow field with a huge, open shelter built under the trees near the road.

"The non-existent airstrip," Ben quipped.

Driving rapidly, they reached the end of the field and realized there was no outlet.

Ben swerved the jeep sideways and they leapt out.

"Run for the woods," he told Alex. "I'll hold them off with this rifle and catch up with you."

The vehicle was approaching rapidly. He could see that it was white, a sedan of some sort with only one person in it. He laid the rifle across the hood of the jeep and began to draw a bead on the driver. Just as he was about to fire, a flashing blue light appeared on the dash and the car turned to the side to reveal the markings of the Adams County Sheriff's Department. It stopped twenty yards away, and a familiar hulking red-headed figure emerged with his hands half-raised.

"Hoke!" Ben yelled. "Thank god you're here!"

He laid the rifle down and nearly ran to the deputy.

Hoke was smiling, relaxed. "You okay, Ben?

"I am now. How did you know we were here? Did Roble call you?"

"Where's the girl? She OK, too?"

"She's fine." Ben's heart was racing. He turned to see Alex, covered with mud and emerging from the woods.

"Hoke, do you know what's going on? Lazard was

going to kill us. Apparently he's running a drug smuggling operation out of..."

"Save it for later, Ben," Hoke cut him off.

Alex was walking up, smiling now for the first time. "Are you all right, Ms. Jennings? Did anyone hurt you?"

"I'm fine, thanks. God, we're glad to see you!"

"And I'm glad to see you two, also. I was afraid these Latinos might have roughed you up. Doc would have been mighty upset."

A sudden wave of terror descended on Ben and Alex as the deputy drew his pistol. "He left real exact orders that you were to be brought back alive."

"Hoke, not you..." Ben moaned.

"Yeah, me, too," he replied as he handcuffed them and shoved them into the back of the cruiser.

They rode in silence for a few moments before Ben spoke. "Why, Hoke? Why are you doing this?" They were just leaving the airstrip, riding more slowly this time.

It took the deputy a long time to reply. "Ben, you know, I've wondered that myself a lot of times. We started off together, but grew up different. When we were kids, we were best buds. But things change, don't they? You're some big doctor now with lots of money, good clothes, fancy car. You don't have any idea what it's like to be a fuckin' peon, sliding by on a twenty-two thousand dollar a year salary, living in a goddamn doublewide trailer and wondering how you gonna scrape up the cash to take your kids to Six Flags. You don't have one fuckin' idea what it's like! So I decided to change it—not that I had much choice to begin with, mind you. Several years ago there was this girl. She was seventeen, I got her pregnant. She went to Lazard to have him arrange for her to get an abortion. He called me—said he was gonna do me a favor. Either I helped him out with something he needed, or he made sure my wife found out. Look, I got three kids. Wanda would eat me alive with alimony and child support. So I said I would, simple as that, only I said this one time. And then the next time he told me he'd make sure I ended up in jail if I didn't work for him. So I did. Now I got a decent car, a decent TV, the wife's got nice clothes and I can take my family to the beach in July. Fuckin' simple, man. You just wouldn't understand."

Alex spoke. "Hoke, people have been killed. My husband was murdered. Susan from the bank, and Greg...." She seemed overwhelmed by it all.

"Shit happens," Hoke said grimly, and was silent as they drove back to the mansion.

CHAPTER
THIRTY-FOUR

THE HUGE HOUSE looked deserted at they drove up. Hoke parked in front and herded them up the steps, through the front door and into the foyer.

"Doc?" he called. No reply. Turning to his prisoners he decreed, "We'll just wait, OK?" He shoved them into the dining room and motioned for them to sit down on either side of the long mahogany table. He took a seat at the head of the table in one of the end chairs.

The great house was silent. In the distance, a clock chimed once. Hoke glanced at his watch and observed, "Three-thirty. Hope Doc's gonna get back soon. I gotta get back to my patrol duties. You wouldn't believe what goes on in this county on a Saturday night, 'specially over in nigger town. Gotta ride around, show a 'law enforcement presence' as they say."

He drummed his hands on the table and looked around the room. "You know, Ben," the deputy continued, "my momma told me one time you lived out here 'fore your daddy cut you off and had you kicked out. Musta' been mighty nice, all this. You must really hate old Doc."

He was interrupted by the sound of a door slamming in the distance, the echo reverberating through the huge house. They could hear footsteps on the marble of the foyer. Troup Lazard appeared at the arched opening.

"Well, look who's come back!" Turning to Hoke, he said, "Good job, Hoke. I'll make sure you're amply rewarded." He turned toward Alex and Ben and grinned. "You two have caused a lot of trouble. So much trouble, in fact, I'm going to have to make a few lifestyle changes."

He consulted his watch. "I've got a lot to do in the next hour and a half, so I hope you won't mind if I skip the perfect host bullshit. At the same time, I want you to know exactly what's going on so you can enjoy every minute of it—your last minutes on this earth, I might add."

"Troup, forget it," Ben blustered. "I called the authorities before I left to come out here. You know that. You're no fool. You know you'll never get away with all this."

"Ben, in a sense of the word, you're right. You have screwed things up royally, but not to fear. I've got a plane arriving to pick me up at five and take me far, far away."

"It won't be far enough," Ben said.

Lazard chuckled. "We'll just have to see about that, won't we?" He glanced at his watch again. "You'll have to excuse me for a few minutes. I've got a bit of packing to do."

Hoke stiffened, "Doc, what did you say? You leaving?"

"Yes and no. I'll explain in a minute. Don't worry, I've got things worked out. You'll be taken care of. Kantt will get you the money as usual."

"I called Roble," Ben interjected. "He's with the feds. It's just a matter of time. They know about you, Troup."

Lazard smiled and sat down at the other end of the table opposite Hoke. "Actually, they don't. But I will admit he works for the government. By the way, that's the solution to an interesting mystery. Mr. Roble and I had a long and very informative talk while you and Ms. Jennings were traipsing across my land and destroying my property. It seems that the government has been suspicious, but they really haven't had any hard evidence on us—certainly not enough for a search warrant, but God knows they've tried. You remember Ortega, of course? He apparently worked with your Mr. Roble and had been sent to infiltrate our organization. We are always looking for a few good men, but we have a strict policy of getting to know our employees before they get to know us. So, we let him work here for a few months. And then he tipped his hand—started asking questions, roaming around the property. When we interviewed him again, we didn't get anything out of him, so I told the boys to get rid of him. They decided he was an innocent fellow wetback and took pity on him. They dumped him in a ditch instead of in the swamp like I told them to. It was a near fatal mistake for everyone. Fortunately he fell under the care of your friend Dr. Carter, who sufficiently mismanaged his case to the point that he didn't make it. Remember the message Ortega was trying write, 'D-E-something'? It was DEA. Your friends work for the Drug Enforcement Administration."

Hoke looked alarmed. "Doc, those guys don't work alone. They'll be back."

"No doubt, Hoke. But after talking with Mr. Roble, who works independently and undercover by the way, I feel certain we've got at least twenty-four hours, maybe more. I don't think we need to worry about *him* turning us in."

He turned toward the kitchen and called for Torrez.

The smiling farm manager opened the door and emerged holding a huge sterling salver covered with a domed lid bearing the D'Ayen coat of arms. He set it down in the middle of the long table.

"Hoke, this is as much for you as anyone, but I thought our other guests might appreciate it. You've got a wife and three kids, don't you? The operative rule here is never, ever get in my way. Never, ever try to double-cross me or sell me out. I may not be nearby, but someone who knows you will. Do you get my drift, Hoke?"

Hoke nodded, nervously now. Lazard motioned to Torrez who lifted the cover from the cover from the tray.

The head of Martin Roble stared sightlessly at Hoke Brantley.

~

Wielding a pistol that he had gotten from Torrez, Lazard nudged his handcuffed prisoners toward the basement. Hoke and Torrez followed behind, the farm manager carrying the tray. In a semi-sarcastic voice, Lazard assured Alex she need not fear another trip to the cellar; he merely wanted them to understand what was going to happen. As they descended the stairs, they saw that the space was brightly-lit, the doors to both locked rooms now standing open. In the room that Ben had not pried open, two men were packing bound stacks of cash into duffel bags. Lazard paused and gestured with his gun, "I have to admit this has been a lucrative business, so much so that I've had trouble disposing of all I've earned. There's nearly five-million dollars in there. Should be enough for me to start my new life."

Ben watched Hoke. The big deputy was staring intently at the cash. He noted that the crates from the other locked room had been moved across the cellar and stacked next to a huge tank. Lazard waved them over and stood in front of it.

"Now, I want to explain my plan to you. Hoke, you listen to this very carefully. You have an important role to play, and I want you to understand exactly what is going to happen." He turned and gestured to the tank. "This is a storage tank for five-hundred gallons of fuel oil. Back in the old days, when this house was heated by wood burning fireplaces, my father had an oil-fired furnace installed as a backup for when the weather was severely cold. When we redid the heating system a number of years ago, I just left it in, in case the newer heat pumps went out. I never have used it and should have had it taken out years ago, but never got around to it. I've often thought it represented a tremendous fire hazard. Even occurred to me that, since this cellar stretches under the entire house, should this tank catch fire and leak, any attempt to put it out would be impossible until all the oil was burned out—by which time, of course, the house would be in cinders. With me thus far?"

He received no reply. Reaching into one of the crates, he extracted an object and held it up for them to see. On the top was a device that appeared no larger than a thick credit card. Extending from it were two wires that ended in a shiny brass object that, in turn, had been stuck into something that appeared to be gray putty. He held it out. "This, in case you don't recognize it, is a timer and battery connected to a small detonator which has been placed in two ounces of plastic explosive. Not enough to really destroy much, but certainly enough to blow a hole in this tank and start a fire in the process. We have just a few grenades and the like that I've stacked here to make sure that the fire spreads appropriately, and to destroy a few documents and some other things I don't want found. Also, I'll ask Hector to set the late Mr. Roble's head here, too. The rest of him is already 'gator bait in the swamp."

Lazard paused, looking first at his watch and then the timer. He pressed a few buttons and the number "75:00" appeared in small glowing red digits on its face. "Now, he continued, I've set this to go off in an hour and fifteen minutes. I'm placing it on the support of the fuel oil tank. It's a quarter-to-four now. I should be departing right at five, so I'll get to watch this all from the..."

"Wait just a damned minute!" Hoke interjected. "You are leaving. What about us? What about all of us who've risked our necks for you? You're taking five-fuckin'-million dollars and leaving us here...."

Torrez put his hand on Hoke's shoulder. "Easy, amigo."

Shrugging it off, Hoke stepped closer to Lazard. "You ain't going no where 'til you tell me what your plans are!"

Casually, Lazard leveled the pistol at Hoke. "What do you need to know, Mr. Brantley? That you'll be taken care of? That I'm not going to leave you to swing on the gibbet while I dance the tango in Buenos Aires? Don't you trust me?"

"Not really," Hoke replied, reaching for his pistol.

Lazard shot him twice, and he crumpled to the floor.

Alex stifled a scream as the deputy's body hit the floor.

Lazard stared briefly at the body. "Such a fool! I'm a Lazard, and my word is my bond." Turning to Hector he directed. "Get his handcuff keys. Take the shackles off of our guests, and stick them back in his belt. Then get plenty of rope and meet me in my study. If my plans are going to work, we need to set the scene carefully."

With his gun he motioned Ben and Alex toward the stairs. "I don't want to kill you now, but I can as you see, and I will if necessary."

He directed them past the men who were now transporting sacks of bundled cash up the stairs. They walked through the kitchen and dayroom to the foyer, then on through the parlor and down the short hall to the study. The paneled room was softly illuminated by the warm rays of afternoon sunlight streaming in through the window. Lazard closed the shutters and switched on several lamps. He motioned for Ben to sit behind the desk, and Alex in a straight chair at its side. Hector appeared with the ropes and they lashed them securely hand and foot to the chairs, Ben's hands to the armrests, Alex's behind her chair.

The pendulum clock on the office wall struck four times. Lazard looked up. "Hector, make sure everything is being loaded in the truck. We've got half an hour yet. I'll meet you out front at four-thirty, which should give us plenty of time to meet the plane and get away by five. I'll keep my friends company here in their final hour."

He poured himself a drink and settled into a wingchair.

"I'm sorry I can't offer either of you a drink," he said. "I do hope you'll forgive me if I indulge. I've got a little time to kill, so I thought I'd tell you about my plans. I'm really rather proud of them, considering the short notice you've forced on me."

Alex spoke, "Dr. Lazard, you don't think..."

Lazard waved her off with his hand. "There's absolutely nothing you can do at this point. No amount of talking or pleading or bargaining is going to change things for either of you. And in case you're thinking about talking me into putting you out of your misery with a quick bullet to the head, you can forget that, too. I want the autopsy reports to show that you were alive when you died in case there's anything left of your bodies. Let me tell you what I've planned and see what you think about it."

CHAPTER
THIRTY-FIVE

"BEN, YOU DON'T REALIZE IT, but you've inadvertently given me a way out of this whole mess. I talk a good game, but I'm not a total fool. I realized that someday this would all have to come to an end. If the cartel kept their end of the bargain, that would be one way. If not....well, suffice it to say I've gone over the options a million times in my mind. I did this to keep from losing everything, to preserve the Lazard name and fortune. And it might have worked, too. I have no heirs—I was going to leave this house and land as a memorial to all that this family has stood for over the years. I was going to call it the Lazard Foundation and direct that this home be preserved for all time as a museum, and that the income from the property be used to fund scholarships and worthwhile projects in the community. It would have worked, Ben. It really would have worked."

He paused.

"And then you came along, like a ghost from the past. I didn't comprehend at first what you knew or didn't know. And, interestingly, you didn't know what you almost found out, but I'll get to that in a minute. Both of you, through your ridiculous quixotic blundering, almost brought me down. In the process though, you managed on one hand to let me find out what the government suspects but doesn't yet know, and on the other to destroy most of the evidence against me. You see, before he died, Mr. Roble gave me chapter and verse about essentially everything the government suspects but can't at this point prove. I realized the one thing that could put me away would be their discovery of our little processing lab we had so cleverly hidden in one of the barns. Well, guess what? It's gone. Thoroughly destroyed by you, however accidentally that may have occurred. *Voilá!* No evidence there."

He took a long pull on his drink.

"So what does that leave? Computer records and files here at the house? The fire should take care of all that. There's one other thing, my bank accounts. If someone as stupid as a bank teller can figure out what's going on, it may well be that the Feds can, too. That's not a certain thing, mind you. With Miller and Ewing firmly in charge at the bank, there's a good chance we'll be able to clean up that mess, also, but it'll take time and careful planning. Roble told me they couldn't connect Ortega's death to me, otherwise, they would have moved on us long ago. His partner, Latham—well, they were suspicious, but in the end they decided it might really have been a hunting accident. But, when Roble turns up missing, that will be three in a row, and they'll surely be after my head.

"Therefore, I hatched a little plan. What would happen if I were dead, and you turned out to be the villain? I *liked* the idea! There are several witnesses at the hospital who will testify you seem to have this thing about me—resentful, disinherited younger half-brother and all that. And Douglas Ewing at the bank will be willing to testify that you, Ms. Jennings, somehow blamed me for your husband's accidental death and had made threatening statements about me. You both have an ax to grind, and motivation to do me harm. So how about this scenario: You two conspire together and then show up out here determined to confront me. There's an argument, I call the sheriff's office—there's already a record of that when I summoned Hoke—or should I say, the late Deputy Brantley. You tie me up and set the house on fire. My body is found in the ashes while you disappear. The town mourns me while every law enforcement agency within a thousand miles is looking for you on a charge of murder. Meanwhile, I'm on a plane to Mexico, then on to Columbia and points south. Sound good?"

"Just great, Troup, but there's one thing you're forgetting," Ben replied.

"Oh? What might that be?"

"Too many bodies. How about Alex and Hoke? How are you going to explain them?"

"Good point, Ben, glad you brought it up. Originally, I planned it this way. Hoke was going to arrive to find that you and Ms. Jennings holding me hostage in my study. He comes in, there's a fight, she gets knocked out, you hit him over the head. When he comes to, you're gone and the house is in flames. He manages to crawl out just in time to save himself. I was trying to do some quick thinking about that. I think we'll change the scenario and have you shoot Hoke. Hector will hear the shots, run in and find you standing over his body. There's a fight, and Alex is knocked out, then you knock him out, he wakes up with you gone and the house in flames, *et cetera.* Sound OK?"

"Like the final act a great tragedy."

"Well, it probably doesn't matter anyway. It's nearly dark and we're so isolated it's unlikely anyone will see the fire. Hector will, of course, wait until the whole structure has collapsed before he calls the fire department. And, since there will be deaths, our dear coroner, Elmo Kantt, will investigate the matter carefully prior to issuing his opinion, relying heavily on the testimony of Señor Torrez, of course. There are some other loose ends, too, but it'll work. Enough people have enough to lose to make it work. I only wish I could be here for my memorial service."

He laughed.

"And Roble?" Alex asked.

"Roble who? As far as anyone knows, he was never here. There won't be enough left after the fire to identify his remains as a separate body—and I suspect by then the 'gators will have taken care of the rest."

"Why are you so sure they'll identify my body as yours?" Ben asked.

"I'm not, and thank you for reminding me."

Standing, Lazard set down his drink and walked over to the desk. "I think you should have this. In truth, it should be yours anyway." Taking the signet ring off his finger, he slipped it on Ben's hand. "If they find your body or whatever's left of it, they'll find that ring. I always wear it. It's been passed down over the years from father to son. That's the Lazard crest engraved in *intaglio* in the stone. I've always treasured that ring." He looked around the study. "Like this room, so full of history. Look at those prints there—Catesby botanicals, early eighteenth century. And my porcelains." He made a clicking sound with his mouth. "Oh, well..."

Lazard studied his watch. "I've really got to be going shortly—but there's one thing I should perhaps tell you, though. There's no real need of course—you'll never have the opportunity to use the information, but you might find it of some ironic interest."

Lazard walked over to the bookcase, removed a book from a bottom shelf, and stooped down to pull a lever. Grasping the edge of shelf, he tugged gently at one side as the shelves silently swung away on well-oiled hinges. In the hidden space behind it an old but secure wall safe stared at them. "Did you know this was here, Ben?"

"No."

"I didn't either. It was one of our father's better kept secrets. I've really got to rush, but I need to open this anyway. I want to make sure nothing in here survives the fire." He kneeled down and turned the combination knob, then pulled downward on the oversized lever attached to the door. The safe swung open. Extracting a thin legal sized folder, he laid it on the desk in front of Ben.

"Do you remember what happened several months ago with Crawford Matthews and that old blind fool, Ollie...Ollie what's her name?"

"They both died the same night," Ben replied, "right after Miss Ollie called me to say she had some information. You were there."

"I was. But, understand me, Ben—they were both old and their quality of life was nil. Can you imagine life in a nursing home? Matthews, of course, had to die, he'd broken a sacred covenant. And the woman—she was blind, a double amputee, no real family. They would have died anyway sooner or later. But when I say that, I fully recognize that what I did was deliberate and outside of accepted procedure. I didn't hurt them, honestly. Matthews went quickly with a little excess IV Versed, and it didn't take much to pop the old woman's neck—she never suffered a moment."

Ben was beyond rage. "Why kill innocent people, Troup?"

"They weren't so innocent. They were like you two. They knew too much. Were there some other way I'd be most happy to let you both walk out of this house this instant, but I can't. You'd talk; you'd tell what you know. They were like you and had tasted of the fruit of the tree of the knowledge of good and evil. They had to die, don't you see?"

Lazard sat back down. "We're short on time. Let me finish part of the story. I'll leave a little reading here for you after I'm gone and you can fill yourself in on the rest. Ben, do you remember what you said the old woman told you on the phone, the essence of her message?"

"Not really."

"I do. She was talking about 'page nine.' That could mean only one thing—Matthews had told her too much. Let me give you the history from the beginning. You were young and probably wouldn't remember it anyway. In 1958, just after you were born, our father called your mother and my sister and me to his law office. Naturally, we'd been upset about his marriage, and when you were born, the combined prospect of another heir and a wife who was younger than us gave us some reason to be upset. You see, Ben, we thought your mother might try to steal the inheritance that was rightfully ours. As it turned out—I have to give him credit—he tried to be fair.

Unfortunately, though, he left this plantation in a life estate to your mother which meant, in essence, she had to die before we could have control of the estate. Since she was our age, that made our ever having control an unlikely possibility. Elizabeth and I argued—furiously, I should add—when she announced she had come to terms with my father's decision. She said that it was his to do with as he pleased, and that he had adequately provided for us financially so we should accept it and get on with our lives. I disagreed.

"Elizabeth died when you were an infant. You never really knew her. I finished medical school and eventually moved home about six years later. By that time my father was ill, and it soon became evident that he didn't have long to live. I recognized that I was the only rightful heir, and I set out to see what I could do to change things. Toward the end, my father was in a great deal of pain, and I controlled his morphine supply. He knew he was dying, and I got him to tell me of his plans to have the trust department of one of the Atlanta banks act as executor of his will. It was easy enough to convince him to change that in favor of his law partner, Crawford Matthews. I argued that he was local, understood the plantation better, and so on. So, my father agreed and signed a brief codicil to that effect. What he couldn't know, however, was that I had reached an agreement—shall we say—with Mr. Matthews. As executor, he would automatically get five percent of the estate which, at the time, worked out to be more than a hundred-thousand dollars in cash, plus the appraised value of some twelve-hundred odd acres of land. You know lawyers—they'll sell their soul for a few dollars. In exchange for his being appointed executor, he agreed to let me have a look at the latest copy of my father's will, and see if we couldn't do anything to thwart his plans to leave the house and lands for your mother.

"Well, Matthews had never seen the will, but knew there was a copy in my father's office safe along with notes to the executor as to the location of the original and a few other instructions I'll tell you about presently. So we opened the safe, found the copy of the will and read it. Ben, can you imagine my shock when I learned that my father had written a totally new will after my sister's death?" Lazard laughed. "He left me, *his eldest son*, the sum of exactly one dollar. He left everything to you, Ben. You and your mother."

CHAPTER
THIRTY-SIX

LAZARD WAS LAUGHING AGAIN, almost as if he'd recalled a very funny story he couldn't resist relating to his eager audience. Ben and Alex weren't laughing, however. They sat in stony silence, having no choice but to listen.

"You should have seen us," Lazard continued. "scurrying around like mice, trying to find the safe that my father said held the original of his will, and then wondering how we were going to open it once we found it—*if* we found it. It was really quite a mystery. In his safe at the law office was an unsigned carbon copy of the will, and a carbon copy of a letter to the executors that made reference to the safe in my study at

Marsellaise Plantation. The letter also referred to a separate enclosed document of which he had not kept a copy that apparently gave the exact location of the safe, as well as the combination.

"It really put us in sort of a dilemma. Since my father wasn't dead, and since we weren't totally sure he hadn't sent a copy of the will to his proposed executors in Atlanta, we just couldn't call them up and tell then to send us the safe combination. That would have been too suspicious! And your mother was here all the time, hovering over things. She had been caring for him day and night. Finally, I convinced her she needed a break and got one of her friends to take her out of town for the day. While she was gone, Matthews and I must have spent three hours in this room trying to find the hidden safe. We had about decided the letter was wrong when I realized there is a rather large unaccounted for structural space behind that bookcase. We took out all the books—again— and there, hidden on the bottom shelf, was a little lever. I pulled it. Imagine our surprise when the whole bookcase swung away to reveal the safe."

He glanced at his watch again. "We still didn't have the combination and didn't want to risk destroying the will trying to open the safe by force. Also, we realized this might be our only chance to get your mother out of the house so we could do what we needed to do. We must have spent another four hours going through every page of every book on the shelf. Finally, in his old worn Bible, I found a series of numbers written in the margin in the Book of Genesis. We tried them and it opened!

"Even then we still weren't in much better shape once we got the safe open. We found two signed copies of my father's will, plus a separate set of instructions regarding the reading of the will and the distribution of several sealed envelopes to certain individuals—apparently personal letters. We grabbed all the papers and took them down to the law office to think about it. For a while we were at a loss as to what to do. My father was completely bedridden by this time, so we didn't need to worry about him finding out we'd been in the safe. We thought about trying to get him to sign a whole new will, but with your mother here all the time, we knew that would never work.

"We were sitting in the conference room at the law office when an idea suddenly occurred to me. I asked Matthews if he still had the same typewriter that had been used to type the will. He did, and we found the solution. You see, Ben, only the last page of the will is signed, and while the signature is witnessed, the witnesses don't know the contents of the document. I realized that all we had to do was simply retype one page. Instead of leaving his estate to you and your mother, we had him leave it to me, his eldest son and rightful heir. You should thank me really. In the original will, he'd only left me a dollar. I made sure that you and your mother got considerably more than that—enough to get started on a new life."

Lazard looked at his prisoners, as if waiting for some kind of response. He was met with silence.

"Well, that was the story of 'page 9.' We simply typed a new page on the same kind of stationary using the same typewriter that had been used to create the original will. We removed the original page and substituted the corrected version. I had no problem placing it back in the safe late one night after your mother had gone to bed. So, when my father died, Matthews dutifully wrote the bank in Atlanta to tell them he would act as executor and to get directions as to how to find the official signed copy of the will. As it turned out, they never had a copy of the original version, so they were none the wiser. Matthews opened the safe in the presence of your mother and several other witnesses and therein 'discovered' a perfectly legal signed document which he probated per its instructions. What do you think?"

Lazard rose and picked up the legal folder that lay on the desk. Removing a document bound in blue legal backing he flipped it open and laid it in front of Ben. "Here's the one of the two originals that we didn't alter—see for yourself what you might have had."

Ben glanced at the will and then at his half-brother. "Why, Troup?"

"Why what?"

"Why on earth would you save this document? What possible reason...."

"For the museum of course. I planned to have my papers sealed for fifty years after my death, and by then it would have been a mere footnote of interest—another convoluted twist in the distinguished history of the Lazard family. There's not only this—the safe is full of family papers going back to Jacques Lazard's original deed from the 1820's. Why shouldn't I keep it? Historians would have applauded me for saving the plantation from the likes of you."

The wall clock chimed the half hour. "It's four-thirty," Lazard said. "Time to go. Hector will be waiting. So long, Ben, Ms. Jennings." He moved to walk out of the study.

"Troup," Ben called after him.

"Yes? Last requests, maybe?"

"One. Out of curiosity. Why did our father disinherit you?"

Lazard laughed heartily. *"That* you'll never know. I'll tell you when I see you in Hell." He turned and left.

Ben and Alex looked at each other. "I can't move," she said.

"Me, either." He looked at the clock on the desk. "We've got half-an-hour if this clock is right."

They began to struggle with their bindings. The only sound was the ticking of wall clock.

Fifteen minutes later, she said, "I can't do it, Ben. I can't get loose. We're going to die aren't we?"

"We'll make it. We've still got time," he said, his own wrists bleeding now from his effort to escape. "Keep trying."

"Ben, I love you. I wanted to say that before...." She did not finish.

That was because they heard a soft sound—more like a dull thump, actually, followed shortly by another. The both looked at the clock. Four-fifty. A dragging sound now from the direction of the parlor.

A moment later they saw a shadow in the short hallway. Both of their mouths fell open when they saw Hoke Brantley, ashen and covered in blood, standing in the doorway.

"Hoke!" Ben almost yelled. "You're alive—thank God!"

The big deputy wavered, zombie-like. He looked like he was going to fall over any second.

"You've got to get us out of here," Ben pleaded. "There's a bomb. We've got less than ten minutes before it goes off."

Hoke grimaced in pain. He staggered into the room. "Ain't no problem. I fixed it."

"The timer? Are you sure?"

"I'm sure." Moving slowly, he extracted a pocketknife from his trousers and began sawing at Ben's ropes.

"Hurry, Hoke! I don't' want to take any chances. I want us out of this house in case he planted a second charge to back up the first one."

His ropes now severed, Ben grabbed the knife and quickly freed Alex. Scooping the folder and papers off of the desk, he pushed her toward the door and turned to find Hoke sinking toward the floor.

Together, they lifted his shoulders and tried to help him up. Finding strength, he managed to stand on his own.

"I ain't dead yet," Hoke mumbled. "Lazard may be a good doctor, but he don't know his anatomy. He gutshot me, and I played dead 'till I knew the coast was clear."

Placing one arm over Ben's shoulders and the other over Alex's, they hurried toward the front door.

In the circular drive, Ben's Taurus was parked next to the patrol car. None of the farm workers were anywhere to be seen. Collapsing on the front seat of his vehicle, Hoke called for backup and for an ambulance. "Don't worry. The rest of the deputies are clean," he reassured them.

In the distance they could hear the sound of a low-flying airplane. A moment later a sleek twin-engined aircraft equipped with auxiliary fuel tanks on its wingtips flew over the treetops and circled around to make a second pass. Through the open doorway, the hall clock began to chime the hour. Far away the sound of a siren wailed.

Hoke peered up at the airplane. "There's the son-of-a-bitch now. He musta' found it."

"Found what?"

"His little bomb. I stuffed it in one of his sacks of money when the men left me alone to take a load upstairs. I know they picked up the sack."

With a deafening clap of thunder, the plane disintegrated in mid-air, each wing with its still-spinning prop twirling erratically in a spiraling motion toward the earth. At the exact place in the sky where the explosion had taken place, a fluffy green cloud had appeared and began to gently disperse earthward, blown by a cool afternoon wind toward the mansion. As they watched in horrified awe, the cloud resolved itself into the individual shapes of hundred dollar bills which began to fall on the house and grounds like leaves after a summer storm.

CHAPTER THIRTY-SEVEN

THE SOUND OF THE SIRENS DREW CLOSER. Across the expanse of meadow in front of the mansion, the wreckage of Lazard's plane was burning brightly in the late afternoon sun, it's oily black smoke carried away on the wind.

Ben turned to Alex. She was filthy, covered with mud from their ordeal in the swamp, the bruise on her cheek now scarcely visible under the grime. "You're beautiful," He said. "Did you mean what you said in there a few minutes ago?"

"I did. I truly did."

He raised his arms to embrace her, and as he did, a piece of yellowed stationary slipped out of the folder he still held in his hand. He stooped to pick it up, and saw it was a handwritten letter. The penmanship was somehow familiar. It had been nearly thirty years ago, but he immediately recognized it as his father's handwriting. With Alex looking over his shoulder, he began to read aloud:

Marsellaise Plantation
February 18, 1959

To my son Troup:

If you are reading this, I can assume that I am no longer living. I have instructed that my executors deliver this letter to you seal unbroken. What I am about to tell you is known only by myself and one other person whose identity must remain shielded and whose silence has been purchased at great cost.

You are by now no doubt aware that I have disinherited you through my nominal bequest of one dollar. You have surely asked yourself why, and you have every right to know, hence this letter.

After your sister's tragic death some months ago, I was most distraught, certainly not an unexpected emotion in a man who has lost forever his beloved child, his only daughter. The circumstances of her death were in themselves strange, and despite the diligent efforts of the Atlanta police, it was ruled to be an accident. Perhaps I should have left well enough alone, but I have never been one to hide from the truth, however painful it may be. After the formal report of the investigation had been issued, I remained unsatisfied. Following discreet inquiry, I retained an individual in Atlanta whose specialty is the sensitive investigation of the most private matters. My charge to him was that every step of the investigation be retraced, every lead followed to its end, and that he devote his full effort to uncovering any new facts that might bear on the matter.

My investigator performed his duties well, and through diligent and concerted inquiry was able to discover certain facts that had been overlooked by the police. I will not bother you with the details of all these, but most prominent among them was the unequivocal fact that a vehicle matching the description of your car was seen parked at Elizabeth's house at the estimated time of her death. He was also able to provide more corroborating evidence concerning your whereabouts at that time, strongly implicating you as a suspect.

In presenting his evidence to me, the investigator suggested that the circumstantial case was strong enough to charge you with murder, should such information be presented to the police. His certainty of this fact left me in a great dilemma. In an untimely way I had lost your mother, the woman I loved, and then my only daughter. Was I to lose my son, too?

After weeks of agonizing thought, I made the decision to forever suppress this shame, and pray that your own self-knowledge of this iniquity would haunt you to your grave. In doing so, I must face my own weakness as manifest by my fear of confronting you. As a father, I cannot bear to look you, my son, in the eyes and ask, Is it true? My comfort is that thin shadow of a doubt we call hope, even in the face of overwhelming certainty.

Please be assured that all evidence that might possibly connect you to Elizabeth's death has been destroyed. At my insistence the investigator has moved from this State, never to return.

At my death, all that I have will go to my beloved Mellie, and thence to my son Benjamin. With this letter, my final and silent communication to you, I condemn you to suffer in the private hell that you have created for me. You have discredited the Lazard name. You are no longer my son.

Lafayette Lazard

CHAPTER
THIRTY-EIGHT

EPILOGUE

From <u>The Macon Telegraph</u>, December 9, 1994-Obituaries:

Hoke A. Brantley

WALKERVILLE — Hoke A. Brantley, 37, of 5241 Mertz Road, Walkerville, died Friday at a local hospital after a prolonged illness. He was the son of the late Herschel and Lilly P. Brantley, and was a Sheriff's Deputy with the Adams County Sheriff's Department. He was an Army Veteran, and a member of the John Conn

Masonic Lodge No. 452 and the Macon Scottish Rite Bodies. Survivors: wife, Wanda J. Brantley, children, Tabatha Brantley, Samantha Brantley, and Krystal Brantley, all of Walkerville. Services: 2 p.m. Sunday at the Mount Moriah Primitive Baptist Church. The Rev. Jimmy Horton will officiate. Davis Funeral Chapel (formerly Kantt's Funeral Home) has charge of arrangements.

From The Atlanta Constitution, April 28, 1995-Georgia in Brief:

Judge rules against Government
in RICO case

Macon—Judge Wilbur Jackson of the US District Court for the Middle District of Georgia issued a ruling today in the controversial case of United States vs. The Estate of Troup Lazard, et al. rejecting the Government's claim of title to more than twenty-four thousand acres in Adams County that had been the site of a recently uncovered international drug smuggling operation. Citing the Justice Department's "unmitigated arrogance" in pursing this claim under the Racketeer Influenced Corrupt Organizations (RICO) Act and other Federal statutes, he awarded ownership of the disputed property to Benjamin F. Pike. In a lengthy and scathing decision, he noted the "clear and undisputed fact" that the defendant properties were originally obtained by "patent fraud" and that the deprivation of the rightful owner of such property "raises serious Constitutional issues under Amendments Four and Seven." When asked about his ....

From <u>The Adams Sentinel</u>, May 9, 1995-Help Wanted:

Farm Help Wanted: Now hiring experienced farm workers for large timber and cattle farming operations locally. Experience preferred, will accept all applications. Competitive salary and benefits, housing available. Contact Jim Wren, Manager, Marsellaise Plantation, Post Office Box 190, Walkerville, GA, 31081

From <u>The Adams Sentinel</u>, February 8, 1996-Social Page:

Birth Announcement

Dr. and Mrs. Benjamin Pike of Marsellaise Plantation, Walkerville, proudly announce the birth of a son, Lazard Wren Pike, on February 1, 1996. He is the grandson of Mr. and Mrs. James Wren of Walkerville, and the late Lafayette Lazard and Mellie Lazard Pike.